Sleep

A marriage made in heaven ...

... a murder made in hell.

M K BOERS

PQP
Purple Queen Publishing

Second Printing: August 2022

Published by Purple Queen Publishing

ISBN#: 978-90-832140-1-6

Dedication

To all those out there that struggle with any or all of the
background topics in this book.
And to Kate Elizabeth

Prologue

It was going round and round, and no matter how high she pulled the sheets up she could still hear it. It had been going for hours, and it was keeping her awake. She was already angry, this just made it worse.

Lizzy hated being laughed at and he'd known that. But he'd carried on, hadn't he? Behind her back and in front of people they'd both known. He'd made her one big fat joke! Fat, yes, there was that word again, one he'd kept using, along with his mate Reedy. They'd loved making jokes at her expense, any kind of put down would do, whether it was about her weight, her inability to have children, her lack of libido, anything to give them a good laugh. They'd laughed a lot, hadn't they? Right in front of her sometimes. And he hadn't cared how upset it had made her – or how angry, oh no, he'd just thrown back his head and laughed. Yes, she was fucking hilarious!

But she's had the last laugh now, hasn't she? Served him right.

It wasn't just that though, there were many things – like the house. He'd never done anything round the house. She would ask as pleasantly as possible, try hard not to nag, but lately it just seemed to spark a row and he'd storm out, leaving her to do it. Then when he'd get back, he'd make out she was playing the martyr, saying she was doing it deliberately herself so she could moan about it later. It made her so angry!

The buzzing was getting louder; it was still going round the bedroom. Then it got caught in the net-curtains, bashing its little body against the glass. The tapping was irritating, getting right inside her head just like they had. She'd had enough!

She jumped out of bed and snapped on the light. It was a huge bluebottle fly. She rolled up a magazine lying on the bedside table and attacked it. It took three hard swats to kill it, even then its little legs still twitched, but it wouldn't be getting up again.

Satisfied, she flicked the light off and hopped back into the warm bed, snuggling down deep. With her anger dissipated, she drifted off to sleep.

Once again, she became aware of buzzing. She didn't know how long she'd slept but it felt brief. There were two of them this time. She just lay there, letting them get the feel of the room, her anger rising.

This was all his fault; they wouldn't be keeping her awake if it wasn't for him. She'd known things hadn't been right between them for years; they didn't talk or touch anymore. And yes she'd let herself go, she knew that too. He hadn't needed to keep saying it. But she'd seen no point in making the effort anymore. She was always too angry and he was too preoccupied.

She hadn't been surprised when she'd found out – she'd known it would only be a matter of time. Lizzy had seen her too, a pretty blonde thing: young, slim – his usual type. But he hadn't been discreet; he'd paraded her round the pubs for weeks and weeks, even snogging with her at the bar. Then the ultimate of betrayals: he'd brought her here, to their home. She couldn't have that, not in her house, not in their bed. It wasn't right. It wasn't fair. He'd known that.

She'd had enough of these two. She clambered out of bed again, this time more slowly giving her body a chance to wake up, and switched on the light. She blinked, waiting for her eyes to adjust, but as she did another fat one came in under the door. She sighed. This was getting ridiculous. She couldn't put up with this.

She opened the bedroom door and stepped out onto the landing. There were plenty more out here. They all seemed to be flying in and out of the master bedroom. The door was ajar giving them easy access.

She walked across the landing and pushed it wider, looking in. This was where they had spent the ten years of their marriage: the first five loving, the last five screaming. The thought made her sad.

The sound in here was no longer an individual buzz, it was more of a collective hum. It reverberated off the walls filling the entire room. She switched on the light.

The sheet had fallen off and with the small top window open hundreds of them had come in, attracted to the scent.

She stood there staring at them lying on the bed, expressions of horror frozen on their faces. They hadn't expected her to come home; they thought they'd got away with it. Had it been the first time? She didn't know. But the freezer knife had surprised them – and herself if she was honest.

It had been a strange sensation when she'd plunged it into his back, not quite how she'd expected. It had been difficult at first, like pushing a knife into hard butter, gaining speed once the surface was broken. When he'd arched his back in response, she'd had trouble hanging on, but she'd persisted until his resistance had slowed and he'd slumped down onto his woman, who'd started screaming hysterically, eager to get out from under him.

It's the only reason Lizzy had killed her. All that noise would definitely bring the neighbours round and she couldn't have that. She'd brought a swift end to it, the gurgling only lasting a few seconds. But it had been a shame; she'd had such a pretty neck.

A fly flew into Lizzy's face jerking her out of her reverie. She couldn't just stand here reminiscing, she had to get them covered up again to get rid of the flies, otherwise she'd never get back to sleep.

Chapter One

The handcuffs were snug. Lizzy sat staring at them. She was used to them now; they were like a piece of jewellery. The movement of the van jiggled them. They put them on her every time they took her some place: today it was the courthouse.

She stared at the back of the guard sitting on the side bench on the other side of the van, outside the cage she was in. He had one hand holding the back of the driver's seat, and the other keeping him steady on the bench. His head was turned to face the driver, watching the road over his shoulder. She was of no interest to him, just another prisoner being escorted.

She ran her eyes over his profile and thought how similar it was to Tony's: Tony had worn a small ponytail too, but his hair had been blond. He reminded her of how Tony had looked when they had first met.

The guard gave her a quick glance. He must have sensed her looking. The flash of violet blue eyes made her stomach jump – they were the same colour as Tony's. For the first time in years she thought of her initial meeting with Tony and all the surreptitious glances he'd given her that night.

She hadn't been able to take her eyes off him as she'd watched him move around the people in the nightclub. The face of each person he approached had lit up as though his smile carried a light that shone on them. He'd been a born charmer and he'd known it. People had loved him and all the women had wanted him.

He'd moved smoothly and carefully, gliding through them, making his way towards her. No one else had been aware of his intentions except her; his eyes darting across at every opportunity, snatching a glance. And she'd made sure her eyes were there to meet his every time; smiling at him; waiting. He was checking she was still there, making sure she knew he was coming, and she reassured him she did.

When he'd finally reached her, she'd been trembling in anticipation. His eyes had looked deep into hers with a longing that had made her giddy and nervous. She'd hoped she would do the right thing and not mess it up. She didn't want to come across as foolish or giggly; she wanted to impress him as much as he had impressed her. She wanted to be more than all the other girls that had swarmed round him on nights out: she wanted to seem cool, calm and collected. And it must have worked, because he'd walked her home in the cold spring night air, all the way to the other side of town. And then he'd called her first thing the next day. By all accounts that had been unheard of and totally out of character for such a lady's man – even his best friend had said so.

Then she'd made him wait a month – a whole month! – before she'd agreed to go back to his place. That had been the clincher, the thing that had set her apart from all the others. Lizzy was no pushover and he'd liked that. And he'd been good that night, very good, which was why she had fallen for him so easily.

She shifted in her seat, the movement causing the guard to look at her again. She didn't make eye contact; she stared at the wall of the cage. He turned away again after a couple of seconds.

She relived the call Tony had made to her just two days after their first night. She could hear his voice in her head: It had been soft, enticing, and eager. They'd been trying to work out when they were going to see each other again. Both of them had been so busy it had been hard to find time.

'If you can't do Thursday, we'll just have to wait until next week,' she'd said.

'I can't wait that long,' he'd replied.

Her stomach fluttered just recalling those words. In the end he'd agreed to shift some things to make time for her. It had been another night of desire.

It'd escalated from there, seeing each other at every opportunity and as the summer had arrived things had become heady. And then there had been the picnic. How could she have forgotten that? It had been their turning point.

He'd lain with his head in her lap looking up into her face as she'd sat forward over him, stroking his forehead.

'You know we can't keep on like this, don't you, Lizzy?'

'What do you mean?'

'It's not enough just seeing you a couple of times a week. I want to see you every day.'

'Okay, so what are you suggesting?'

'Move in with me?'

She raised her eyebrows, and smiled. 'Are you sure you want to do that?'

'I've never been so sure. I love you Lizzy.'

And that was it: she was sold; she was all in.

'I love you too, Tony. Let's do it.'

As the police van came to a stop at another set of lights, the sound of a siren distracted her. At first she thought maybe they wanted to get her to the courthouse in a hurry, but it was just an ambulance careening past them, going the other way.

The flashing lights brought her back to the night of her incarceration. She didn't know who had called the police, but they'd come with sirens blaring. She'd rushed downstairs to the front room to find it alight with swirling blue lights. For a second she'd expected music, as though she was about to be picked out by a spotlight on a dance floor, but then the thumping on the front door had killed the illusion.

As the van jolted forward with the light change, her mind shifted back to her reminiscing and to the first night in their new home. They had decided not to move into either one of their existing homes; they'd wanted to do it properly instead. They'd found a new place and chosen it together: a nice three-bedroom semi with its own driveway and garage.

They'd settled in well and found an easy rhythm. They'd created date nights and nights in together. Their first holiday abroad had been thrilling, both enjoying the same type of beach holidays: part lazing on the beach, part discovering the history of the Greek island they had picked. It had worked; they were in sync, which meant it was only a matter of time before the next step.

Lizzy paused. It had been a long time since she'd recalled any of the softer, gentler feelings she'd had towards Tony. She hadn't dared, it hurt too much. Plus she'd been too consumed with rage. But that rage was gone now – she'd quelled it.

Chapter Two

Lizzy felt the van slow down to a stop and saw the steps of the courthouse through the windscreen. She saw all the people gathered there, and as the van pulled up, the noise of their anger.

Tony's modelling career had been a great success. He'd gone from small town factory worker to most billboarded face in the north of England. Scouted through photos in the factory catalogue, he'd gained a lot of popularity over the years. It had given him a minor celebrity status. His death had come as a shock to many people – especially when it had been at the hands of his own wife.

The guard raised his eyebrows at her and held up a blanket. She looked at him stone-faced and then at the blanket. If nothing else it would protect her from the spit.

She lowered her head as she stepped out of the cage and he swept it round her as the back doors opened. He clutched her shoulders helping her out.

The roar increased as she came out, the blanket blocking her view of them. She was grateful for that, but knew the journey up the steps was going to be one of humiliation.

It was like walking through a lightning storm as camera flashes went off left and right, streaking through the material of the blanket, heating up her face. When she reached the courthouse entrance, she sensed a gathering of people behind her and heard the warning voices of police telling them to keep their distance. Then the silence of the marble foyer inside deafening her once the doors closed. Someone pulled the blanket off, leaving it to rest on her shoulders and she saw her legal team standing there waiting for her. Everything was hushed inside as they manoeuvred her into one of the side rooms for the briefing.

Lizzy hadn't held onto much of what was going on around her; she didn't much care. This was only her third time in court and up until now she had just been going through the motions. But coming out of the briefing room into the main courtroom she caught sight of who was here to watch and became interested.

She hadn't seen her in-laws for a long time and they looked older. She held eye contact with her mother-in-law as she was led to the dock, feeling her contempt. Lizzy didn't look away, she wasn't going to give her the satisfaction, she was worth more than that.

After the ritual opening comments on both sides and address to the jury, Lizzy watched her brother-in-law take the stand. He had always been lacking in any intellectual nature, but his similarities in mannerisms and facial expressions to her late husband sparked her memories. She even wondered if the suit he was wearing was the one he had worn at their wedding. It wasn't as though Jim was a man who owned many suits; it was probably the only one he had, it was certainly the only one she had ever seen him in.

The speech he had given on their wedding day was much like the one now: monotone and dull. Back then everyone had smiled and laughed in the correct places and toasted alongside him, but when he had got drunk later and become obscene, Tony had had to take him outside and put him in a cab. He'd been bitter, even jealous of his brother's natural charm and luck in life. But now that bitterness was turned on her as he pretended a love and loyalty to his brother.

Despite his nasty revelations about her, she smiled. His presence had triggered a memory she had buried long ago: a memory that had carried her through some tough times.

She could still see Tony trying to get through the door of the hotel suite with the box in his arms while she lay flat out on the honeymoon bed engulfed in volumes of silk, netting and taffeta provided by her wedding dress. She'd laughed as he'd heaved it over to the bed and dumped it next to her, enjoying the light spinning of the alcohol haze she was in after their wedding reception.

'What is it?'

'You have to open it to find out.'

'Now?'

'Of course now!'

'What have you bought me, Tony?' She struggled to sit up and clutched at the box to steady herself. It had flowers all over it, and a big bow on the top. She pulled at the bow, making a mess of it, and had to waste time unpicking it to finally release the box. The lid popped up and pink packing chips fell out everywhere. She dug into them and rummaged around trying to find what was inside.

Tony had plonked down on the bed next to her, laughing as she scrambled.

'I thought it was heavy, the way you were carrying it.'

'Gotta keep you guessing now, haven't I?'

She finally came across a small box in the midst of it all, and dug it out carefully. It was wrapped in silver paper and sealed with a red heart shaped sticker. She glanced at Tony and he just grinned, giving her his winning smile.

Lizzy carefully opened the present, taking her time. Inside she found a beautiful white gold locket, on a fine white gold chain. She opened it up, but it was blank inside.

'Turn it over.'

On the back was inscribed: 'To Lizzy, Queen of my Heart. Tony.'

She couldn't keep her eyes from welling up, and laughed lightly with embarrassment as she wiped away the tears. He leant over and gave her a tender kiss.

'I left it empty. I thought you might want to put photos of our children in there.'

She gasped and looked at him wide-eyed. They had never really spoken about children. He knew she had wanted them but hadn't allowed her to draw him out on the subject. She knew that an ex had miscarried his child and it had upset him, so she had never pushed it.

She touched his face, running her fingers down his cheek to his lips, letting her tears flow freely. She kissed him then with what felt like her entire soul, and that night had been the most emotional night of their married life as they continually reaffirmed the love and desire they had for each other all night long.

Chapter Three

There was a short recess, or 'tea break' as Lizzy liked to think of it, where she was left in an empty room to stare out of windows that were too high to see anything but clouds. She nursed a cup of tea. It was a large majestic room that echoed every breath, and since she was cooped up in a small cell for twenty hours a day over in the psychiatric wing of the prison, she indulged in its size by walking round it, listening to the sounds a large space makes.

She used the time to prepare herself for whatever came next. It would be a day of witnesses and character assassinations, and she had no idea who was going to be called next, but after having his family sprung on her, her overtaxed mind reeled at the possibilities.

When they finally called her to return, she had zoned out a little, trying to distance herself mentally from all the possible people that would be taking their pound of flesh. She shuffled along between the two Court Security Officers, staring blankly ahead of her. Court days exhausted her, she just wanted them over. She didn't really care about the outcome; she just wanted to stop having to go over the last ten years of her life – especially the last five – and keep having to face the people who had let her down.

This time Lizzy caught a glimpse of the next witness before she entered the courtroom. Sue's blonde hair and large size were unmistakable as she squeezed through the double doors. Lizzy felt her stomach lurch on sight of her and knew this was going to be a difficult one to listen to. She had expected Sue to show up at some point in the proceedings but that didn't make it any easier. She could already hear the stream of lies that would spew from her mouth. In her experience two-faced bitches never told the truth no matter the oath they swore.

Once Lizzy was seated in the dock again, Sue was called to the stand. When Lizzy saw her close up she was given a moment of respite: the pallid skin tone and scraped back hair were a clear indication of a hangover – some would say she was even a little green round the gills. Lizzy's mouth twitched for a second as she suppressed a smirk. Maybe Sue had a conscience after all and needed some Dutch courage the night before to face her. How else had she found the nerve to come here today and talk against a woman who'd once been her best friend? And not just any best friend, but one that had laid herself on the line for her time and time again until she had uncovered the ultimate betrayal.

Lizzy's eyes followed Sue's every move as she walked up to the witness box, but Sue avoided even a glance in Lizzy's direction. Lizzy thought that was a shame; Sue was missing out on her expression of disdain.

Sue was asked all the standard questions; name, age, occupation and how long she had known the accused. Lizzy actively listened this time, wanting to hear exactly what she had to say and how she said it. Lizzy even pulled the notepad she'd been provided onto her lap, pen poised at the ready. Her solicitor noticed the movement and glanced at her from his place behind the barrister. She had a feeling there would be things to contest and she had to write them down fast for him to pass on when it was their turn to question her.

Then the first key question came: How had they become acquainted? Lizzy wanted to know how Sue remembered this.

'We met in a nightclub one night. Tony and I were friends, and he introduced her to me.'

Lizzy's lips twitched again. He had done nothing of the sort. Sue had approached her that night on her own, having seen her with Tony a few times and asked if they were officially together. Sue had been friendly alright, but had actually warned her off Tony and told her he had a reputation with women. This hadn't been news to Lizzy, Tony had told her that himself. She'd told Sue she knew all about his past and was only seeing how it went at this stage.

Sue was asked by the barrister if she had known Lizzy well, Sue replied that they had become close friends. But when asked if they were still close Sue explained that their friendship had come to a halt a few years ago when Lizzy's behaviour had started getting worse. When asked what she meant by that Sue described how Lizzy had become unhappy and regularly complained about Tony; how she'd started to get paranoid about Sue being with him behind her back. The barrister asked her if there was any truth in that and she immediately denied it, saying she wouldn't do that to Lizzy even though she had been Tony's friend first.

Sue said it so sweetly it made Lizzy sick to her stomach. She started to write furiously on the paper, her solicitor leaning back slightly ready to take a look at whatever she was writing. The story poured out on the paper as her mind spun back to the day the betrayal was revealed.

They had been on holiday together, a week in Spain. It was an attempt to get Lizzy out of a low period, a return to the good old days of girls' nights out, all drinking together again. There had been eight of them in total, all good trusted friends who she'd known for several years.

They were at dinner on their last night, talking about their single years and the lads they had known; what they were up to now and who had slept with who back then.

Sue had been talking about her "romps" as she referred to them – of which she'd had plenty – when she'd started giggling about one in particular.

'It was so big I didn't know what to do with it! I told him 'It's the size of a bottle of bud!' He said, 'You suck on plenty of them, so you shouldn't have any trouble with this then!' I laughed, and said 'So do you Tony, but I didn't think it was your thing – does Wayne know about this? You ought to warn him before your next work trip!' We both had a good laugh at that.'

The conversation stopped dead as the girls all held their breath and looked at Lizzy. Lizzy felt like the breath had been snatched from her.

'You mean Tony, as in my Tony?'

Sue's face flushed despite the heavy foundation.

'No, no, this was another Tony, Tony Johnson, you know, the one I always talk about.' She'd tripped over the words as they flooded out, avoiding eye contact.

'What? And he worked with a Wayne too, did he?'

'Yeah, yeah. Down at the factory – Griggsey's – remember?'

Lizzy shook her head slowly and looked down at her plate, pushing it away from her.

'Sue, don't lie to me, you're no good at it and you'd be better off coming clean.'

Sue flushed again and everyone waited in silence for her to confess.

'It was before you were around, me and him used to muck about. There was nothing ever in it; I would just go back with him from time to time.'

'So it was more than just a one off then?'

'Yeah, about 5 or 6 times – just before he met you.'

Lizzy looked at her, no longer sure if she could trust anything she was saying. 'Lizzy, I'm telling you the truth. I know I should've mentioned it before, but there was never really a good time, plus it was no longer relevant once we became good friends.'

'Once we became good friends? That was all part of the plan though, wasn't it? Befriend her and she won't suspect a thing? For all I know you could be sleeping with him behind my back now! I know someone is!'

'Don't be ridiculous, of course I'm not! Lizzy, you're one of my best friends. Plus I'm still in love with my husband, despite all his faults! I ain't got time to be Tony's bit on the side!'

Lizzy let it drop, not wanting to put a dampener on the dinner. But the truth came out later that evening when Sue was steaming drunk and talking about her last time with Tony, claiming she'd only wanted to see if he'd still take her back.

Lizzy had asked her what she was talking about, and Sue had covered her mouth and giggled, feigning embarrassment.

'Shouldn't have said that, should I? You were away in Ibiza at the time with your mates – you'd only been seeing him a couple of weeks and you hadn't slept with him yet, so I thought, why not?' Sue's giggle turned into a full hearty laugh.

Lizzy felt like she'd been slapped in the face. She no longer heard the deafening rave music in the bar, or the babble of shouted conversation from everyone around her. She could only hear Sue's laugh, which had always been filthy, as though she'd just heard a dirty joke.

She'd stood staring at Sue, anger turning her nose up and her mouth down. Sue had stopped laughing and returned the stare, then said exactly the wrong thing: 'What?'

Lizzy had gone for her.

She'd grabbed Sue's hair on either side of her head and yanked her off the stool she was sitting on. Then she'd dragged her out of the bar, kicking and screaming.

Once out in the street, Lizzy had let her get back on her feet and swung at her with a full fist, punching her clean across the face and sending her flying across the bonnet of a parked car. The black-eye and bruised cheekbone it left would be visible for weeks.

Lizzy had laid into her, tapping all the rage and bitterness that had built up over recent years, using Sue as a punching bag to let it all out. In the end the other girls had had to pull her off, holding her back until she'd calmed down. The fight was over – along with their friendship and the holiday. Lizzy had known she'd gone too far. She'd packed her stuff that night and gone to the airport, sitting there until their flight took off twenty-four hours later.

Lizzy could still remember the feeling of satisfaction of seeing the state of Sue's face at the boarding gate. Sue had given her a black look, and when she'd stepped forward to speak to Lizzy the other girls had quickly flanked her, making sure there wasn't going to be another fight before they boarded.

Sue had had tears in her eyes when she'd spoken, and Lizzy remembered her saying, 'There was no justification for what you did!' Lizzy had chosen not to respond, and in fact hadn't spoken to Sue since.

She had no plans on speaking to her now either, not that she would be allowed to – there was no fraternising when you were a prisoner.

She looked at Sue all these years on, her make-up showing in the ageing lines on her face, still trying to fit into clothes that weren't quite big enough for her, and – on this particular occasion – looking rough. Lizzy hadn't understood then and didn't understand now what Tony had seen in her.

Chapter Four

Even now, whenever Lizzy saw Sue she thought about what Tony and her must have looked like in bed together. She imagined Tony's hands all over her and her eager for him. She remembered how Sue talked in great detail about the sex she'd had and wondered how much of it had been about Tony.

What had made it worse was that when they'd returned from their holiday the lads had found out about the fight, and verified it all: they'd all known about Sue and Tony, it had been general knowledge. So how come no one had told her?

Tony had been unremorseful when she'd questioned him, simply stating the same as Sue: they hadn't been sleeping together yet, only seeing each other, as though that made it alright. In fact he had been quite blunt about it and said, 'You didn't want to go to bed with me, Lizzy, and you know what I was like back then: if another woman made a play for me while I was out and I was pissed, I couldn't say no. And Sue was someone I'd been with a few times, so it was no great shakes.'

No great shakes? She'd been devastated by the knowledge. She'd spent evenings just watching him watch the TV, remembering how life had been when they were first together, how in love they had been, totally consumed with each other. But yet all that time she had been naïve not knowing that he had slept with one of her best friends behind her back even right at the beginning. If that was the case, how many others had there been?

Thinking of their beginning always brought her back to a night when they were first living together. It had been one of their "stay-at-home" date-nights, when they would take it in turns to do something romantic for each other at home. He'd made her a special meal and even set the table with candles. After they'd eaten, he'd reached over and taken her hand, and said, 'Lizzy, I love you so much. I never thought it was possible to feel this way about anyone.'

Had that been a lie then?

As she listened to Sue's voice up there on the stand in the courtroom, the final image came to her, the image of how she had dealt with his lies: the knife in his back. And yet for so many years he'd been the one twisting the knife in hers.

Lizzy was brought out of her thoughts by the gavel hitting the block, and she realised they were breaking for lunch. She was returned to the room where she'd spent the recess.

A sandwich and drink were brought to her and she ate it whilst watching her solicitor go through the notes she'd made during Sue's questioning. It was their turn to cross-examine after lunch, and he smiled at Lizzy as he read it.

'There's a lot to go on here. Hopefully we can discredit her with some of this.'

Lizzy gave him a small smile in return. It would be something to see Sue squirm after all these years.

They finished their lunch in silence and the Court Security Officers came to fetch them.

Sue was already on the stand again when Lizzy came in and for the first time they made eye contact. Again Lizzy refused to break first, staring her down. Sue tried to challenge it initially, but eventually gave in; fussing with her hands in her lap as she waited to begin.

Lizzy's barrister approached and introduced himself, starting with a strong opening question.

'You say that you were friends with Mr Dyson, and he introduced you to Mrs Dyson. Is that correct?'

'Yes'

'But you were more than 'just friends' with Mr Dyson at one point, weren't you?'

Sue hesitated. 'Well that depends what you mean.'

'Miss Andrews, did you have sexual relations with Tony Dyson?'

'Yes.'

'Did you have sex with Mr Dyson after he started dating Lizzy Dyson?'

Sue faltered again. 'Yes, but they weren't sleeping together.'

'And how did you know this?'

'Well, he told me and so did she.'

'After he introduced you, do you mean?'

'Yes.' Sue's face was starting to turn red.

'Is it correct, Miss Andrews, that he didn't actually introduce you, that in fact you approached Mrs Dyson yourself one night in a nightclub and introduced yourself, and opened a conversation about Mr Dyson?'

'Well it could be; I can't remember the exact details.' Sue fidgeted, looking uncomfortable.

'Is it true that after you became friends – even close friends, going out and meeting up with Mrs Dyson regularly – that you still had sex with Mr Dyson?'

The red flush on her face deepened and spread across her chest.

'Yes.'

'Would it be fair to say that you became friends with Mrs Dyson to stay close to Mr Dyson, as you knew he was serious about her?'

Sue fumbled over a response as the prosecuting barrister shouted 'Objection!' and the judge responded 'Sustained'.

'I'll reword, your honour. Would it be fair to say that you befriended Lizzy Dyson solely due to your relationship with Mr Dyson?'

'Initially, yes.'

'Did it change then?'

'Yes, I got to know her and I got to like her.'

'But it didn't stop you from returning to his bed?'

Sue looked down at her hands and mumbled, 'No.'

'So in fact you lied this morning when you said you didn't have a relationship with Tony Dyson behind Mrs Dyson's back, didn't you?'

'Well no, it wasn't a proper relationship and once they were sleeping with each other it never happened again.'

'Did you have a relationship with him behind her back, yes or no?'

Sue huffed. 'Yes.'

'Did you ever tell Mrs Dyson that you had slept with Mr Dyson?'

'I thought about it, but in the end I didn't, no.'

'Did anyone else know that you had slept with Mr Dyson and were continuing to sleep with him?'

She glanced down at her hands. 'Yes.'

'Who else knew?'

Sue looked wide eyed. 'I don't know lots of people, I suppose.'

'You suppose? Did you know for sure that others knew?'

'Yes.'

'How?'

'Because people talked.'

'Was it just talk or did they see you with Mr Dyson?'

Sue's tone became resigned. 'People saw us; we were quite open about it. But it was on nights that Lizzy wasn't out, or was away on holiday.'

'So in some ways you flaunted it?'

Sue stated 'No!' as the prosecuting barrister shouted 'Objection!' and Lizzy's barrister said, 'Withdrawn.'

'But you didn't worry that others would tell her?'

'No, not really.'

'You went on holiday with Mrs Dyson and several other female friends to Ibiza in 2010, is that correct?'

'Yes.' Sue let out a sigh and rolled her eyes. She knew where this was going.

'All the ladies that were on that holiday, except Mrs Dyson, knew that you had slept with Mr Dyson, didn't they?'

'Yes.'

'And one drunken night, you let the cat out of the bag, so to speak, and inadvertently told Mrs Dyson that you had slept with her husband, didn't you?'

'Yes.'

'Do you want to tell the court what happened that night?'

'I can't really remember much of it.' Sue's eyelids fluttered.

'Did you tell Mrs Dyson that you had knowingly and deliberately slept with Mr Dyson behind her back?'

'I might have.'

'Yes or no?'

'Yes.'

'And what was Mrs Dyson's reaction to this?'

'She punched me.'

'Just one single punch?'

'Well …' Sue sat back slightly, looking up, trying to remember. 'It was quite a big fight, and several punches were thrown, one of which sent me across the bonnet of a car, so no there were several.'

'And have you spoken to each other since that night?'

'No, well she hasn't spoken to me. I tried to speak to her before we flew home.'

'To ask her to apologise, is that correct?'

Sue gave a surprised look and glanced at Lizzy. 'Yeah, and so she should, there was no call for that!'

'No call for that? Did you apologise for sleeping with

Mr Dyson?'

Sue was silent.

'Miss Andrews?'

Sue shifted in her seat. 'No.'

'What was the state of their marriage at that time?'

'Objection, hearsay.' The prosecuting barrister interjected.

'Miss Andrews was best friends with Mrs Dyson and knew her well. I am trying to establish the possible state of Mrs Dyson's mind at the time, Your Honour.'

'I'll allow it.' The judge looked at Sue.

'Not very good. They were having problems and Lizzy didn't trust Tony.'

'Didn't trust him in what way?'

'She thought he was having an affair.'

'And was he?'

Sue pulled a face. 'I wasn't sure at that time.'

'At what time?'

'When we went away on the holiday.'

'Were you sure at any other time that he was being unfaithful to her? Beside when you were sleeping with him at the beginning of their relationship?'

Sue looked at her hands. 'Yes.'

'When was this?'

'The last couple of years before ...' she glanced at Lizzy, 'he died.'

'He was having an affair with one person, or multiple affairs?'

'One person.'

'And you knew this person?'

'Yes.'

'Was it the deceased, Miss Sally Bryant?'

'Yes.'

'Did you know her personally, were you friends with her?'

'I knew her to speak to occasionally, but we weren't friends.'

'Did you tell Mrs Dyson about their affair?'

'No, I didn't.' Sue looked at Lizzy with genuine remorse in her eyes and added, 'And I'll always regret that.'

Lizzy hadn't taken her eyes off Sue the entire time and didn't blink when Sue spoke directly to her.

'Miss Andrews, is it true that Lizzy Dyson suffered five pregnancy miscarriages?'

'Yes.'

'Were you friends during this time?'

'Yes, we were close friends when she started having them.'

'But you became more distant during the last two miscarriages, is that correct?'

'Yes. By that stage I didn't know what to do or say anymore. It was so awful.'

'And would you say it affected her state of mind?'

'Objection!' The prosecuting barrister sighed. 'Miss Andrews cannot possibly know what Mrs Dyson was thinking.'

'No, but as a close friend she would have had an idea, if they spoke about it. Did you talk about it, Miss Andrews?'

'Initially yes, and I tried to be there for her, but with each one she just seemed to get worse.'

'"Get worse', what do you mean by that?'

'She was emotional, depressed, desperate. She became consumed with trying to have a baby.'

'Was that difficult for you?'

'Yes.'

'What did you do?'

'I saw her less and less.'

'So your friendship started to breakdown?

'Yes.

'Was the holiday you took together before or after the miscarriages?'

'After.'

'So in some ways this was a reunion?'

'Yes, we had hoped that it would help her come back to herself, sort of like the good old days.'

'But that didn't happen, did it?'

'No.'

'Instead you announced that you had slept with her husband, in front of a group of friends, who already knew even though Mrs Dyson didn't, is that correct?'

Sue looked humbled hearing it stated like that. 'Yes.'

'So would it be reasonable to say that this would be upsetting?'

'Yes.'

'That it might be difficult to trust your friends again after that?'

'Objection! Assumption,' the prosecuting barrister stated.

'Withdrawn. On your return from the holiday, did Mrs Dyson continue to have contact with the other girls that were on holiday with you?'

'No, she withdrew from all of us and became a bit of a recluse. I hardly ever saw her out socially after that.'

'Did that surprise you?'

'No, not really. Everyone was talking about it.'

'It?'

'The fight we'd had. How she'd reacted when finding out about Tony and me.'

'Did you speak to Mr Dyson about it?'

'Briefly, yes.'

'What did you say?'

'I apologised for letting it slip, and said I was drunk.'

'What was his response?'

'He didn't seem to care. He even thought it was funny that she'd hit me.'

'So he was not remorseful about it?'

'Tony?' Sue gave a laugh. 'No, Tony was never sorry about that sort of thing.'

'What sort of thing?'

'Playing around.'

'Was it normal for him to play around then?'

'Before he was married, yes. He never had just one girl on the go, there were always several.'

'But that changed when he met Mrs Dyson?'

'Yes, in the early days.'

'"In the early days?' Did that change while he was married?'

Sue looked confused. 'Well clearly! He ended up having the affair with Sally, didn't he?'

'And there were no other affairs that you knew about.'

'No.'

'Was Mr Dyson open about the affair? Did others know?'

'Yes, lots of people knew. He didn't really keep it a secret. I'd seen him out with her a few times, at nightclubs. They didn't hide the fact that they were together. They would have their arms round each other and kiss and stuff.'

'Did you know when Mrs Dyson found out?'

Sue laughed. 'Everybody knew when she found out!'

'Can you explain what you mean by that comment, Miss Andrews?'

'Lizzy went for her in the pub.'

'This was in The Angel public house, is that correct?'

'Yes.'

'And you say "went for her"? What do you mean by that?'

'She attacked her; she grabbed Sally by the hair and started to punch her. The whole pub witnessed it.'

'Was Mr Dyson present?'

'Yes, he was desperately trying to pull her off Sally.'

'Did he succeed?'

'Eventually, but it took more than one person.'

'How long was this before his death?'

Sue pulled a face. 'It's got to have been six months, maybe more.'

'So despite this, he continued his affair with Sally Bryant.'

'Yes. Nothing changed.'

'Thank you, Miss Andrews. I have no further questions at this time.'

Chapter Five

Lizzy's face flushed when Sue brought up the fight with Sally Bryant. She hadn't forgotten that night; in fact she could remember every detail of it: seeing them in The Angel, and how Sally had been all round him at the bar. It had been the last straw when she'd seen Sally's hand fall to his bum. That was when she'd had to do something. She recalled grabbing Sally's hair and the thump as they both fell to the ground. She wasn't proud of what she'd done. She felt deep shame. And Tony had drilled it home to her when they'd got back that night, highlighting exactly what she had known for some time.

'Lizzy, what the fuck were you thinking?! You're seriously losing it and I don't know how much longer I can put up with this.'

'You'd like that, wouldn't you? An excuse to leave me and go off with her!'

'This is not about her, Lizzy, this is about you and your irrational behaviour. What the hell were you doing there anyway? You told me you were sick, that you didn't want to go out?'

Her eyes had burned with fury as she'd looked at him, but she hadn't opened her mouth. She hadn't want to confess how she'd been following him for months whenever he went out, staying hidden in the shadows to see exactly who he'd been with and what he'd been up to. She hadn't been stupid – although he'd liked to have thought she was — she'd known all about his other woman.

Tony had put his hand on her forehead. 'Maybe you should have a lie down, Lizzy, maybe you're sick.'

Lizzy had slapped his hand away. 'Fuck you, Tony! I'm not sick. I'm trying to find out what my husband is up to! I'm trying to find out what slut he's been shagging this past year and a half! I'm trying to find out what she's got that I haven't.'

'Fucking rational thinking that's what!' Tony had screamed in her face.

He'd stepped back, trying to restrain himself. 'A woman who is soft and loving and gentle, not angry all the time, not cold; not someone who has given up on herself.'

'And of course I'm sure she does marvellous things to your dick, too, doesn't she?' Lizzy had spat the words.

The glare Tony had given her had cut her dead. He'd stepped back further to the kitchen table and slumped down on a chair, putting his head in his hands.

'Lizzy, it's never been about that and you of all people should know that. There is no one who can top how you and I used to be, and I would do anything for us to be like that again.' He sat back and looked at her. She hadn't moved from the corner by the back door. 'But it's never gonna be, is it? I think we seriously need to talk about getting a divorce.'

Lizzy's breath had caught in her throat. They'd never mentioned divorce before, or separation. It had never really crossed her mind, no matter how bad things had been between them.

She'd bolted out the kitchen and run up the stairs. He hadn't follow her.

Lizzy's barrister jumped up and shouted, 'Objection', jerking her back to the courtroom. Sue had left the stand

and now there was a doctor of sorts sitting in the witness box.

Lizzy had never seen her before, but it seemed the prosecution thought she knew something about Lizzy's state of mind – or at least the state of mind of women who had lost babies. The lady talked about their feelings of loss and grief, especially with multiple losses, how feelings of failure or that their bodies had let them down could start to consume them. She said that much of it hinged on what support they had around them and what therapy was offered.

When it was Lizzy's barrister's turn to cross examine he established that this doctor had no personal knowledge of Lizzy or what she had been through, but clarified how it might affect someone's mental state and how it might display: self-loathing, depression, anxiety, withdrawal from social events, cutting off family and friends.

Despite it going in her favour, Lizzy didn't like hearing how it had caused her downfall. She didn't like being reminded that the loss of her babies might in fact have driven her to kill their father. She didn't like thinking about her loss at all, or that she wouldn't be able to visit them anymore, or that there might not be anyone to tend to their little graves.

'Mrs Dyson?'

Lizzy's eyes focused on the man in front of her – it was Mark Haygarth, her solicitor. She looked round to find the courtroom empty. The guards were waiting at the doors.

'Mrs Dyson, it's time to go.'

She looked at him blankly.

'It's over for today, we'll be back again in a few days.'

Lizzy staggered as she stood up, readjusting herself to accommodate the handcuffs. The solicitor helped her and she let him.

'It went well, I think, no one taking sides yet. Your brother-in-law helped us, and then your friend's clear betrayal.'

Lizzy had no clue what he was talking about, but he continued on regardless.

'He tried to make out he was a devoted brother, but we blew holes in that. Then she tried to make out she was a loyal and trustworthy friend and we derailed that. And the doctor ended up giving evidence to support our side.'

Lizzy suddenly stopped and let out a raucous noise. The solicitor's lips twitched unsure if it was a laugh, his eyes shot round the room at the last remaining people for reassurance. He found none.

Then she spoke, the startled look in his eyes indicating it was a sound he wasn't used to. In the few months he'd been her counsel she'd only spoken a couple of times.

'And a fat lot of good it'll do, won't it?'

'I don't get your meaning?'

'He's a liar, she's a liar, they're ALL liars!' She could feel her eyes opening wider, lighting up with rage. His eyes shifted; he glanced at the security guards who had registered her tone too and were on their way towards them.

'And no matter what they say, or who the jury believes I don't have a chance in hell, do I? – Well, in fact I do, it'll be the only place for me!' This struck Lizzy as funny, and she let out peels of uncontrollable laughter that bordered on hysteria.

The guards escorted her out from behind the desk, but she didn't stop. She couldn't. They continued to escort her out of the courtroom, and by the time they reached the main foyer everyone was watching her.

Her solicitor told them to stop there and wait for her to collect herself before facing the press outside. Seeing her in this state would not help any of them.

Slowly it died out, her cheeks wet with tears; everyone including Lizzy unsure if they were real tears or just from laughing so hard.

The guard offered the blanket and she reluctantly conceded to lowering her head once again for the trip to the van. This time they moved her more quickly, fearing that people outside might have heard the laughter and be incensed by it. The roar of the disgruntled crowd implied that they might have, although they didn't seem to be more abusive.

She rushed up into the van, tripping up the steps and finding herself prone, only managing to grab the side of the inner cage at the last minute and haul herself into it, landing on the bench inside. She caught her breath as she was locked in, the back doors slamming shut seconds before it pulled away.

Chapter Six

On the journey back to the prison Lizzy returned to her stone-faced pallor. The laughter had taken it out of her and her mind could no longer filter anything she'd seen or heard that day. Being locked away in the psychiatric wing of a prison for a couple of months meant she wasn't used to all the bustle and interaction with other people. The flood of emotions it brought with it was overwhelming. Reliving her humiliation and having it exposed publicly left her raw.

By the time they reached the prison Lizzy felt near comatose and kept her eyes down as they frog marched her back to her cell. Once locked inside she lay down and fell fast asleep, finding comfort in being left alone at last.

She was jolted awake by a scream, which she initially thought was in her nightmare, but when a second one followed she realised it was just Jeanie down the hall having another bad night. She turned over to try and go back to sleep but her mind was awake and racing with events from the day.

Lizzy couldn't get away from the doctor's testimony about how miscarriages affected women. It made her think about hers. She recalled the excitement they had both felt knowing they were pregnant the first time and revelling in the knowledge that no one else knew. Although this turned out to be fortunate with the miscarriage ending just shy of the seventh week. They recovered from this by believing what everyone said: that it was common with the first pregnancy and it didn't mean they wouldn't be able to fall again. But when the second one went the same way, doubt began to set in. It had been Christmas Eve as well and had overshadowed their entire Christmas.

Lizzy remembered standing in their bedroom looking out the window staring at nothing, hugging herself and wondering what it was she had done wrong this time. She'd taken all the vitamins, eaten all the right foods, avoided all her favourites – the soft cheeses, the pate – and made sure she was in tip-top condition. She couldn't understand it. Tony had joined her, slipping his arms round her waist and pulling her into him from behind, resting his chin on her shoulder. He hadn't spoken, knowing that no words could help this time, just his presence was enough.

They'd had no idea at the same time the following year on that exact same date they would be reaching the twelve week milestone of their third pregnancy and ready to announce it to the family on Christmas day. It had removed the shadow they had feared would be permanent over the festive season, making it one of the most joyous Christmases of their marriage. But the excitement of what the New Year would bring was cut short by the end of January, when Lizzy had gone into labour.

She recalled the pain and the blood, and rushing to the hospital. But the faces of the doctors and nurses had remained expressionless, just the odd shift of the eyes at each other indicating what she already knew – the baby wouldn't survive. The minor torturous labour she'd gone through exhausting Lizzy to the point where she could barely speak when Tony had arrived, rushing into the room just in time to see the miniature baby appear, small enough to fit in his palm – a baby girl. They'd called her Amber.

That was when the cracks had started to appear and the hope had begun to fade. The aftermath had left Lizzy bedridden and unable to do much other than cry. And by the second week Tony's patience was wearing thin and he'd refused to comfort her anymore.

'You've got to pull yourself together, Lizzy, there's no point in moping. Go to the doctors after the next check up and get all the tests done, let's see what's going on.'

'I can't have babies, that's what's going on.'

'You don't know that for sure, you've got to get all the facts first.'

'What about you?'

'What about me?'

'You might need some tests too.'

'Well if I do, then I have them, but babe, continuing these baby blues ain't going to help us now, is it?'

Lizzy hadn't replied, feeling hurt by his lack of sympathy, but also feeling he would view her as foolish or childish if she continued. For the first time in their marriage Lizzy withheld her feelings and started looking at Tony through eyes that weren't quite as adoring.

However, looking back now, she considered that his change had begun during her second pregnancy when he had landed his first modelling job.

Having worked for years in factories, it had been huge for Tony. He'd said it had made him feel validated and recognised as more than just the good-looking guy round town. He'd felt like the world could see that he had potential at last and it was no longer Lizzy who was the only one who believed it.

The photo shoots had started small in the local area, but as his face had become known his popularity had spread and he'd been asked to go on photo shoots all over the country, spending nights away here and there. If it encompassed a weekend then Lizzy went too. And they'd worked out that it was on one of those weekends that they had conceived their third baby.

Lizzy smiled as she remembered. They'd attended their first charity gala, which Tony had been personally invited to. That night she'd seen him grow as an individual as the other guests were given the opportunity to see him as more than just a face in a magazine. His agent had taken him round and introduced him to all the influential people, all the main donors. They'd found out who he really was and what he was about, listening to his point of view and his thoughts on world events. That night Tony had realised he was someone of worth and his opinion did matter, that he was more than just a pretty face.

When they had gone to bed that night he had made love to her with so much emotion: touching every part of her with a renewed curiosity and looking deep into her eyes as though seeing her for the first time. She remembered holding his face between her hands when he was on top of her and seeing the depth of his soul shining through those violet blue eyes. She'd stroked his blond hair back and kissed him with a passion she didn't know she had. Lizzy had given every ounce of her heart and soul to Tony that night, completely vulnerable, yet completely secure in their love for each other.

This had made the revelation of their third pregnancy six weeks later more poignant. She had convinced herself that it had to be right this time, that it was destined to be.

Tony had been elated by the news, convinced that this was it for them too. Lizzy even remembered him coming home from work that day with alcohol-free wine and chocolates for her and a huge bouquet of red roses, an extravagance he would never have risked before the money from his modelling career had started coming in. She'd beamed at him when she'd opened the door.

'Are those for me?'

'No, they're for the baby,' he'd said with a sly grin.

Lizzy had laughed as she'd taken them from him, rubbing her tummy and feeling so hopeful that their lives were turning around at last.

And as Christmas had approached Tony's confidence had grown, taking on more and more jobs until he was able to resign from his day job at the shoe factory. He'd also started to receive a lot of fan mail and they'd spent many evenings laughing over some of the things in them. It had scared Lizzy a little, making her unsure whether all this attention might lead to her losing him, but he'd reassured her that although he enjoyed the fun of it, it would never be anything he could take seriously.

'Don't be silly, they're just letters, Liz, just people being hopeful, either to get a piece of me or my money.'

'Yeah, but you never know, if you met one of them or something.'

'Met one of them? Are you mad? I'm not about to do something that stupid.'

'You never know, you might meet someone at one of those mixer things you go to?'

Tony frowned at Lizzy and shook his head.

'What do you think, Lizzy, that I'll go off with just anyone? I love you, you mean the world to me, and we're about to start our own family. If anything, this is the time for us to enjoy everything we've worked towards.'

'Yeah, but often when people get famous they get all swept away with it, you know, all the parties, the drinking, the drugs, and then the women.'

'I'm a bit long in the tooth for that now, Liz; I did most of that in my twenties. I'm lucky to be getting this kind of attention as it is in my thirties; it's only because mature men are in fashion. It won't last long, Lizzy, so we have to make the most of it while we can. And I'm not stupid enough to give up everything we've built together for a short ride.'

By the time Christmas had come, Tony had become a local celebrity and life was good for them.

Thinking back now she hadn't really considered at the time how much the loss of their third child had affected him – just as she had shut herself off, so had he. The hospital had suggested counselling and they had gone, but Tony had only lasted a couple of sessions, saying that sitting and wallowing wasn't going to change anything – it wasn't going to bring Amber back. In truth Lizzy knew that opening up was hard for him; he was a doer not a talker. She'd gone on her own a couple more times, but not being able to share it with him had left her feeling even more bereft, so she'd stopped. And as the year had gone on, Tony had done something, he'd started going out and drinking, more and more. She believed it was behind his attitude change toward her, why he'd started to become so disrespectful – that and spending more time with Stuart Reed.

Chapter Seven

The clang of the feeding slot opening and a tray being shoved into the cell cut into Lizzy's memories. At the same time it threw one up a memory of a defining moment that illustrated how much Tony had changed.

They were in The Peacock on a Friday, a good six months after they had lost Amber. Lizzy was with the girls on one side of the pub and he was with the lads on the other, until one of them sauntered over. Stuart Reed, or Reedy as they called him, was an old friend of Tony's from his youth, who had returned to live in the area a few years before and started spending more and more time with Tony. He was a bit of a stirrer, loving to twist things up between people, saying things he shouldn't and generally being a big mouth, and that night he had turned it on her.

'Hey, Lizzy, Tony's says it's too big, is that true?'

She smiled but her forehead creased.

'What you on about, Reedy?'

'He says you ain't putting it to good use.'

The girls giggled, but Lizzy wasn't buying into it.

'Sorry Reedy, you're gonna have to spell that one out for me.'

'The car, Lizzy, the car, what else would I be on about? You know that big four wheel drive he bought, for when you had the big family? Bit of a waste now, ain't it?'

He walked away fast, laughing, but the girls were wide-eyed, the smiles wiped clean off their faces. Lizzy was furious and followed him back to Tony.

She watched Tony try and wipe the smile of his face as she approached. He failed.

'You think that's funny, do you? Him taking a pop at me about not providing a family?' She pointed at Reedy, her finger an inch from his face. He pretended to bite it. Tony giggled at him and took another swig of his beer.

'Answer me, Tony, I'm serious.'

'Oh calm down, Lizzy, he's just having a laugh. You take it too personally; you know what he's like.'

'Yeah, he's a fucking arsehole and we all know it.'

This wiped the smile off Tony's face.

'Hey! There's no call for that, we're just having a laugh.'

'Yeah, at my expense, and I'm not having it, Tony.'

His eyes turned cold as he looked at her.

'There's a lot you're not having these days, ain't there Liz?'

Lizzy was so shocked she couldn't find words to reply. Even Reedy's smile faltered. She blinked; her eyes big as she looked at him, waiting for some sense to return. But he held her glare, even taking another swig from his beer bottle as he did so. She spun round and stormed off.

She grabbed her glass from the table and downed her drink in one.

'We're going.'

None of the girls uttered a word, just stood and drained their glasses too, grabbing their coats as they followed her out.

Tony watched them leave, his cold stare unchanged, and Lizzy returned it.

That night he'd tumbled in at 4am, waking her up as he fell on the bed. He passed out, his snore stopping her from being able to fall back to sleep again. It was the first time Lizzy had come home alone on a night they were both out together and she hadn't liked it.

Lizzy chewed the overcooked meat and vegetables that had been served to her through the door without really tasting them. She heard some noise in the corridor and knew it wouldn't be long before it was time for the daily exercise and interaction with the other inmates. In the beginning she'd hated going out there, but now a few months on, she'd grown used to it.

By the time they opened her cell door Lizzy was ready to take a walk. There was only one courtyard, and unless you wanted to hang out in the corridors or the bathroom, it was the place to be.

Lizzy took the seat furthest from the building. There weren't many because the point was to walk about and stretch your legs, but having been out already that morning she didn't need to. She sat and enjoyed the evening light, which was fading faster now that they were passed the mid-summer point.

Carlene came to join her, sitting down with a sigh and watching the other inmates in silence. Lizzy didn't mind her company, she was calmer than the rest and quite rational – and she too was here because of a man.

They took solace in their common ground despite the different roads that had brought them there. Carlene had said enough for Lizzy to know that she'd been driven beyond her breaking point too. Only Carlene had had a small family depending on her, and the battle of keeping sane under physical and emotional abuse had been lost after he decided to start in on the children too. The blood on Carlene's hands had been shared with two of her children, and the burden of knowing that had kept Carlene out of mainstream prison and locked away in here, where there was a slim chance of some kind of help.

'How'd it go this morning?' Carlene knew Lizzy had been to court.

'Hung out to dry as usual.'

Carlene nodded. 'Nothing new then.'

'Just another 'friend' stepping forward to remind me I'm no good.'

Carlene took a breath in over her teeth.

'You don't want that shit getting you down. If nothing else, this teaches you there's only one person who can stand for you, and that's you.'

'I ain't getting much of a chance at that.'

'What'd your solicitor say?'

Lizzy laughed. 'He had hope. He thought we had 'blown holes' in some of what they said, but it's not like it's going to do me much good in the long run.'

'Might give you a chance to get out some day.'

'To what though? More screaming hordes spitting in my face? More betrayal and turned backs? Nah, I'm safer staying in here.'

'I get that Lizzy, but you can't think that way. You get out, you can start again. Go somewhere new, build something else.'

'I need a point, Carlene.'

'You're the point, Lizzy. You deserve better than that.'

'Do I? Didn't he too?'

Carlene shook her head. 'Gotta stop looking back. What's done is done. Accept it, and move on.'

'But is it fair for me to move on after what I did?'

'You've acknowledged what you did. You feel regret. You'll carry it the rest of your life – like me. But don't let it dictate who you are, don't let it make you a victim. You did it to stand up for yourself. You need to still do that.'

'You've got it sussed, Carlene.'

'No sister, I ain't. I'm struggling with it too. Every time one of my kids comes and sees me in here I go through it again. And knowing two of them are also in here some place doing time for me?' Carlene shook her head. 'I don't know if I will ever get past that one.'

Carlene's situation put Lizzy's in perspective; she only had herself to worry about, only herself to be accountable to. It was only on court days that Lizzy had to face anyone, and today had shown her that when she did, she wasn't going to take it lying down.

'I looked them all in the eye today, Carlene. His parents, his brother, it wasn't as hard as I thought.'

'There you go.'

Lizzy wanted to feel proud of herself, but it felt inappropriate in the face of what she had done – and especially where she was. Was it really a strength to look people in the eye after you had taken their beloved away, or was it just pure arrogance? She just needed them to understand there was reason behind her madness – and it was madness, a complete sickness. Now she was on all the pills, anti-depressants and anti-psychotics, she could think more clearly, could see it more easily. Although really did that help?

'They changed your meds, didn't they, Carlene? How's that going?'

'Yeah, much the same though, doesn't help that much. I mean, what can after what I've done?'

Lizzy gave a faint smile. Carlene couldn't be more right. In some ways she thought remaining in her deep dark rage and depression would enable her to cope better with what she had done – clarity of mind wasn't all it was cracked up to be. But she knew that being doped up wasn't either.

They sat in silence until the bell rang and then walked inside together. They gave each other a squeeze of the hand before they went to their separate cells.

Chapter Eight

Back in the silence of her cell, Lizzy took the sleeping pills they'd handed her when she'd gone in, and lay down hoping for more sleep. She'd slept heavily when she'd come back from the court and that was an unusual treat.

She let her mind wander back to when there had still been hope for their marriage. Despite his snide remarks on social occasions about her weight, and not caring about Reedy's cutting remarks, the couple of sessions in grief counselling had sparked something in Tony and he'd made attempts to connect with her and bring some warmth back to their marriage.

Lizzy remembered how special he had tried to make their next Christmas – the last good Christmas they had. She'd come home from work that Christmas Eve to find him already home, table laid, candles burning and him in nothing but a tiny serving apron and a dickie bow. He'd had a tea towel over one arm and a bottle of sparkling wine ready to serve.

'How long have you been waiting like that?' she'd laughed.

'Long enough. I've put the heating on,' he'd replied, his winning smile sparking her in all the right places.

He'd taken her by the hand, taken her bag and coat from her, and proceeded to serve dinner, teasing her all the way through with glimpses of what was to come.

By midnight they were lying together naked on the lounge floor in front of the fire, both exhausted and satisfied. He'd wrapped her up in the blanket from the back of the sofa and held her tight.

'We've got to remember this is about us, Lizzy, not about having a baby.'

'But it was what we both wanted.'

'Yeah, but we don't have to make it all that matters.'

'True.'

He kissed her softly then, stroking her hair as he did so. She had never felt so loved and cared for by anyone. Then he'd got up and taken a small box out from under the tree and handed it to her.

'It's not Christmas yet.'

'No, but I want you to open this now. It's waited long enough as it is.'

Lizzy sat up and took the tiny box, pulling the bow, letting it fall away with the paper. It looked like a ring box, but inside was something far more touching.

'I bought one each time you were pregnant. I didn't know what to do with them after we lost the last one, but after talking to that lady I realised there might not be anymore and it's important to me that you have them. So I got them set into something you can wear.'

Lizzy's forehead creased with curiosity as she opened the box, and inside she found a white gold pendant, with an L engraved in the middle, set with three pink diamonds. Her eyes filled with tears.

'Tony, it's beautiful!'

'Just like you, Lizzy.'

He kissed her gently on the forehead. 'Will you wear it?'

'Of course I will; I might never take it off again.'

He helped her do up the clasp at the back of her neck. The gems glistened in the firelight.

Lizzy put her hand to his cheek and stroked his brow with her thumb.

'Thank you, for making me feel so special.'

He smiled and kissed her gently on the lips, lying her back down and moving on top of her, his passion rising again.

Afterwards they lay watching the lights on the tree dance their jig and the ornaments twinkle in the reducing light of the dying fire. Only when the heat started to fade did they climb the stairs to bed, falling in and cuddling up tight to sleep in late on Christmas day.

Lizzy wondered what Christmas in prison was going to be like. She gave up trying to sleep and got up, walking round the cell to stretch her legs and take a pee in the tiny toilet in the corner. Then she went over to the window high up on the wall, and glimpsed the night sky. She didn't think it would be much different from this.

The following day was broken by a visit from her solicitor. He did all the talking informing her of their next court date scheduled for the end of the week.

'I'm considering putting you on the stand, how do you feel about that?'

Lizzy sat quite still, her hands resting in her lap. She looked at his face, his soft young cheeks and unwrinkled eyes, not a crease to be seen on his forehead; the hazel in his eyes making them appear bright. He couldn't have been much over twenty-five, twenty-eight tops.

'Lizzy, can you hear me?'

'Yes, I can hear you, Mark. Do you think it's a good idea? Do you think there is anything I can say to make this better?'

He sat back, blinking, her clear tone surprising him.

'I don't know. I just thought maybe you might like the opportunity to give your side of things.'

'My side? What side is that then? The psychotic, paranoid, betrayed wife, or the sad, childless, barren victim of other people's betrayal?'

'What's your truth, Lizzy?'

It was Lizzy's turn to blink. No one had ever asked her that before. And did she know the answer? She wasn't sure she did.

'I mean, you and I both know you're going to have to serve time, but maybe putting you on the stand, giving people the chance to get a glimpse of who you really are might make the difference between life and a chance at parole.'

'Not much of a choice, is it?' Her tone was soft as she looked down at her hands.

'But at least it IS a choice.'

She looked at him, knowing that she should feel grateful; knowing that people in her position shouldn't have choices, but the victim inside her wanted a 'do over'.

'Will I need to go on the stand on Friday, then?'

'No, we will need to do some prep for it. It'll be the next court date and probably the final one before the jury's decision. I should think it will be next week sometime, but we won't know until Friday.'

'So what will Friday be about?'

'Much the same as Monday, more witnesses speaking for the prosecution and a couple for us.'

'Who's speaking for us?' Lizzy was not aware that anyone was in her corner.

'We have your sister as a character witness …'

'My sister?' Lizzy hadn't thought her sister would be supporting her.

'Yes, she wants the jury to know who you really are, not the person you are being portrayed as in the media or in the courtroom.'

'But I haven't seen her in years.'

'I know, she told me. She said that she feels partly responsible because she wasn't there for you when you needed her most.' Mark hesitated, giving Lizzy a careful look. 'After you lost your last child.'

'Have you met with her, then?'

'Yes, she approached me. She's been at all of your court appearances.'

Lizzy shook her head, her eyes squinting as she pulled a face. 'I don't understand, she hasn't written or visited or anything. Why now?'

Mark shrugged. 'Family loyalty, maybe? These things often make people stop and think. She didn't really say why you two weren't in touch, is there anything there I need to know?'

Lizzy let out a breath. 'Gosh, I don't know. I haven't thought about it in some time. We drifted really, rather than had a row or anything. She was never keen on Tony, she made that clear. Someone with his reputation, she didn't trust him.' Lizzy snorted. 'Turns out she had good reason. And so she kept her distance. She moved away with her husband's job too.' Lizzy's eyes faded a little. 'Let me think about it, Mark. If there's anything I'll let you know. Will we be meeting again before Friday?'

Mark sat up, gathering his papers together. 'I wasn't planning on it, but if you want me to, I can? Otherwise I'll see you Friday morning at the courthouse.'

'Friday will be fine.' Lizzy tried to stifle a yawn with her hand. 'I'm sorry, I get so tired these days with any interaction.'

'I saw that on Monday. You get some rest and think about what you want to say if I do put you on the stand.'

Mark stood, coming round the side of the table to Lizzy as she stood. He looked at her with a small smile and put out his hand to shake. She took it. He said, 'It was nice to finally chat with you properly; it's a big improvement on the semi-comatose woman I've met so far. I think it's a good sign, and it gives me confidence we can win our plea of diminished responsibility. Take it easy Lizzy, and I'll see you Friday.'

'Thanks, Mark.'

It had been a long time since anyone had spoken to Lizzy that tenderly and with sympathy in their voice. She even managed to return a small smile.

Chapter Nine

Lizzy came out groggy and disgruntled the following morning when she was called to see another visitor. After a night spent tossing and turning with thoughts of her sister, and how little contact they'd had over the last few years, she half wondered if it might be her visiting, although really she expected it to be her solicitor. So when she saw the bottle-blonde sitting in the visitor room the surprise shut her down, forcing a stone-faced expression, and her stomach tightened as she approached.

When Sue saw Lizzy coming into the room she stood up with a jerk, almost toppling the chair behind her. She looked nervous and shaken. Lizzy wasn't used to seeing her like that, she'd only known the cocky overconfident girl who used to take the lead in most things.

'Lizzy, you agreed to see me.'

Lizzy raised an eyebrow but didn't speak. Clearly Sue didn't know that her attendance wasn't optional and she was never informed who she was about to see.

When Lizzy slipped into the seat opposite, Sue sat down too, shuffling her seat up to the table and leaning on it, her hands outstretched as though wanting some sort of contact.

'You're probably wondering why I've come, aren't you?'

Lizzy remained silent, only looking at her more closely, keeping eye contact even though Sue's eyes flitted all over the place.

'I felt bad about Monday. It wasn't right to give evidence against you. And well …' Sue fumbled. 'I just, I dunno, all those questions and the way your solicitor put things, I sort of looked at it all a bit different, I suppose.'

Lizzy raised her eyebrows but still didn't open her mouth. This seemed to encourage Sue.

'I suppose I never really thought about me and Tony as a betrayal on you. I'd slept with him first and then watched him chase after you. It was never about you, it was more about finding out if he would still have me. And he would. Dunno if that says more about me or him?' Sue snorted. It was a laugh Lizzy had heard many times.

'When I first saw him with that Sally I was shocked, Lizzy, I really was! I didn't expect him to ever do that to you, not like that, not round town. And she didn't seem to care either. And I want you to know I told him too, I asked him what the fuck he was doing with her, but you know what he was like Lizzy, no one could tell him. He just laughed at me.'

Sue's fingers were twisting and turning the whole time she was speaking. Lizzy looked at them to try and still a hysterical laugh that was building in her chest.

'A couple of the lads didn't like it either, and there was a row one night about it.'

Lizzy looked at her face again. These kind of details interested her. Sue registered the look and carried on.

'It was Eddie and Nathan, they thought it was uncalled for. It actually caused a scuffle between Tony and Eddie, and Nate tried to step in, but they're both so much bigger than him.'

Lizzy could see it in her mind: Eddie was a good foot taller than Tony and the same width ways. They'd been best friends for years and she'd noticed a cooling off between them, but Lizzy had put that down to Tony's modelling jobs getting in the way at weekends. And Nate, he was much shorter than most of the lads – although his barrel size gave him weight that people didn't mess with.

'Eddie told Tony he was being a "fucking twat" if I remember right, and he even turned to Sally and called her an "unscrupulous bitch" before walking out. Nate had shrugged at Tony and said "Sorry mate, I agree with him. This is well out of order" and that was that. And well, if they couldn't make a difference I know us girls wouldn't get through to him. I know some girls talked about having a go at her too, but really none of us knew her, and … well … if that was what they wanted to do it wasn't really up to us.' Sue stopped, her eyes sad and imploring as she said, 'And none of us had seen you either, so we just thought, well, let sleeping dogs lie or whatever.' She paused. 'I'm so sorry, Lizzy.'

Lizzy still didn't speak. She just looked at Sue and let the emotions wash over her, refusing to allow them to show on her face. It was painful to hear and to think about; knowing they had all known, but there was some comfort in hearing that even the lads didn't like it. She had imagined they had patted him on the back, even envied him a little bit – and maybe a couple of them had even tried it on with that Sally woman, thinking that if she put out with one married man, maybe she would another.

It also explained why Reedy had been around more, he'd been okay with it: approving, thinking it was what she deserved. Tony would have needed at least one person to make him feel okay about it.

Sue sat back a little. 'That's all I came to say really, Lizzy. I don't know if it makes any difference, but I needed to say it to you – to your face. I've been a shit friend to you for years now, and I haven't got an excuse really.'

Lizzy still didn't speak.

'How are you, Lizzy? What's it like in here? Are you alright?'

Lizzy grunted a half laugh through her nose.

'Am I alright, Sue? What do you think after what I've done?'

Sue looked down at her own hands, not knowing how to respond, so Lizzy carried on.

'But yeah, it's okay in here. Not as bad as you'd imagine. But then they've got me locked down for a good twenty-two hours out of the day.'

'Shit that must be hard.'

'Nah, actually I quite like it, although I'm told I'm not supposed to.'

Sue smiled. 'Yeah, but I get that maybe being alone is what you need right now with everything going on. If he hadn't been doing all that modelling there wouldn't be half this fuss.' Lizzy thought about the crowds they tried to protect her from at every trial. 'I was so stunned when I first heard, and all the gossip about it and then the papers. It's made it all so messy. After the court case on Monday I realised that you were just human like the rest of us, and hurting more than any of us had realised.'

Silence fell between them. Lizzy knew that Sue was trying to make it alright between them, but she didn't know if it ever could be, or even if there would be a point to it. But she knew it had taken a lot for her to come here in person and say it all.

'Thanks for coming, Sue, you're the only one that has.'

Sue stared at Lizzy. 'Really? None of your family have been?'

'Well, there's only my sister really, not heard from my brother in years, he lives in Italy, and well mum's in the home now. I found out yesterday my sister's going to be a character witness for me on Friday, but she hasn't made any contact with me. I did wonder if it would be her when they told me I had a visitor.'

'I'm sorry to hear that, Lizzy, I thought you had more support than that.'

Lizzy gave a sharp laugh, causing Sue to jerk back.

'Support? No, there's been none of that for years.' Sue looked guilty again and Lizzy was starting to find it tiresome. 'It's done now, Sue. I made my bed, now I've got to lie in it.'

Sue gave a tight smile, and shuffled herself together as she stood. Lizzy remained seated.

'I'd best go then. I'll be there Friday. I'll be sitting on your side.'

Lizzy bit her lip so she didn't say "so you can gossip about it all to everyone after?" knowing that Sue was trying her best to make amends the only way she knew how, even though it was too late. She smiled at Sue and said, 'Thanks for bothering, Sue.'

'You're welcome, Lizzy, it's the least I could do.'

The guard had come over to escort Sue out and Lizzy waited to be taken to her cell. This had put her head in a spin, and she looked forward to the quiet isolation to process it in.

Chapter Ten

Lizzy heard the door lock and let herself physically relax. She lay down on the cot and let Sue's visit flood her mind. She imagined all the scenarios of what Sue had described, seeing them all in the pub, their expressions, their outrage back and forth. She hadn't thought anyone had really noticed what was going on with Tony and his woman – and least of all cared. Although by that time she'd withdrawn from them, no longer trusting any of them anyway – and none of them had proved themselves worthy of her trust either. Sue's friendship was long gone, and Lizzy had befriended a younger crowd from her work who had no association with her usual group. It made it easier. They didn't know any of her personal history and she could pretend she was someone else.

She remembered one of the first nights she'd gone out with them and how she'd bumped into a couple of members of her old group. They had looked a bit shocked, even put out that she was out with other people, but they hadn't said anything, just watched her from a distance, heads together gossiping.

For a while it had been good, it had been refreshing, but slowly Lizzy had tired of their youth, of their giggles over lads. She had gradually stopped going out with them, until eventually she was sitting in on her own watching telly on a Friday night. And it had been on one of those nights that she'd had her suspicions confirmed.

She'd watched Tony get ready to go out, preening and primping in front of the mirror in the hallway. He'd made more effort than usual that night and she'd commented on it.

'You look all dolled up.'

'Got to make a good impression,' he said, while slicking back his hair with some gel.

'On who?'

He threw her a quick glance. 'No one in particular, just the public at large. I've got a reputation to uphold.'

Lizzy laughed. 'You've always had a reputation, Tony, that's nothing new.'

'Funny, Liz, you know what I mean.'

'Yeah, but who's all the aftershave for? And that's the expensive stuff, isn't it? Thought you saved that for special nights?'

'Every nights a special night when I'm out on the town.'

Lizzy gave him an incredulous look. 'Yeah right.'

The doorbell rang and Lizzy had answered it. Reedy had been on the doorstep, giving her one of his inane grins. She didn't speak and left him at the door as she returned to the lounge. He'd stepped inside and she'd listened to them in the hallway.

'You ready to go, Tony boy? She's ready and waiting.'

'Shhh, you idiot! Not here!'

'Oops.' Reedy had giggled. 'Forgot you don't want her to know.'

'What? 'course I bloody don't, what are you, stupid or something?'

'It's not like she would give a shit.'

'You wanna fucking bet?'

Reedy had walked to the front door. 'Come on, let's get out of here then.'

Tony had grabbed his coat, and shouted, 'Bye, Liz.'

She'd mumbled, 'Bye' back as she'd sat there absorbing what she'd just heard. The minute she'd heard the front gate shut she'd raced up the stairs. Her first thought had been to go out after them, but she hadn't been sure she'd find them and she hadn't wanted to risk him seeing her either – not at that point anyway. So she'd looked round their bedroom and thought about where she might find something, anything that would tell her more about what she'd just heard.

She'd started with the wardrobe, going through the pockets of all his jackets, and come up with nothing other than a few business cards and some cash, so she'd gone downstairs and had a look through the coats on the coat hooks by the door.

It was in one of them that she'd found her first piece of "evidence": a tissue with lipstick on it. It had definitely been lipstick, she'd been able to smell it. Had he wiped it off her, or himself? There had been no telling. Tony had liked to carry tissues, always wanting to appear chivalrous in times of need. Lizzy scoffed at the idea now; he'd been far from that those last few years.

And then there had been the clincher, in his inside pocket: a comb. To most people it would have meant nothing, but as his wife, Lizzy had known it wasn't Tony's. It'd been lilac and not a small stubby one like most men carried, but a long handle one – that was how she'd spotted it, poking out of the top of the pocket.

Lizzy's stomach had sunk with the discovery. If he'd been carrying her comb how long had this been going on? How personal had it got? Tony hadn't been the kind of guy to carry round girls items, she'd known that for a fact.

She'd taken the comb into the lounge and sat there looking at it. She'd wondered whether to leave it out for him, let him know she'd found it, or even ask him about it. But no, if she'd done that he would have just lied and been on his guard. She'd wanted to find out exactly what was going on and she'd only be able to do that if he didn't think she had any inkling about it. She'd thought it was crazy that he didn't already know she suspected what with the increasing nights he'd spent out overnight claiming to have crashed at Reedy's house, let alone two trips to modelling shoots in London on his own. When she'd called to speak to him at one of the hotels, the surprise and confusion in the receptionist's voice when she'd said it was Mrs Dyson calling had been blatant proof something was up. Lizzy hadn't been stupid. He could keep pretending all was right in their world and in their marriage, even though they'd both known it wasn't. But being lied to wasn't something she would tolerate, and infidelity? That was a deal breaker and he'd known it.

Lying in the darkening cell, hearing her dinner being shoved through the slot, Lizzy felt the anger rise again, the anger she had felt for years before the fateful night that had put her here. And in truth it would never be gone; there would always be a part of it left within her. It had driven her for so long; it had enabled her to function in a way that might not have been rational, but had got her through some of the worst of the hurt. Although right now it was only going to stop her from getting some sleep.

Lizzy got up and ate the food they'd passed through. Then she sat cross-legged on the floor by her cot and closed her eyes, focusing on her breathing, pushing all other thoughts out.

Her therapist had recommended that she do this daily. She'd been dubious it would really work and her first attempts had been half-hearted, but once she began it grew on her. She still didn't do it very often, but after a day like today, when everything had been uncovered, laid bare, leaving her feeling raw, it was the only thing that soothed her. She breathed slowly. Every time she became aware she was thinking about it again, she stopped and went back to her breathing and gradually let it go. Tiredness swept in where the anger had been and she crawled back onto the cot and let sleep take her, slipping into a deep slumber she'd not reached in weeks.

Chapter Eleven

In the morning it was therapy time. They had initially put Lizzy in group therapy but she'd been too tight lipped for their liking, letting others do all the talking, so they'd assigned a personal therapist to her in the hope she'd open up.

'How's your week been, Lizzy? You've been out to court I gather?'

Lizzy shuffled in the plastic seat and tried to look out of the window but it was too high, she could only see clouds.

'Yeah, another trip down memory lane. Another reminder of the animal they all see me as.'

'Do you really think they see you like that?'

She looked at her therapist, with his bright orange jumper screaming its colour at her, against his olive pallor, giving him a sickly glow in the dull light. The lines on his face told her he wasn't as young as he used to be.

'Should I care how they see me?'

'You're deflecting. Tell me how it went for you.'

She searched the clouds outside for the answers before responding.

'Not much different from the other times. Chained up like I'm some kind of wild beast who'll take a chunk out of anyone that passes; listening to them all lie about what a wonderful guy he was, and how dreadful I was to him. They even had a classic this time, dredged up an old friend of mine to give evidence against me.'

'Was that hard?'

Her sharp gaze returned to his watery grey eyes.

'What do you think? Of course it was. And then she turned up here yesterday, pleading her case, wanting to be friends again, or at least wanting to be forgiven.'

'And did you?'

'She hurt me such a long time ago, but hearing her on the stand blaming me for it all, it felt like it had only just happened. But then yesterday she told me the trial had shown her a different perspective, like she finally saw me for the first time and all that he had done to me. And she told me things that made me realise that I hadn't been the only one thinking what he was doing wasn't right, and that was odd, like all that time I thought I was alone with it, and I hadn't been. I dunno …' Lizzy looked out of the window again. 'She apologised, even said she had been a shit friend. Can I afford not to forgive her?'

'What do you mean?'

'I never imagined Sue of all people would come and say that to me – not after everything that had happened between us, and then with her giving evidence against me. So it's a big deal, and I can't take that lightly, and holding onto the bad feeling doesn't help anyone, does it?'

The therapist shook his head slightly and smiled. 'No, it doesn't.'

'I have to let it go, I have to let it all go, but it's hard.' She sat up straighter and said, 'I meditated last night.'

He raised his eyebrows. 'That's good.'

'Yeah. It was all spinning and the rage came up again. Haven't felt that in a while.'

'What were you thinking about?'

'The night I found out he was cheating. Finding her comb in his jacket pocket. How it made me feel to think that he was getting intimate with someone else.'

'What do you think that rage is about?'

'Hurt, fear, betrayal. Disappointed that I didn't mean enough to him anymore to stay faithful. He'd been hurting me for so long; this was like the final straw. After that night I could no longer try and think nice thoughts about him, be loving and warm. On the outside they all thought I was shaping up at last, but in fact on the inside I was burning up with rage. Although he knew it – yeah he knew it.'

'How did you think he knew it?'

'That's when things started to get physical – violent, not sexual. That's when I started pushing him like I would never have dared before.'

'What do you think you were trying to achieve by doing that?'

'I think I was hurting so bad on the inside I wanted to be hurt on the outside too. I wanted to make him feel bad, I wanted to hurt him, emotionally and physically. I wanted him to share in my rage too.'

Lizzy gave a wobbly sigh and tears sprung into her eyes. 'I drove him so hard too, the nights he relented and struck me I could hear him later, pummelling the punch bag in the basement. One night he came up and his hands were covered in blood.'

'What did you do?'

'I saw him in the kitchen, rinsing them off and went to the bathroom cabinet to get the salve and bandages. He let me bandage them for him. He didn't speak and neither did I. A silent truce.'

Lizzy pulled a tissue out of the box on the table, and brought it up to her nose, letting the tears fall untouched.

'For a moment there I thought we might turn it around, you know? Might try and mend things, but days later he was out with her again.'

'How did you know?'

Lizzy grunted a sarcastic laugh into the tissue as she wiped it across her nose. 'He went out all dolled up, pretending to be out with Reedy as usual. I followed them to her house.'

'And they didn't see you?'

'I dunno, and I didn't much care by then. I was on the moped I used for work, had my helmet on, so I wouldn't be too obvious. Depends if he was looking, I don't think he much cared even if he was.'

'You couldn't be sure of that.'

'Yeah, well it doesn't matter much now anyway, does it? He's dead. I killed him.'

Her therapist raised his eyebrows, blinking at the statement.

'Well I suppose that's one way of looking at it.'

Lizzy laughed. 'Is there any other way?'

He smiled. 'No, no there's not really. But if he was punching punch bags after a fight with you, it shows he had some emotion about it. And letting you dress his wounds, that's sort of like letting you heal that pain in some ways. Had you expected him to stop seeing her after that? Had you discussed the affair with him?'

'Discussed it with him?' Lizzy eyes were wide. 'I screamed it at him a few times, but he refused to deny or confirm it; he'd just keep saying, "I'll only talk to you when you stop screaming at me. You're not rational when you're like this." But it only made me worse, and afterwards … well, either he walked out or I did, either from the room or the house. There'd be no discussion after. None.'

'So in some ways you were both ignoring it.'

'Well, he was.'

'But by never trying to talk to him calmly about it so were you, weren't you?'

Lizzy gave him a black look. 'Don't you fucking start.'

He put his hands up. 'Sorry, sorry. I'm just trying to understand what communication there was outside of the fights. What did you talk about?'

'Just day to day stuff: my work, his work, where he was off to next for a modelling job; food shopping, news, any gossip about friends. But we didn't see a lot of each other, we never sat in together to watch something. If I was watching telly, he'd be on the computer, or vice versa. Neither of us would make an effort to talk about anything.'

'So how would the fights start?'

'Usually about him going out: I wouldn't want him to go, or me wanting to know where he was going. Occasionally he'd try and get me to go out with the girls – try and relieve his guilt, I reckon. He hated me sitting in all the time. Dunno why though as it was perfect for him to carry on with his woman.'

'And the two of you never went out together?'

Lizzy pulled a face. 'It was very rare; only to big opening gigs or events to do with his modelling. I saw less and less of my friends over the last couple of years, so I didn't go out round town much. I cut myself off, I suppose.'

'You suppose, or do you think you did? And why do you think you did?'

'I did, and it was a combination of things really, starting with losing the babies – by the third one everyone seemed a bit tired of it. They didn't want to know anymore. The last two just sort of topped me off and it all went downhill from there.'

'There was no one you felt you could turn to?'

'No. I exhausted all my friendships, with family too.'

'And you didn't seek help? Counselling of some sort?'

'We had a few sessions after we lost Amber, our third. But I couldn't face it after we lost Daniel, our fifth and last. I was so lost in it all.' Lizzy wiped her hand over her face and let out a big sigh. 'I couldn't really think straight, and once I knew about the affair my main focus became tracking Tony.'

The therapist nodded and glanced at the clock. 'Times up I'm afraid, but you did really good today, it was great to finally hear you talk about some of this stuff.' He grabbed his diary. 'I see you're in court tomorrow. Do you still want to meet Monday? Or would you prefer to bring it forward to Saturday?'

'Monday's good. I have no idea what Friday's going to throw up, so it'll give me time. And my solicitor wants me to take the stand too.'

'What, tomorrow?'

'No, at the next court date, the last one before the judge makes her decision.'

'That's pretty big. Are you okay with that?'

'We discussed it and he thinks it will mean the difference between a chance of release or life inside for good.'

Her therapist raised his eyebrows and pursed his bottom lip. 'Yeah that's quite major. Do you want to?'

'I think I'm ready, and really at this stage it can't hurt, right?'

'Well, there is that.'

He stood up and put out his hand. 'Good seeing you today, Lizzy; it's good to hear you finally do some talking. I'll see you Monday.'

'Thanks Doc.'

'It's John.'

'I know, but I prefer Doc.' She smiled and he returned it.

'It's nice to see your smile too, makes you look so different – younger.'

Lizzy laughed. 'Bet you say that to all the girls.'

'Just the ones in the psychiatric wing.' He winked.

Chapter Twelve

Lizzy left her therapy session laughing and it felt odd. After a few seconds she stopped. She was in prison for murdering her husband and his lover, laughing with her shrink seemed inappropriate.

Talking about Tony and their fights brought back so many images, but the one that stayed with her was the one after she'd come home from the hospital, after the fifth and final miscarriage. Having reached twenty weeks with this one she'd thought they were going to make it. Even Tony, who had distanced himself after the fourth, (which had only reached eight weeks), had started to talk about baby things. He mentioned baby furniture and started talking about ideas for the nursery, wanting to revamp it entirely, calling it a fresh start.

Then the horror had started and they'd rushed to the hospital. They didn't speak a word through the whole process but he hadn't left her side: sitting with her and breathing with her, squeezing her hand, supporting her where needed, and when the baby had come out, his face, the sorrow and the joy. He'd handed their little boy to her and there had been nothing but tears and him stroking Lizzy's hair. No words. Daniel's beautiful silent face, tiny but perfect.

And she hadn't spoken for more than a week. She couldn't, not even at the funeral when Daniel was laid to rest with his sister, Amber. Tony had removed everything remotely baby-related from the house. She had no idea where he took it but it didn't need to be discussed, it just needed to be gone. The first words she had spoken were a whisper one night.

'I can't do this again. It's over.'

He'd put his arm round her and brought her into him, kissing her softly on the head and rubbing her back. He'd whispered, 'Okay' back, and that was that. No further discussion.

And although that had been what Lizzy had initially wanted – no further discussion about babies or having a family, a couple of months down the line she'd wanted to discuss their relationship and what this meant for them. But Tony hadn't.

'What does this mean for us? It doesn't mean anything for us.'

'Shouldn't we think about adopting, fostering – or splitting up?'

The last caused him to pause as he came back into the bedroom from the en-suite bathroom.

'Split up? Why should we split up?'

'Maybe you'd like a family with someone who can have babies, whose body hasn't failed her.'

'Don't be silly, Liz, it's never been just about the babies and you know that.'

'Yeah, but what's the point of us, then?'

'Point? What are you talking about? We love each other, that's the point of us.'

'Yeah, but what are we going to do now?'

Lizzy came out of the bathroom and got into bed, cuddling up to Tony.

'I don't get you, Liz. Nothing has changed between us, things are the same. We just carry on.'

'Well, do you want to adopt or foster?'

Tony put out his bottom lip as he thought about it for a moment. 'I've not really thought about it, but my gut feeling is no, not really. It takes a long time and hoops to jump through, and … I dunno.'

'We could look into it and at least find out …?'

'If you want to do that, Liz, then go ahead, but I'll tell you now, I'm not keen to jump into anything straight away. After losing Daniel, we could do with a rest, maybe a holiday. Kick back for a bit.'

'Okay.'

Lizzy had let it go but deep down she was disappointed. She wanted them to be parents, to be a family. And eventually she started pushing for it. He'd come home and she'd give him all the research she had printed off that day, wanting him to read it immediately so they could talk about it. The fourth time she did this, he got annoyed.

'Enough with this Liz! I thought I told you I didn't want to do this right now. I want to take a break from all this kid and baby stuff.'

'But you told me to look into it?'

'Yeah, YOU look into it. I'm not interested.'

'So you don't want to do this, then?'

He looked at her, a frown furrowing his eyebrows. 'Did I stutter? No, I don't want to do this, not right now!'

'Or not ever.' She mumbled as she took the papers over to the bin.

'What?' He turned to face her. 'What did you say? Why are you pushing me on this, Liz?'

'I need to know. I need to know if you want this or you don't. I need to know if we are EVER going to have a family together.' She tried not to shout, but her volume rose.

Tony rolled his eyes. 'Liz, we've just lost our fifth child – FIFTH Liz! Does that sound like it's going to happen to you?'

Lizzy's stomach clenched. 'So you are saying no to this, then?'

'If you keep on pushing me, I will.'

'I just need to know, Tony, I need to know what we're going to do.'

'Do? Nothing at the moment, Liz. I think we need a rest, don't you? We've just lost our fifth child, we need a breather.'

'You think I don't know we've lost our fifth child, Tony? You think I don't feel that every second of every minute of every day?' Lizzy tried to control her voice. 'You think I don't know this means I've failed you, that I've failed us?'

Tony winced and walked over to her, trying to put his arm round her, but she pulled away, refusing to let him comfort her.

'How do you think I feel walking round feeling totally shit about myself all day, every day? Seeing other people with children, pregnant women with another one in the buggy, showing off how fucking successful they've been! How do you think it feels to know that I can never do that, that I will never be able to carry a child? Hmmm, have you any fucking clue, Tony?'

'Liz don't,' Tony said. She knew he wanted her to stop, but she couldn't.

'And you want to take a breather, you want to have a rest? You threaten to say you won't look into any other way we could become parents because I'm pushing you? Thanks for that, Tony, thanks for that. It's alright for you, the big model, everyone thinking you're so hot, and there's nothing wrong with you, is there? Your boys work just fine, you can get me knocked up no problem. And what must they all be thinking, huh? What must they all be saying? What's he doing with her, eh? What the fuck is he wasting his time on her for when he can have anyone he wants, and they could probably give him ten live babies if he liked!'

Lizzy was screaming by this point, tears streaming down her bright red face. Tony had remained silent while she'd escalated.

'And you can just carry on, can't you? Go out drinking with the lads, have a few beers, it'll be fine. They'll all pat you on the back, tell you what a good bloke you are to stand by a woman who is clearly so totally un-fucking-worthy of you, who's been nothing but a burden to you for years now. Reedy taking the piss out of your nice big family car, telling you, you should get rid of it, like your wife. He probably does say that, doesn't he? That I'm a waste of space and you should get someone else?'

Tony's nostrils had flared and she could see his hands were clenched into fists.

'You don't know shit about my friends, so don't start in on them. This isn't about them.'

'Oh, it's not, is it? It's fine for them to bad mouth ME, but it's not okay for me to say a word against them! Where does your loyalty lie, Tony, hmmm? It's not with me anymore, is it?'

Lizzy had moved right up to him, shouting into his face. He hadn't stepped back, and his face was set in a sneer.

'So I have to be happy with "We'll take a breather Liz; we need a rest. We'll talk about it after." Like fuck you will! You just want some time to assess the situation, and fuck off out with your mates.'

'Don't keep pushing me, Liz!'

'Or what? What you gonna do?'

She was up in his face, her eyes burning into his. He'd stared back, his eyes dilated with rage. She'd known that look; she'd seen it a dozen times, when he'd been about to take a swing at someone, but she hadn't cared.

He'd broken eye contact and shoved her back so he could step past her, grabbing his coat off its hook in the hallway and marching to the door.

'I'll be back later, when you've calmed down.' He'd shouted, slamming the front door, her rage ending with it as though the two had collided.

She'd stood there feeling sick – mostly from shame, but anger had been mixed in too. How dare he walk out the door!

Chapter Thirteen

It was shame now more than anger that consumed her as she lay thinking about it.

Her thoughts were temporarily interrupted by screams from further down the corridor. Jeanie was off again; her ranting and screaming fits had become a regular occurrence. Lizzy wondered if she was claustrophobic or scared of the dark – not that the guards cared. If she went on for long enough they might come and sedate her. She'd seen Jeanie out in the yard a couple of times but never spoken to her. She didn't speak to many of the inmates, Carlene was really the only one. Carlene knew Jeanie but hadn't gone into detail about her story, just that once they'd found the body parts hidden in the loft she'd been sectioned. Carlene had mentioned it because she believed there was a man behind it – Carlene believed there was a man behind every woman being in here. Lizzy thought that was a bit extreme.

As the screams subsided to sobs, Lizzy knew Jeanie was finished for the night and tried to imagine what it would be like to feel trapped in here. Lizzy didn't feel trapped at all, she felt safe. She felt protected from the outside world – a world which had overwhelmed her for the last few years. In here the paranoid thoughts no longer ran rampant through her mind. She no longer had to think about what others might be doing behind her back, what they might be thinking about her, or saying about her. They no longer mattered. She didn't have to think about all the areas of her life where she was failing. She could gather her thoughts without arguing with them, and without creating little scenarios of imagined arguments with all the people who had let her down, whom she'd felt betrayed her. She didn't have to do any of that anymore because she no longer had to see any of those people, and it was such a relief.

But what did taunt her were the memories of Tony and how she had behaved, and how he had responded. She had never expected him to treat her with such disrespect after all they had been through. She'd deserved better than that, or thought she had. She'd been prepared to consider that it was his way of coping with it all, especially after the fifth and final miscarriage. That year had been particularly bad and she had been so awful towards him. But he had known she was struggling and he had stepped away from her rather than forward. The more she seemed to need him, the more distant he had become. And each time they'd been out together his snide remarks and nasty comments seemed to have become more and more personal, right up until that final time, at the charity ball in London. She was done after that. It had been the last event she'd gone to with him.

Attending had been especially hard for her due to her weight gain over that year. She had failed to take off any of the baby weight since the pregnancy in the spring, and comfort eating afterwards had only added to it. The dress she had bought had been designed to cover most of it, or at least divert the eyes away from it, but her self-esteem had been at its lowest point. And with him looking a million dollars and the cameras going mad to get shots of him, it had been hard being on his arm.

People had shouted at her to move away so she didn't 'ruin' the shot, but she had reassured herself it was just because they'd wanted him alone in it. She had even thought she had heard a press photographer shout, 'get out of the way fatty' but she couldn't be sure, there had been so many people calling out. And Tony had obliged them all, leaving her at the side to watch as he posed alone and with other celebrities.

The fixed smile on her face had hurt that night.

At their table, all the women had looked perfect: not a crease on their skin let alone a belly roll in sight. Lizzy had been glad for a table to hide hers behind. And after dinner when the music had started, Tony had been pulled up to dance with more than one woman and she had remained seated watching him enjoy the night.

It had been towards the end when it had happened. Tony had returned to the table sweating a little, having danced a fast number with some hot Brazilian beauty. He'd stood next to her, picking up his drink to refresh himself. Another man seated at their table with his wife had asked the fateful question:

'Aren't you going to dance with your wife, Tony? Surely she deserves a spin on the floor.'

Tony had laughed, and given him a wink as he'd said, 'I like someone a bit lighter on her feet, if you know what I mean.'

The man had blinked and said, 'I'm not quite sure I do.'

'Well it's not so easy to move round a dance floor when you're with someone carrying that much weight.'

The man had looked shocked and glanced at Lizzy wide-eyed, expecting a reaction, but Lizzy had remained expressionless. Her gut had clenched and her breathing hitched, but she had sat tight, careful not to show how much his comment had sliced through her and willing her eyes not to allow a tear. But she couldn't smile at the man.

Instead his wife had spoken for her. 'That's a little uncalled for isn't it, Tony? It's been a rough year for you both I understand?'

She'd looked at Lizzy with sympathetic eyes and Lizzy had had to take a deep breath to keep control of her emotions, although Tony's next words had shut her down completely.

'Yeah, it has, but you've got to get over it some time and move on. You can't just let yourself go. Stuffing your face ain't gonna make it any better now, is it?'

The woman's jaw had actually dropped and the man had sat forward as though about to speak, but Tony had winked again and returned to the dance floor before he could.

Lizzy had known she couldn't stay after that. She'd gathered her purse and mumbled, 'Excuse me' as she'd left the table. She hadn't been foolish enough to go out the front entrance with the press still out there, instead she'd gone up to one of the doorman in the foyer and asked if she could hail a cab from a side entrance, claiming she wasn't feeling well and needed to leave as soon as possible. It hadn't been far from the truth. He'd been courteous and quick, and she had been in the back of a cab within minutes, not quite sure where she was going. Knowing Tony wouldn't come after her, she'd decided to go back to the hotel, again making sure she went in via a back entrance, and asked for another room, a single room that she would pay for herself.

No one queried her reasons, the look on her face had been enough, and before she knew it she was alone in her own room overlooking the busy West End Street. She knew he wouldn't try and find her as she had explicitly asked them at reception not to give him her room number. Again they hadn't questioned it, just written it down and reassured her that all of the staff would be told.

After a restless night, she'd checked out early, the only question asked: did she want to leave a note? She said they could tell him she'd checked out if he asked, but she doubted he would. And once home she'd cried with wild abandon, knowing he was unlikely to be back anytime soon. She'd been right: he'd rolled in at gone midnight, steaming drunk.

From that point on there had been no more talk only shouting, broken by a silent truce through Christmas until New Year. The hurt grew into resent, fuelling rage in both of them. And once she'd confirmed his affair it had turned physical.

Lizzy had thrown the first punch, not expecting it to make much of an impact, but it had shocked Tony so much he had responded in kind, leaving her with a shiner he had the decency to be ashamed about.

After the disaster of the holiday with the girls the previous spring, Lizzy had already distanced herself from her friends, so there'd been no one to turn to. And despite finding new friends, she didn't want them to know what was going on, so she'd started distancing herself from them too. She couldn't get her mind free of the turmoil her crumbling relationship was creating. She had retreated into her own little place of rage and spent most of her time stalking them.

The upside of this new obsession was weight loss: Lizzy had started going to the gym and pulled herself together – or so she wanted people to think. The reality was that she'd refused to sit by and be ridiculed as the one who let herself go. She'd refused to let him mock her anymore – especially his mate Reedy who was coming round their house more and more. His malicious back-handed comments went deeper each time, not that she'd let him or Tony know that, but she used each one to keep motivated. She was going to look good and flaunt it in their faces. She was going to make them all wonder what was wrong with HIM for going off with other women.

Lizzy lay on her cot and looked down at her body. If anything she was skinny now, but with little appetite and restricted food it couldn't be any other way. She sighed and rolled over, knowing she had to try and get some sleep with the busy day ahead. She worked to block more memories, and the effort finally wore her out enough to drop off.

Chapter Fourteen

The journey to the courthouse was uneventful, although Lizzy thought the crowd seemed much bigger this time. No doubt the press were escalating the story as it wouldn't be long now before there was a verdict.

Lizzy's solicitor was in the foyer waiting for her, and they sat in one of the little side rooms waiting to be called in, going over who was giving evidence today. Lizzy felt like she was waiting to go on stage for the next act in a macabre production, even though she was only a spectator.

When she was brought into the courtroom, Sue was indeed there sitting on her side next to two of their other friends, Hayley and Dawn. They all smiled at her, but she only made eye contact, her gaze pulled instead to the other side of the courtroom where a new set of people were sitting. Lizzy looked at the full range of Tony's friends, and of course Reedy in the front. He gave her a welcoming sneer as she stepped up into the dock. Lizzy wished she had taken more than one sedative that morning to calm her nerves. She wanted to dull her senses completely; this was going to be a rough day.

First to the stand was Eddie Johnson. Lizzy hadn't noticed him when she'd glanced across all the lads faces, but when he sat down in the witness box he looked straight at her. He neither sneered nor smiled, but the very fact he was a witness for the prosecution told her he wasn't on her side.

After the preliminary questions they got right down to it, Eddie going over his friendship with Tony: how it had developed, how well he had known him and what sort of person Tony was. When Lizzy's barrister stood up to cross examine, he was holding the sheet of notes Lizzy's solicitor had given him that morning. Once Lizzy had heard Eddie was going to give evidence she'd told Mark about Sue's visit.

'Mr Johnson, were you aware of Mr Dyson's infidelity?'

'Yes, I was.'

'With more than one woman, or just with Miss Bryant?'

Eddie's eyes shifted to Lizzy.

'With more than one woman.'

'Mr Dyson was unfaithful to his wife with more than one woman during their marriage?'

'Yes.'

Lizzy couldn't help but sit forward, this was news to her.

'Did they go on during the entire marriage?'

'No, only towards the end.'

'Was there a trigger for this, do you think?'

'Objection, hearsay!'

'Your Honour, Mr Johnson was Mr Dyson's closest friend. I am just trying to shed light on what might have changed in their marriage to cause this.'

'I'll allow it.'

'Mr Johnson?'

'Yeah, Tony and Lizzy were having problems at home, and this was Tony's way of dealing with it, I suppose.'

'Did he discuss this with you?'

'The problems between him and Lizzy?'

'Yes.'

'Not really. He'd make the odd comment about how she was being unreasonable, and how things weren't good, but no details.'

'Did he talk about the women he was unfaithful with?'

'Oh yeah, Tony always did that.' Eddie smiled.

'And you were okay with it?'

His smiled dropped. 'Well, the odd one nighter, yeah.'

'But you didn't feel this way about his affair with Sally Bryant?'

'No.'

'Can you tell us why?'

Eddie shifted in his seat. 'To begin with I thought it was just gonna be a couple of times or something, but when he started taking her out regularly I thought he was taking it a bit far.'

'Did you say anything to him about it?'

'Yeah, loads of times.'

'And what was his response?'

'He'd laugh it off, say it was nothing to worry about.'

'Was he discreet? Did he take Miss Bryant out in public?'

'At first he was discreet, but after a while he started to take her out round town where everyone could see it going on.'

'Did you have a problem with this?'

'Yeah, I thought it was out of order.'

'And you told him that publicly, didn't you? In fact you almost came to blows over it, is that correct?'

Eddie raised his eyebrows and glanced at Lizzy again. 'Yeah, it is.'

'Can you tell us about that, Mr Johnson?'

'Tony was out again with her – Miss Bryant – and he was getting all fresh with her in the pub, snogging and stuff, it wasn't necessary at all; they were making a show of it. I told him to leave it out, and he didn't like it. We'd both had a bit to drink so there was a bit of a scuffle, and another friend stepped in to break it up.'

'And what happened after?'

'Nothing. I walked away.'

'Did you remain friends?'

'No, not really. We didn't go out again after that.'

'So in fact his affair with Miss Bryant caused the end of your friendship?'

'Yeah, I suppose you could say that, but I thought he'd eventually end it with her and come round at some point.'

'Did you have any personal contact with Mrs Dyson through this period?'

'No, I didn't really speak to Lizzy unless she was out with Tony.'

'Did it occur to you to call her and let her know what was going on?'

'No. Tony was my mate, I wouldn't do that.'

'Not even after your friendship ended?'

'No. It was his business.'

'Thank you, Mr Johnson, I have no more questions.'

Eddie stepped down and Lizzy watched him go. He didn't glance at her again but he remained in the courtroom, taking a seat at the back. The prosecution called the next witness. Lizzy wasn't looking forward to hearing this at all.

Chapter Fifteen

Stuart Reed smiled as he was called and looked straight at Lizzy. She looked away, her stomach churning at the thought of what nasty little pieces he'd be coming out with. She pulled the notepad towards her, ready to start scribbling.

The prosecutor covered all the standard questions and Reedy started answering. There were so many lies Lizzy had to force herself not to burst out laughing, instead using the notepad to stifle what she really wanted to say. He did a good job of making out that Tony had turned to him about everything, and depicted Lizzy as some devil from hell who caused Tony endless misery. She couldn't be sure that Tony hadn't done that, but she knew Reedy better, knowing how he loved to stir and twist things up to get a rise out of people, running off before he could be held responsible for any of it.

One of her first encounters with him socially had taught her this. It had been in the early years of her marriage, and Reedy had returned to the area, acting like the new guy in town. Tony was oblivious to Reedy's nasty little ways, or pretended to be, but he'd struggled to make excuses for this one.

It hadn't been long after she had lost their first child, and she hadn't been aware that Reedy had known about her pregnancy. Lizzy had been careful about telling people, she hadn't wanted the world to know. Just a handful of people giving her sympathetic looks and continuously asking her if she was alright was enough, along with the overcompensation of trying to hide any pregnant women in her proximity from her sight line. It had been tiresome in the early days and not necessary. Back then she'd still believed that having a child was possible and that most women went through it. And it was that night in Henry's Bar, their usual starting point so she'd only been on her second beer, that she'd found out what he was really like.

Tony was with him at the side of the bar and they'd been there a while. Lizzy had walked in with the girls and briefly left them to go and say hello. She'd put her arm around Tony's waist and given him a quick kiss when he'd leaned back to greet her. She registered Reedy's jeering look as they had pulled away but ignored it, returning to the girls, ready to order a drink.

Lizzy even remembered what they'd been gossiping about when he'd rudely interrupted them.

'He didn't?!' They were giving Jackie the low down on who he was.

'He did. Left her stranded; couldn't have given a toss!' Hayley flicked a glance at him, her nostrils flaring. She saw Lizzy approach. 'He's hanging round with Tony a lot, how do you feel about that, Lizzy?'

'Dunno yet. Tony doesn't say much about him. Seeing as they're old mates, I suppose it's like nothing new for him. It's usually only Eddie who comes by the house, mostly Sundays–'

'Eddie lives with someone, doesn't he?' Jackie interrupted.

'Yeah, but they're not getting on. But then Reedy showed up last week.'

'What, really? What for?'

'Well, I think he thought he could get Sunday lunch, but I told Tony that wasn't happening. He didn't stay long.'

'What did Tony tell him?'

'I'm not sure, but Tony wasn't bothered. He's not into feeding the five thousand as he would put it. Eddie's different, he's his best mate.'

Dawn nudged Lizzy. 'Hold up, he's coming over?'

'He probably just going for a piss.'

Lizzy was right. He nodded his head and touched an imaginary hat as he passed them and said, 'Ladies.'

They smirked at him, and then looked at each other giggling.

'I think he looks alright,' Jen piped up.

Lizzy almost spat out her mouthful of beer. 'Oh Jen, you'll have anyone!'

'Don't be so cheeky! He's got a nice smile, nice eyes, and he's in shape.'

'Oh Jen, no! You couldn't!' Dawn scrunched up her face.

'What?' Jen was trying to defend her decision. 'What's wrong with him?'

'What's wrong with him? Haven't you been listening? He treats women like dirt.'

'I only want to shag him, I didn't say I wanted to marry him!'

They all laughed at this. And that was when it happened.

Lizzy felt a hand on her waist, and lips by her ear say, 'It looks like you lot are having a good time. The boys had better look out.'

Despite their conversation, the girls all giggled at him; Jen flicking her hair back and giving him a big smile. Lizzy replied on their behalf.

'No boys allowed when we're out.'

'So I've heard.'

'What do you mean?' Lizzy pulled away from him so she could look at him, happy to move his hands off her.

'You young ladies need more than just us lads to keep you satisfied.'

They roared with laughter, but Lizzy's eyebrows twitched.

'I dunno, some of you can do a good job, when you want to.'

'Yeah, but it's not up to muster though, is it, Lizzy?'

'How do you mean, Reedy?' Her smiled wavered.

He started to walk away as he replied. 'Well, if it didn't stay, it can't have been much good in the first place, can it?' Then he grinned at her and winked, leaving her with a frown on her face.

'What did he mean by that?' Dawn was watching him rejoin Tony over her shoulder.

Lizzy took a slow sip of her beer and said, 'I'm not sure.'

Jen opened her eyes wide. 'Oh you don't think he means …?'

Lizzy looked at her, realisation dawning. 'No! He couldn't have. That would mean Tony's told him.'

'That's possible. Tony's never cared much about keeping things private,' Dawn said, taking a swig from her bottle of beer.

Lizzy finished draining her bottle. Dawn was right, when she'd first met Tony and heard the rumours about him, he hadn't been bothered about admitting to them; he had no shame.

'But it's a bit bloody off, blurting it out like that though,' Jen said, forgetting how charming she'd found him just moments ago.

'He couldn't give a shit, look at him.' Lizzy tipped her empty towards Reedy and Tony laughing about something. 'I'm gonna have a word and get another round in, who wants one?'

They all did, so Lizzy took their bottles back up to the bar and sidled round by Tony. He finished what he was saying to Reedy and a couple of other lads, and turned to her, leaning on the bar.

'Alright, Lizzy?'

She smiled at the wink he gave her. 'I was, until your mate came out with something I didn't expect.'

Tony glanced back at the lads. 'Who? Reedy?'

'Yeah. Did you tell him about the baby?'

Tony looked puzzled. 'I'm not sure, might have, why?'

'He just made some snide remark about it, saying you couldn't have been up to much otherwise it would have stayed.'

Tony frowned, his eyes going out of focus. 'Does it really matter?'

Lizzy pulled back her head and looked at him. 'How many you had?'

Tony gave her a dopey smile. 'A fair few, but still got room.'

She shook her head at him and smiled. 'I'll tell you about it tomorrow.' She ruffled his hair as he continued to smile and then Reedy butted in again.

'Oh look at the love birds. Cooking up lots of love, but not much else.'

Tony looked at Lizzy, his expression slowly changing to one of confusion. He looked round. 'What you on about, Reedy?'

Reedy slapped him on the shoulder. 'Nothing mate, you just carry on.'

When Tony came back to face her, Lizzy raised her eyebrows. 'See?'

'I don't know what he's on about babe, just ignore him.'

She nodded and gave him a quick peck before collecting the fresh beers and returning to the ladies.

She didn't know then that those last three words would be something she'd hear repeated dozens of times over the next few years, most of them in defence of Reedy and his behaviour. And even now, even though Tony was gone, Reedy was still here, in her face, making her feel bad – still getting the upper hand. She never thought it was possible to loathe someone so much.

Chapter Sixteen

The prosecutor continued to ask questions and Reedy continued to tell the courtroom how difficult Lizzy had made Tony's life, while her solicitor tried to quash his comments.

'Mr Reed, would you say that Lizzy Dyson showed aggressive behaviour towards her husband many times prior to his death?'

'Objection. Hearsay!'

'Overruled.'

'But Your Honour, relevance?'

'It's quite relevant, Mr Davis, in light of the reason why we are here.'

'But this is Mr Reed's opinion, not actual fact.'

'You'll get your chance to establish that during your cross examination.'

Lizzy's barrister sat down and let out a sigh. He didn't like what Reedy was doing at all. Lizzy fluttered the notepad pages to catch her solicitor's attention. He glanced back at her from his seat in front of the dock and saw what she was waving. His strained expression relaxed and a small smile tugged at the corner of his mouth as he took the ripped out sheets and read down her list of responses. He slipped out his mobile phone and tapped in a text.

The courtroom had fallen silent, so the judge prompted. 'Answer the question, Mr Reed.'

'I believe she did. I saw Tony with bruises on his body and cut hands on more than one occasion.'

'Did Mr Dyson tell you his wife had caused all of them?'

'He indicated she did, yes.'

'Can you give us an example of what he would say?'

'I'd mention the bruises and ask what had happened and he'd make some joke about the little woman not being happy with something at home.'

'Did you personally witness any of this aggression?'

'Yes, I did, although it was directed at me, not at Mr Dyson.'

'Can you elaborate, Mr Reed?'

'One Sunday afternoon I'd gone round to their house, you know, just to see what Tony was up to and whether he wanted any help with anything. We were in his garage, fiddling with one of the motorbikes he was doing up, and she'd come in to check on him. She seemed to get upset when she saw I was there. She started ranting furiously about how I couldn't just walk in and make myself at home; that I was there too often and I wasn't welcome.'

'What was Mr Dyson's response?'

'Initially he tried to calm her down and stuff, and then she started shouting at him. In the end he'd had to take her back into the house.'

'Did he come back out?'

'Yeah, but only after half an hour or so, and he looked pretty shaken up. He was rubbing his shoulder.'

'Did you ask him about it?'

'I asked if everything was alright and he'd laughed saying that it must have been something she'd eaten that morning. We'd both laughed about it.'

Lizzy snatched the notepad back up as soon as Reedy had mentioned that particular day and started writing again. She looked as though she wasn't paying much attention but she was listening to every word, in fact she was correcting a story that was being told wrong: with each of his responses, she wrote the correct version. She could see it all in her mind's eye, how it had really unfolded that day. She had indeed gone into the garage that afternoon to offer them both drinks. She had known that Reedy was out there, but what she hadn't anticipated were the things he would say to her.

'Hey, Lizzy. You keeping the little man fed and watered are you?'

'I thought you guys might like some drinks, yes.'

'No, I don't mean that, I mean up in the bedroom.' Reedy had stuck out his tongue and made a hip gesture. Tony had glanced at him and giggled.

'That's none of your business.'

'It could be if you liked. I'm always up for a threesome.'

Lizzy had looked at Tony. He'd just snorted, shaking his head.

'I wouldn't touch you with a barge pole, Reedy. You disgust me,' she'd said.

'Oh yeah, but I'm sure you wouldn't mind a change of scenery every once in a while though, eh Lizzy? Must be getting tiresome with our boy Tony here.'

Even Tony had looked at him. 'What you on about, Reedy?'

'Ah come on, it's got to be hard work trying to make babies all the time, surely you could do with a break sometime, and I could stand in. And well it wouldn't matter if I knocked you up now would it, Lizzy? 'Cause it's not like you'd manage to keep it.'

That's when Lizzy had lost it and even Tony had stood up, wiping his hands and frowning at Reedy. He'd let her handle it and hadn't got involved, letting her list all Reedy's failings and call him things that had even made Tony wince. But at the end, when she had told him to "Fuck off", he'd remained and simply responded, 'Gladly, if you can guide me to your mates house – Jen, isn't it? She's got the hots for me, hasn't she? I could happily sort her out.'

'You keep your fucking hands off her, Reedy, she's doesn't deserve scum like you!'

'And how you going to stop me?'

Lizzy had attempted to launch herself at him but Tony had pulled her back. 'Come on, Lizzy, enough now. Let's just calm down a bit.'

Tony had taken her back into the house and they'd had a discussion where it was decided that Tony was going to ask Reedy to leave and not come round on Sundays anymore. And Reedy had left within a couple of minutes of Tony going back out to the garage.

As the prosecution came to the end of his questioning, Lizzy's solicitor slid a folder of papers onto the barrister's desk. Mr Davis took a quick look at it and Lizzy was sure his expression relaxed slightly.

'Mr Reed, can you tell us where you were employed when you first met Mr Dyson?'

Reedy's eyes flicked to Lizzy's for a moment, then he said, 'At Griggs, in the factory.'

'And how long had you worked there?'

'A few months.'

'You were new into the area, weren't you?'

'I'd been away for a bit, yes.'

'Where had you come from?'

'Petersford.'

'Why did you leave Petersford?'

'I got divorced.'

'And sacked, isn't that correct?'

The prosecution stood up. 'Your Honour, how is Mr Reed's work history relevant here?'

'I'm getting to that in a moment if you'll bear with me, Your Honour.'

The judge nodded. 'Please answer the question, Mr Reed.'

'Yes, I was fired.'

'Can you tell the court why you were fired?'

Reedy looked down at his hands. 'Embezzlement and fraud.'

'To quite a hefty amount if I'm not mistaken – in excess of a hundred thousand pounds?'

Prosecution stood up again. 'Your Honour, Mr Reed's previous convictions don't apply to this case; they have no bearing on his relationship with Mr Dyson.'

'Make your point, Mr Davis.'

'Mr Reed, is it true that the owner of this company had a fifteen year old daughter who became pregnant by you, and which you refused to take accountability for?'

'Objection!'

'Mr Davis, Mr Reed is not on trial here. Can you please explain to the court where this is going?'

'I am trying to establish the character of the witness, Your Honour, and show the court that he has a history of lying, stealing and low moral integrity.'

'You're treading a thin line here, Mr Davis, but I'll allow it. Mr Reed, please answer the question.'

'Yes it is, but there were extenuating circumstances.'

Mr Davis raised his eyebrows. 'Can you explain to the court what they were?'

'The baby wasn't mine.'

'And you proved that, did you?'

'Well, no, not in the end. She got rid of it.'

'Were you a part of that decision?'

'I told her I wouldn't have anything to do with it or her, if she had it.'

'And your relationship with this girl, was this before or after your divorce?'

'I was separated at the time.'

'So you had a relationship with a minor while you were still married? Did you have children in your marriage?'

'Yes, three.'

'And what are their ages?'

Reedy sat back, looking up, using his fingers to count.

'You don't know your own children's ages?'

'I haven't seen them in a while.'

'How long is 'a while'?'

'I dunno, about six or seven years, maybe longer.'

'And why is that?'

"Cause my ex-wife won't let me.'

'Because you were violent towards her and the children, isn't that correct?'

'Objection!' The prosecution's face had turned very red.

'Overruled. I want to hear this. Do you have proof, Mr Davis?'

'Yes, Your Honour, I have police and hospital reports showing domestic violence against the children and wife.' Mr Davis took the documents to the judge, who looked through them.

He looked at Reedy. 'Continue. Mr Reed, please answer the question.'

'Yes.' Reedy's hand went to his face and rubbed it.

'And were there any extenuating circumstances for that?'

'Objection!'

'Withdrawn. So if I understand this correctly, Mr Reed, you were married for what, was it seven years?'

'Yes that's correct.'

'And during that time you were physically and verbally abusive to your wife and children, then you moved on and took advantage of a minor and in actual fact committed statutory rape on a girl, whose father you then embezzled.'

'Objection.' The prosecution said, although more calmly this time.

'Sorry what are you objecting to? I was just summing up what the witness has just told us.'

'Overruled. But Mr Davis, can you please make your questions more relevant to the case at hand?'

'Yes, Your Honour. Mr Reed, you recounted a story to the court about a Sunday afternoon in Mr Dyson's garage, claiming that Mrs Dyson was aggressive towards you, is that correct?'

'Yes.'

'Can you tell the court what it was that caused Mrs Dyson to get so upset?'

'I don't remember.'

'Did you suggest that you go to bed with her to alleviate the boredom they must be feeling while trying to become pregnant?'

'I don't remember.'

'And that it wouldn't matter if she fell pregnant by you, because she wasn't able to keep a baby – referring to her first miscarriage?'

'I don't remember.'

'Could it be possible?'

'Anything's possible when a woman's screaming at you.'

'But she wasn't screaming at you until after you said these things, was she? And in fact Mr Dyson asked you to leave that afternoon and not return on a Sunday ever again, isn't that correct?'

'Yeah, maybe, something like that.'

'Something like that? Can you be more specific?'

'Tony came out of the house and said that he didn't want her getting upset anymore and thought it was best I leave, and that maybe Sundays weren't a good idea to come round.'

'And is it correct that you made several lurid remarks to Mrs Dyson about her miscarriages, and her inability to maintain a pregnancy, when out on social occasions?'

'I could have done. It sounds like me.'

'It sounds like you? What do you mean by that, Mr Reed?'

'When I'm out drinking and had a skin full, I tend to say what I think.'

'And you've never considered that this might be upsetting?'

Reedy shrugged.

'Mr Reed, you referred to seeing cuts and bruises on Mr Dyson's body and hands, is this correct?'

'Yes.'

'What did Mr Dyson do for a living?'

'He worked in Griggs with me, in the finishing department, and did modelling.'

'Finishing? What does that involve?'

'Finishing off the shoes, cutting off excess pieces of heel or leather.'

'Would you use a knife doing this?'

'Yes.'

'And is it true Mr Dyson liked to box?'

Reedy knew where this was headed and sighed. 'Yes, he did.'

'In fact he had a punch bag in the basement, didn't he?'

'Yes, he did.'

'And as I understand it, you even sparred with him a couple of times at the gym, is that correct?'

'Yes, it is.'

'Was he any good?'

Reedy gave a small smile. 'Yeah, he knocked me out twice.'

'So, is it at all possible that Mr Dyson's cuts and bruises could have been either work or boxing related?'

'I suppose they could, but he told me otherwise.'

'So he told you that Mrs Dyson had hit him, in those exact words?'

Reedy pulled a face. 'No, not in those exact words, just that they weren't getting on, that they had been rowing. He would come over to my place all sore. I wasn't stupid I could put two and two together.'

'So there is no possibility that he could have been sore from a bout with his own punch bag in the basement, or from a visit to the gym?'

Reedy sighed. 'Yeah, it's possible.'

'Thank you, Mr Reed. No further questions, Your Honour.'

'You may step down, Mr Reed.'

Reedy didn't walk back to his seat with as much enthusiasm as he'd left it, and when Lizzy's barrister sat down, he gave her a side glance with a half smile. Lizzy didn't smile outwardly, but she was laughing on the inside.

Chapter Seventeen

The judge called a recess for lunch. Lizzy was taken to one of the side rooms in the courthouse where her solicitor joined her for lunch. Some plain sandwiches and refreshments were brought in to them and Lizzy tucked in despite her handcuffs. They were a luxury compared to the limp equivalents she received in prison.

Mark smiled at her. 'That went better than I thought after everything he came out with.'

'I knew he'd be a tough cookie. But how did you get those police and hospital reports?'

'Preliminary checks on all witnesses. That's why the prosecution didn't object. They knew about it, and really once he started saying you were aggressive I had to produce them. But you gave me the rest, especially that underage pregnancy.'

'But what if they had asked you to produce papers on that, could you have?'

'Definitely. I sent a text to my assistant as soon as I read your notes. Her father filed a complaint, but it didn't seem to be followed up after all the mess of the embezzlement. How did you know about that?'

'He bragged about it one night when he was drunk, and he'd told Tony too. I don't know if he did time?'

'He did eighteen months of a five year sentence apparently. He got off lightly because he gave names of other involved.'

'That sounds like Reedy. Were they allowed to bring that up though? I didn't think previous convictions were admissible or something?'

'Mr Davis didn't refer directly to the conviction, he was going for the underage pregnancy and Mr Reed not fulfilling his moral duty, but he was just building up to the divorce really, and the reason behind it. He managed to get it all in.'

'How the mighty fall and all that?'

Mark laughed. 'Yeah, something like that.'

'So who's going to be up there this afternoon? You didn't say this morning.'

'That's it for the prosecution, now it's our turn. Your sister is speaking on your behalf, and one of your friends – Hayley Robins.'

Lizzy raised her eyebrows. 'Wow they're all crawling out of the woodwork now, aren't they?'

'Mrs Robins approached me two days ago.'

'That'll be Sue's work.'

Mark frowned. 'I don't follow.'

'I told you she came to visit me at the prison after the hearing on Monday, all guilt ridden, remember?'

Mark coughed round a mouthful of sandwich. 'Oh that's right. I'm still surprised; I didn't expect that after her testimony.'

'Yeah, it came as a bit of a surprise to me too. Seems she's done a full turnaround and here today with the girls.'

'I noticed that. It's a good thing though, the more show of support the better.'

'And you still want me to take the stand next week?'

'I think it could work well for you. Have you thought any more about it?'

'Yeah, I have. I want to. After all this talk about me, I think I should at least speak. Not sure what I should say though, nothing in my head sounds right.'

'What do you mean?'

'Well it's not like it was okay what I did, not at all, and

I don't want to sit up there and make any excuses for it, I don't think that will fly.'

'You just have to tell them the truth, from your heart.'

'What that I loved him more than myself?' Lizzy's eyes filled with tears, she wiped at them. 'Sorry, these meds make me so emotional.'

'No, no, it's fine. It's good to see some kind of emotion. You've been out of it since … well since I first met you, but this last week you seem to be sort of waking up. And you've given me so much input. I hadn't expected any of that. I thought this was going to be an open and shut case – excuse the cliché.'

Lizzy smiled. 'I know. I think it was that hysterical fit on Monday, you know after the hearing? I dunno that seemed to just sort of clear it all out of me.'

'So it's not all the meds then?'

'Well no. I suppose not. Although I'm on lighter ones now. But they haven't changed them for the last few weeks – that I know of, they look the same.' She laughed lightly and sat back.

'You've done well.' Mark nodded towards the platter of sandwiches where only one remained.

Lizzy grinned. 'Yeah, I was hungry. You don't want to try prison food, you really don't. Although it keeps your weight down.' She patted her stomach.

Mark ate in silence while Lizzy looked round the formal, wood-panelled room, and up at the corniced ceiling and high windows. 'I miss clouds.'

'What?'

'I miss seeing clouds. I'm locked up for 22 odd hours a day and it's the clouds I miss the most. I used to spend a lot of time cloud watching, either from my bedroom window or the kitchen window. I miss them.'

Mark chewed his last mouthful. 'I've never really thought about them. But then I've never really thought about what it must be like being shut in a room all day every day. How you coping?'

'Really well actually, I don't mind it.'

Mark raised his eyebrows.

'I like the quiet and not having to think about other people or what I have to do every day. It became such a struggle at the end, just getting out of bed and knowing I had to face other people – even if it was just Tony. Every time I stepped out of the house I felt like people were watching me, as though they knew all my business and were talking about me all the time. I bought more and more stuff online, even food shopping, so I didn't have to go out. And if I went out, I'd drive a long way to another town where no one knew me, so I could shop in peace. But there'd always be a little voice whispering in the back of my mind telling me I might bump into someone I knew.

'There was all this noise in my head, all these paranoid thoughts all the time; it was really hard to focus on anything. I would find it exhausting and it would make me so angry. Everything I did made me angry, because it cost time or energy. And if I had to do anything for anyone else it made me worse – especially for Tony. It was like a burning inside me every time I saw him. It wouldn't matter whether he was pleasant or not; I would find every word he spoke irritating. It would rub me the wrong way and develop into a screaming fit. Some days he just wouldn't speak, and if I started he'd walk away. Occasionally he'd try and respond, but it never ended well when he did.'

Lizzy wiped a tear away. Mark handed her his handkerchief.

'This is exactly what you need to say on the stand, Lizzy, it's what they need to hear.'

'I'm not sure I can say all that again, exactly the same way.'

'It doesn't need to be exact. We'll find a way. I'll draw up some questions with Mr Davis that might help you go over it again.'

'I might digress into how I felt he treated me when we were out.'

'So? That's what we need. You can maybe describe some specific instances too. I'll draw something up and we'll go over it on Monday when I see you. I've asked for an extended visit.'

'And they've agreed?'

'They have to really, it's your trial.'

Lizzy felt a flutter in her stomach. Would this be a good idea? Could she finally make herself heard? Make others understand what she had been through? She didn't know, but she was grateful for the opportunity. And in the end it didn't really matter what any of them thought, because it didn't change anything – it didn't change what she'd done.

Chapter Eighteen

Hayley Robins was called first. Her walk to the stand looked confident despite her petite stature. She sat down and flicked her blonde hair over her shoulders, reminding Lizzy how she was someone who wasn't to be trifled with. Many people thought because she was little and genteel looking they could push her about – they couldn't have been more wrong.

Mr Davis established how they had been close friends before Lizzy had met Tony, and how Lizzy had been careful at first with Tony due to his reputation for being a womaniser.

'How did you know the deceased?'

'I'd known Tony for years, ever since I started going out drinking. He was also friends with a guy I was seeing so I got to know him a little bit.'

'You were friends.'

'Sort of, he would chat in passing, but not about anything serious.'

'Did you introduce him to Mrs Dyson?'

'Sort of. I pointed him out to her because he'd recently split up with someone. They liked the look of each other. But Lizzy wasn't his usual girl.'

'What do you mean by that?'

'He was into taking them home with him that night, you know, and Lizzy wasn't up for that. I think he liked that, made him respect her. He liked the chase.'

'Would you say they had a rocky relationship?'

'No, not at all. They got serious pretty quick – certainly by Tony's standards. They moved in together after just six months, and everyone could see they were both in love with each other. There was no question about that.'

'When would you say things started to go wrong for them?'

'After the miscarriages – particularly after the third. Lizzy started coming apart.'

'Can you explain to the court what you mean by that?'

'It was such an awful thing, to lose your baby at four months. They were both devastated, everyone was. We'd all believed they'd have a baby successfully up until that point, but that sort of rocked everyone. And although we all tried hard to help her get over it, it never quite worked. She tried coming out with us on Friday nights, but she'd go home early, not being able to have fun or let go. Or sometimes if someone was pregnant or something, she couldn't handle it. And then when she lost the last one, the fifth one, at almost five months. It was dreadful.'

Hayley's eyes shined with tears, and Mr Davis gave her a moment as he formulated his next question. 'I believe there was a funeral, did you attend?'

'Yes, we all did, in fact half the town turned out.'

'What do you remember most about that day?'

Hayley tried to speak, but a tear ran down her face. Mr Davis stepped forward and handed her a hankie and she took it. She cleared her throat and said, 'The little coffin, it was so tiny. And the silence. No one spoke, no one could. It was like someone burying their hopes and dreams.' Hayley shook her head and brought the hankie to her nose.

Lizzy sat and listened, trying to remain numb. She couldn't feel anything, not here in this courtroom, not now, but as Hayley's voice broke so did something inside her. She could feel her stomach churn and she fought the lump in her throat. Her face was set, every muscle tense.

If she moved she would start sobbing, she knew she would. She looked through Hayley. The images coming to her as Hayley described it: Tony's hand clasping hers like a vice, not daring to let go; his rapid shallow breaths as he tried to keep from breaking down; her eyes fixed on the little booties embossed on the coffin lid; the stifled sobs and sniffles of everyone around her. She'd held her stomach so tight it'd hurt, but she'd rather that pain than feel the one in her heart. As they'd walked away from the graveside, Tony and Lizzy had clung to each other, neither speaking, neither able. It was the most difficult day of her life – nothing prison threw at her changed that, with the exception of one thing: knowing she'd taken the life of her babies' father. The very thought he was no longer there by her side came crashing in and she couldn't take a breath for a couple of seconds.

She focused on the talking, and released her breath slowly. The subject had moved on.

'When you came back from the holiday, had things changed between you?'

'Not initially. I still called Lizzy and went round to see her; nothing had changed in our friendship.'

'Had you known about Mr Dyson and Miss Andrews?'

'Yes.'

'And that it had gone on behind Mrs Dyson's back in the beginning?'

'Yes.'

'And you hadn't told Mrs Dyson?'

'No. I never really thought to. It was in the past, and no longer an issue. I never thought it would come out that way.'

'What way?'

'Well, on holiday, and Sue wasn't particularly sensitive about it.'

'Did you discuss what happened with Mrs Dyson when you got back?'

'No, it was said and done, and that was that. I knew

she wouldn't have anything more to do with Sue.'

'Did it make things difficult?'

'Sometimes, although Lizzy didn't really come out with us after that holiday. Occasionally we would go for a drink on our own, but really I only saw Lizzy if I went round or we went out shopping together.'

'So Mrs Dyson distanced herself from you at that time?'

'Yes.'

'Were you aware she was doing that?'

'Yes, I was, but I didn't really stop it, it seemed to be what she wanted.'

'Did you know about Tony Dyson's affair with Sally Bryant?'

'Yes.'

'How did you become aware of it?'

'They started going out round town together and made it clear to everyone it was going on.'

'Were you shocked?'

'Not really.'

'Not really? Can you explain that?'

'Rumours were out that Lizzy and Tony were having troubles, and no one was surprised after everything that had happened. Lizzy didn't come out anymore. She'd put on a lot of weight and she just didn't seem to care.'

'Did you at any time think to inform Mrs Dyson about what was going on?'

Hayley's eyes darted across to Lizzy for a second before she replied.

'I picked up the phone to call her on several occasions, to tell her, but every time I chickened out. And I even went round a couple of times with the intention of telling her, but still couldn't do it.'

'Why was that, Miss Robins?'

'Lizzy wasn't in a good way. She was quite distraught and felt everyone was against her. I just felt it would have been too much for her.'

'You didn't think she already knew?'

'She spoke about her suspicions that he was sleeping with someone and would get quite upset when talking about it, so I thought maybe she did. But in some ways it was her upset that stopped me from confirming them. I was worried she would do something silly.'

'What like kill her husband?' The courtroom inhaled at the statement, but nobody objected.

Hayley's mouth opened into a small 'o'. She breathed, 'No, no, I never thought she'd do that, if anything I thought she might kill herself.'

'So you thought Mrs Dyson might have been suicidal?'

'Well, she was busy blaming herself for it all: the loss of the babies, the fights between them, her not bothering enough about herself, and coming up with all the reasons why she had failed him as a wife and mother.'

'Did you see a lot of Mrs Dyson during this period?'

Hayley paused. 'No, only a few times, and to be honest, each time I saw her it put me off. I no longer knew what to say or do for her.'

'So why have you come forward and asked to speak on Mrs Dyson's behalf today?'

Hayley sighed. 'I just wanted to sort of try and put her side across, I suppose. Stand up and be the friend I should have been years ago. She deserved better than that. I failed her – we all did.' Hayley looked at the other girls sitting at the back; a couple of them put their heads down. 'None of us stepped up and were the friend we should have been, and well I suppose I'm trying to make that right, even though it's a bit late. Lizzy went through hell burying two children, and then Tony backed away from her – we all did. It wasn't fair.'

'Thank you, Miss Robins. No further questions, Your Honour.'

The prosecution's solicitor stood up and buttoned his jacket, giving Hayley a shark's smile – nothing but teeth. She didn't return it.

'Miss Robins, you have testified that Mrs Dyson was not in a rational state of mind when you last saw her, is that correct?'

'Lizzy was upset, but I didn't say she was irrational.'

'But you said you were worried she would 'do something silly', does that not indicate irrational?'

'I was worried she would do something silly to herself, due to her sadness, not due to any mad or strange thoughts.'

'But even that might be considered irrational, no?'

'It might.' Hayley shifted in her seat.

'What did you think Mrs Dyson might do if you had told her about the affair Mr Dyson was having?'

'I thought she would leave him or get in another fight with him. I thought she might be angry at me.'

'You didn't think she would seek revenge?'

'No, Lizzy's not like that.'

'Not even after what happened during your holiday?'

'What? Her hitting Sue? That wasn't revenge. She didn't think about it, she just did it – under provocation.'

'But you hadn't seen much of Mrs Dyson the last eighteen months or so prior to Mr Dyson's death, is that right?'

'No.'

'Until the night she came out and launched an attack on Miss Bryant, is that correct?'

'Yes.'

'So you couldn't say that she hadn't planned the attack on Miss Bryant?'

Hayley looked at him with a frown. 'I can't say that, but I do believe it was unlikely.'

'And would you consider the attack irrational or someone seeking revenge?'

'In the moment it might be irrational, 'seeking revenge' is a bit strong. The woman was flirting and getting physical with her husband in a pub, in her face! I think she might have had good reason for it.'

'But would you agree that Lizzy had been showing unstable behaviour prior to Mr Dyson's death?'

Hayley glared at him. 'Unstable maybe – but not enough to murder someone–'

The solicitor cut her off. 'Thank you, Miss Robins, no further questions.'

Hayley sat there watching him return to his seat, her nostrils flared. She didn't move until the judge told her she could step down. She continued to glower at him until she walked past him.

Lizzy felt for her, knowing she had done her best, and looked round as she sat down, pressing her lips together and giving a slight shrug in sympathy. Hayley gave her a sad smile in return. It was enough for Lizzy to know that they were trying to support her. It might be a bit late in the game, but it was better than never. And she hadn't expected it – not from any of them.

Chapter Nineteen

There was a fifteen minute recess and Lizzy was taken to a different side room, smaller than the others, with no windows. They gave her tea and biscuits. Mark joined her briefly.

'I'm hoping your sister does better than that.'

'It wasn't good was it?'

'Her intention was good and I think that came through, but generally, no. She depicted you as falling apart beforehand and already being of unstable mind prior to the killing. I really don't want them to go down the pre-meditated route.'

'But it wasn't.'

'I know that and you know that, but we have to prove it at this stage.'

'So no "innocent until proven guilty" then?'

'You've pleaded guilty to murder, Lizzy, so that doesn't apply. But if we want a chance of release or any kind of leniency we have to show it was diminished responsibility. We have to show that you found them and did it in that moment.'

Lizzy saw the knife in her hand again, the blade and its different pattern on either side to give two options for cutting through frozen meat. She had pulled it out of the drawer without a thought, only hearing them going at it upstairs. Her head had been filled with the sound: Sally's cries resounding through the house, his grunts occasionally interjecting. Lizzy wasn't a screamer; she made noises in the right place, and the right kind of noises according to Tony, but she had never screamed, never had the urge to. Did he enjoy that? Did he prefer that? It wasn't a surprise they hadn't heard her come home.

The snapping of fingers appeared before her eyes. 'Lizzy? Lizzy? Come back, we've got to go back in now.'

She blinked and shook her head. 'Sorry, I'm here.'

Chapter Twenty

Upon entering the courtroom again Lizzy saw her sister in the front row. She looked a little drawn and there were grey flecks in her dark hair that weren't there the last time Lizzy had seen her, but the tight little smile she gave Lizzy reached her eyes and helped Lizzy relax.

She was called to the stand straight away and strode to the box with a confidence Lizzy envied.

Mr Davis stood up and started the preliminary questions, asking her to state her name and her relationship with the defendant.

'Lucinda Jarvis. I'm her sister.'

'How long is it since you have seen Mrs Dyson?'

'Six years.'

'And can you tell us about the last time you saw Mrs Dyson?'

'I visited Lizzy in hospital after her third miscarriage. It was awful news and I came as soon as I heard.'

'Did the visit go well?'

'Yes, Lizzy and I always got on.'

'But you didn't go to her after the last two miscarriages, why was that?'

'I was out of the country when Lizzy had her last miscarriage. My husband was working abroad, in Hong Kong on a project, and I had joined him for his last year there. I wasn't able to get back quickly. I called her and she told me not to worry, and said not to come.'

'But you didn't see her upon your return, was there a reason for that?'

'I maintained telephone contact with Lizzy, but we both seemed to be caught up in our own lives – or that's how it seemed – and we drifted. When I moved back I was still living quite a distance from her, in the West of England, so visiting never came about.'

'When was the last time you called Mrs Dyson?'

'Probably about two and half years ago.'

'And did that call go well?'

'Not as well as I had hoped. We ended up arguing.'

'What about?'

'Tony, her husband.'

'Can you tell the court about the call?'

'Lizzy expressed some concerns about him cheating on her. She had said he didn't want to consider adoption and she felt they were drifting apart. I had voiced my opinion of him and it hadn't gone down well.'

'Your opinion? And what was that?'

'I had never really taken to Tony. I found him aloof and a little arrogant when I first met him: a bit of a charmer, with a bad reputation, someone I didn't quite trust, and that had never changed really. I was always concerned that he would lose interest in her. And after they had lost so many children it didn't surprise me that his eye had started to wander.'

'If you argued, did that mean Lizzy defended him?'

'Yes she did. She told me that I didn't know him well and had always resisted getting to know him; that she didn't think I was being fair on him.'

'How did the call end?'

'Lizzy put the phone down on me.'

'Did you try to call her back?'

'No. I knew my sister; she was angry and there was no point trying to say anything further.'

'And you had no further contact after that time?'

'We exchanged emails when our mother had to go into

a home, but that was about it.'

'You have another sibling, is that correct?'

'Yes, a brother, Marcus, but he lives in Italy. We only exchange Christmas cards now really.'

Mr Davis paused for a moment. 'Mrs Jarvis, can you give us a little background on your childhood and family set up?'

'Yes. Our father died when I was 12 and Lizzy was 8. He had lung cancer and over the last two years of his life, he was pretty much housebound. My mother cared for him and we did our best to support her. His loss was major for all of us, but Lizzy was affected the most: being the youngest, she'd been his little girl and they adored each other. Our brother, Marcus, who was 10 at the time, tried to compensate as the male figure in her life but it didn't really work, although they were close for a while. Lizzy had accepted it by the time she became a teenager. And although our mum worried she might go off the rails, she was alright.'

'Off the rails? What did your mum mean by this do you think?'

'She thought Lizzy would be easily led by men, easily influenced and likely to get herself into trouble, especially without a father to love her. She worried that Lizzy would seek love and attention from any man that would give it, but Lizzy didn't.

'Lizzy was "alternative" as we called it back then; she liked to rebel against the norm. She always hung around with a group of people that were much older than her. But although she looked like she might get into trouble, she never did. I think she just liked the company of people more mature than her because she'd had to grow up more quickly with dad dying. She'd been through more than most children her age.'

'You mentioned your mother is in a home now, when did she fall ill?'

'Our mum suffers from dementia. It's similar to Alzheimer's, but hers was brought on by strokes. She had several mini strokes that even she didn't know about, until one large one when I was in my early twenties and Lizzy in her late teens. Her condition declined steadily until she was unable to function properly and that's when Lizzy arranged her transfer to a nearby home.'

'Did Lizzy have to make all the arrangements herself?'

'No. Some years ago now, when mum was still cognitive enough, we'd looked round a few together and decided on this particular one, because it was not too far from Lizzy – or Marcus at the time. Mum knew she was going to get worse and need help eventually so it was the right thing to do.'

'Your mother sounds like a very responsible, conscientious woman.'

'Yes, mum always managed everything, always thought about the future, always had a plan. Nursing your husband through his death, and managing three young children couldn't have been easy, but mum always made us feel like everything would be okay and that there were no problems we couldn't face. She was always there to help us and give advice.'

'Was she there for Lizzy after her miscarriages?'

'Yes, every time. It was one of the reasons I didn't pull out all the stops to fly back for the funeral of Lizzy's fifth child. She told me mum was there with her and it would be okay.'

'But your mother was showing signs of dementia then, wasn't she?'

'Yes, she was, but it was more in the physical area of her life at that time: she had trouble moving around and being able to complete tasks, making big decisions about things. At that time her memory was still good as I understood it. Although it wasn't long after that it started to deteriorate.'

'Lizzy was the main person taking care of your mother

at the time?'

'Yes. She went round to mum's daily on her way home from work, and would do shopping for her on weekends and arrange help for other things. Mum has a brother in the area too, our Uncle Peter, and he also supported Lizzy, by taking mum to any hospital appointments and shopping and stuff.'

'Where was your own brother at this time?'

'Abroad. Marcus left home when he was eighteen and went off travelling round the world, working in all sorts of places. He used to send postcards regularly and then he settled down in Italy. Now it's became Christmas Cards and the odd email. He's married now and has a couple of children of his own.'

'But you've never met his family?'

'No. He sends photos with Christmas cards, so I know what his family looks like, but that's about it.'

'So he wasn't involved in any of the decisions about your mum and her care, and he hasn't been around to support Lizzy or you, with anything going on in your lives?'

'No.'

'Does he know about Lizzy's arrest and this court case?'

'Yes. He responded last week to an email I sent him about it.'

'And his reaction?'

'Shock. He has asked me if I wanted him to fly over.'

'What did you tell him?'

'I told him that if his sister meant anything to him, he should.'

'And has he responded to this email?'

'No, not yet.'

Mr Davis paused again, giving the court a chance to absorb this information.

'Do you have children of your own, Mrs Jarvis?'

'Yes, two daughters of ten and twelve.'

'Did you have any troubles conceiving or carrying your children to term?'

'No, none at all.'

'Did you find it difficult to relate when Mrs Dyson lost her children?'

'No, not really. I understand how much a mother loves her baby from the moment she finds out she is pregnant. I might not be able to relate to the feelings of loss directly, but with how intensely I love my children, the thought of losing them at any stage would be quite unbearable.'

'Did Mrs Dyson have a lot of contact with her nieces?'

'In the beginning, yes, because I lived close by, but we moved away for my husband's work when they were small, just two years old and six months, so after that it became less frequent.'

'How old were they when they last saw their Aunt?'

'Let me think, probably about four and two, just before we moved overseas the first time. We came to their wedding, and then we visited once more just before we left.'

'Do you think the lack of contact and visits might be due to Mrs Dyson finding it difficult seeing them once she had lost her own?'

'It's possible. We did talk about meeting up again after her third miscarriage, but it never actually happened.' Lucy paused. 'So, yes it could have had a bearing on it.'

'And knowing you had no problems having children might have also been difficult?'

'Oh yes, definitely. She would often say how there must be something wrong with her, because I had no problems.'

'How did you respond to that?'

'I told her it was rubbish, that I could have had the same problems and that it was luck of the draw. Millions of women lose babies and then go on to have healthy children.'

'Did Lizzy believe that?'

Lucy shot a glance at Lizzy. 'I think she wanted to, and with the first couple she might have, but with each one it became more and more difficult.'

'And did you find it difficult to speak to her about it?'

'Sometimes.'

'Do you think that might have been a reason why your contact with her eventually stopped?'

Lucy's bottom lip extended as she thought about it. 'Maybe, I've never really thought about it. When you live far away and you have your own family to look after you get busy. And after our last phone call ending so badly, we reverted to email contact, and then it would only be about important things, like mum.'

Mr Davis took in a deep breath. 'Why are you here today, Mrs Jarvis?'

'Despite our lack of contact over recent years, I wanted to come and support my sister; let people know who she really is.'

'And who is that?'

'A feeling, emotional, sometimes sensitive person, who has only ever been kind and caring towards others. She tried her hardest over the years to try and bring our families together, and I think she was right that in many ways I resisted it, using her husband and our geographical distance as an excuse. She's been the one left to look after our mother too, which she's always done without a word of complaint.'

'How did you find out about her arrest?'

'The police called me, as since our father's dead and our mother's in a home, I'm her next-of-kin.'

'Were you surprised by the news?'

Lucy leaned forward, her eyes widening. 'Surprised? That's putting it mildly! I never imagined or believed that Lizzy could be capable of such a thing! And I still didn't believe it until I read about her pleading guilty in the newspapers – and even then I had to call the authorities to verify that it was true.'

'You haven't visited Mrs Dyson since her arrest?'

Lucy's eyes flicked to Lizzy and then to the floor in front of her.

'No, a part of me believed that they would find out it wasn't really her that had committed the crime and she would be let out.'

'And that it would all blow over?'

'Yes, something like that.' Lucy fidgeted in her seat.

'Is there anything you would like to say to the court, Mrs Jarvis?'

Lucy looked at the individual faces of the jury for a moment, and then turned back to Mr Davis.

'I don't believe my sister is a bad person, and I don't believe that her actions were calculated or pre-meditated in any way. I believe she was responding to a situation that was hurting her and she had no other way of stopping it. I love my sister and will always regret not having been more supportive of her in her time of need. And I will also always wonder, if I had been, would this have ever happened?'

Mr Davis gave Lucy a small smile. 'Thank you, Mrs Jarvis. No further questions, Your Honour.'

The prosecution's solicitor stood up, remaining behind his desk as he spoke.

'I just have a couple of questions. Mrs Jarvis, would it be correct to say you had a bias against Mr Dyson?'

'Yes, I suppose you could say that.'

'And did Mr Dyson do or say anything to you, in the time you knew him, to support this bias?'

Lucy turned her mouth down. 'Not directly, no.'

'And everything that gave you reason to dislike him was hearsay or gossip?'

Lucy sighed. 'Yes, I suppose it was.'

'Thank you. No further questions, Your Honour.'

Lucy looked less certain of herself as she stepped

down, but still managed a small smile for Lizzy who was busy wiping away her tears. She hadn't imagined ever hearing her sister saying any of that.

There were no further witnesses and the court was adjourned until the following week.

Chapter Twenty-One

Lizzy was taken out to one of the side rooms while the court emptied and everyone left. Then she was taken out to the van, but it was at the back entrance this time due to the amount of press and public crowding the front entrance. As the van drove out it was spotted and Lizzy was startled by the sound of items hitting the van. She covered her head in response as though it were possible for them to reach her. She was grateful she hadn't had to face them in person.

When she arrived back in the prison, she was allowed to join the other inmates outside for their late afternoon stroll in the courtyard. She enjoyed the opportunity to stretch her legs outside after being in the courtroom all day, and to see the clouds, which were changing colour now the sun had started its descent. The faint apricot tinge made her feel nostalgic for wide open spaces, and she was reminded of a time when she used to go for picnics when she was a child.

They used to drive out into the countryside and try and find the most remote field, sometimes walking for what seemed like hours to find one. And then they'd lay everything out and sit back and enjoy the views, listening to local wildlife and embracing the fresh air. Even after her father had passed, they still went on them, and even though they all missed him they still had fun. Her brother would run about collecting bugs in a pot and sometimes she'd follow him. If there was a copse of trees nearby they'd explore it, sometimes building dens and playing house. They were carefree days, where there were no other thoughts in her head than what was in front of her at that moment; where she had nothing else to think about but the ant crawling up her arm, or the spider wrapping up a fly it had caught in its web. She would sit for ages watching birds circling or flying from tree to tree as she ate her sandwiches, with the sweet sound of her mother's voice in the background as she talked about something with her sister.

Seeing sunsets were special moments now too, knowing that she would be confined to a small space and restricted from going outside for many years to come.

Carlene was also doing a round in the courtyard.

'You've been out all day at court, haven't you?'

'Yes. I think they thought I could do with a stretch.'

'Yeah, it can be tough sitting there all day. How'd it go?'

'Not too bad; seems I'm gaining support.'

'Really? That's great news!'

'Yes, my sister testified on my behalf and some old friends I didn't expect to see were sitting on my side.'

'Your sister? She's never been to visit you though, has she?'

'No, I only found out earlier this week that she was planning on being a witness. I didn't expect that.'

'So it went okay?'

'Yeah, it was good; brought up lots of memories though.'

'Good or bad?'

'Good ones, but it makes me sad to think how much time we've wasted so unconnected from each other. Such a waste.'

'Yeah it is.' Carlene looked round at the others. 'We all feel that.'

'How about you, did you have any visitors today?'

'Yeah, I got to see my kids, the ones over on the other side of the prison.' Carlene smiled, but didn't make eye contact.

'Did it go well?'

'Yeah, but I hate not being able to touch them.' Carlene turned and Lizzy could see her eyes shiny with tears in the late sunlight. Lizzy rubbed Carlene's arm in sympathy.

'Let's take another walk round and you can tell me what they've been up to.'

Lizzy enjoyed the distraction from herself, listening to someone else talk about their problems and upsets and emotional upheaval for a change. For a moment she didn't have to think about what she had done and how everyone was responding to it. It reassured her that she wasn't alone in the frustration of trapping herself in a situation she couldn't change, and losing control of her life. Handing her life over to others to dictate was the hardest part of being here. It was nice on a temporary basis to get away from the day to day mundane chores and stresses of life, but when she realised it was going to be like this day in and day out for years and years to come it was a whole other story.

Carlene's predicament was one Lizzy couldn't conceive. The emotional pain Carlene was experiencing knowing her own children were doing time for her was unimaginable. And then facing them through glass where the two prison buildings met, and only being able to speak to them through a phone, it became tougher still. It gave Lizzy a chance to try and be supportive of another, to try and be the one to console. It made her feel she had some value again; it gave her a purpose.

They eventually sat down when Carlene couldn't control her sobs, and Lizzy put her arm round her and rocked with her knowing no words could really help. In its own little way it was therapeutic after the day she had had, helping her clear her mind and have physical contact with another human being.

By the time the bell rang Carlene was over the worst, and they walked inside together ready for a night of rest.

But despite wanting to rest, it didn't come easy to Lizzy. Thoughts of the day churned over in her head: Hayley's description of her state of mind, her sister reminding her of family and how scattered they had all become, and worst of all Reedy.

She tried hard not to think about him. She tried hard to not hear his condescending tones; the way he'd always talked down to her as though she was worthless. But then he despised her especially after that night.

She'd spent years trying to suppress the memory of it, particularly after Tony's reaction of disbelief. And today it had felt like he was trying to get some kind of revenge for it, get his own back on her. But it hadn't worked: he'd forgotten how much he'd told her.

In some ways it had been Tony's fault too – not only for befriending him, but for thinking she would be safe in his company while he was away for the weekend on one of his first modelling jobs. 'He'll look after you if you need anything, Liz. He's a good bloke.' How little Tony had known – or wanted to know.

Reedy had checked on her that Saturday morning, first with a call, then popping round on his way into town. It had been that visit that had first sent up red flags, as he had stood there in the kitchen talking about his ex-wife.

'She never understood me.'

'What do you mean?'

'She couldn't have cared less about me; it was all about the kids.'

'But that's how it should be, shouldn't it, Stu? Kids come first.'

'Nah, but this was different. It's like she'd got what she wanted and I was no longer of use to her.' He stood there cradling his mug of tea against his chest with one hand, the other stuffed deep in his jeans pocket. Lizzy sat at the kitchen table.

'Did you try and talk to her?'

'Talk? She wasn't interested in anything I had to say. Whenever I tried she'd start screaming at me and get all angry. I couldn't stand that.'

'What did you do?'

'Scream back mostly, or walk out.'

'And now she won't let you see the kids?'

'No, claims I was abusive, claims I hit her and the kids.'

Lizzy took a sip of her tea and said, 'Did you?'

'She just wouldn't shut up sometimes, Lizzy, she didn't know when to stop. And the kids would start that dreadful crying. I tried hard, I really did, but I've never had much patience.'

'Do you miss them?'

'I don't miss her.'

'No, the kids.'

'She barely let me near them, I don't really know them.'

'So you came down here to make a fresh start?'

Reedy smirked and took a swig of his tea. 'Yeah, you could say that.'

Lizzy's brow twitched. 'What do you mean?'

'I had to get away, got some young girl in trouble – didn't help that she was the boss's daughter either.'

Lizzy's eyebrows went up and Reedy laughed. 'Yeah, serves me right for messing about with someone underage.'

Lizzy broke eye contact, her eyebrows still raised as she took another mouthful of tea.

'Like them young, do you?'

Reedy pursed his lips. 'Oh I dunno, it's not about age really, it's about what they have to offer. I'm not a fussy man, Lizzy.'

As she looked at him, he flicked his eyebrows at her in

a flirtatious way and she laughed, unsure if he was winding her up or not. She changed the subject.

'You going out tonight, Reedy?'

'Yeah I am. You're out with the girls, aren't you?'

'Yeah, it's long overdue.'

'You had better behave with Tony away.'

Lizzy laughed. 'You don't have to worry about me.'

Reedy grinned. 'I'll be keeping my eye on you.' He looked at his watch. 'Speaking of which I'd best get moving.'

He put his mug down on the table and leaned towards her, so close that Lizzy pulled back a little. 'Thanks for the brew, Liz, I'll see you later.'

'Bye.'

She'd watched him go down the hallway and out of the front door, a sick feeling settling in her stomach. She knew there was something about him that unnerved her, but she put it down to his over familiarity. He always stood too close or touched her – a hand on her waist, or round her shoulders, always in full view so no one could read anything into it. She decided it was just his way and her being oversensitive to it, so she hadn't thought anything more of it.

Chapter Twenty-Two

That night Reedy had certainly kept an eye on her, and when she'd planned on staggering home with a skinful after the clubs shut, he had intercepted her at the take away where she was taking the edge of her drunkenness with some chips and gravy.

'I'll walk you home, Liz.'

'No, you're alright, I can find my way.'

'I'm sure you can, but I'd rather make sure you get there safely.'

'Don't be so bloody silly, Reedy.'

She'd laughed and the girls had laughed with her, although Jen had piped up. 'Go on, let him, Lizzy, he's just trying to be a gentleman.'

They'd all giggled at that and he'd grinned inanely at them, refusing to go anywhere without her.

'Oh, alright then.' She'd thrown the rest of her chips in the bin.

Dawn had looked at her reproachfully. 'Eh, what you doing? I'd have had them if you didn't want them, are they no good?'

'Oh, sorry. Just I suddenly feel a bit sick, must be too much on top of the drink.'

She'd given Dawn a soppy smile and a half hug.

'I'd better get gone, seeing as my chaperone is waiting.'

'Ooo la la!' Jen had called and they'd all given a raucous laugh.

The grin on Reedy's face hadn't changed and Lizzy took his arm, needing support in her high heels as she staggered away, still laughing.

She hadn't paid much attention to his chatter as they walked home, the blindness of the alcohol causing her to focus on her footsteps as though they were the only thing in her life. She'd only caught the edges of him talking about his loneliness and how he missed having someone in his life. She'd responded with sympathetic noises.

As they'd approached her front door, she'd let go of his arm to search for her key, and expected him to step back as she opened it, but he hadn't, he'd pushed in behind her as it swung open and shut it behind them. It'd caught her off guard, and when she'd tried to turn, he'd spun her up against the wall, pushing his groin against her arse and grabbing at her body, nuzzling her neck.

She'd never sobered up so fast in her life.

Her arms were raised so she'd brought them down hard, both elbows slamming into his sides as she stamped a stiletto-heeled foot down hard on one of his booted feet. He let out a satisfying shout and reeled back. She wasted no time turning and swiftly brought a knee up to his groin. He fell forward onto the floor, totally unprepared for her attack.

'With my husband, do you really think I wouldn't know how to handle myself? Self-defence was one of the first things he got me into. Now get the fuck out of my house!'

Lizzy had swung the front door open and pulled him up, dragging him to the door. He hadn't had it in him to protest as he'd found his feet and stumbled out still bent over as she'd slammed the door shut. She'd slid both bolts across and put the chain on, leaning against it for a second. Then she'd run to the kitchen and checked the back door, making sure everything was locked there, too, and then done a quick run round the house, going into every room and checking all the windows. She'd ended up in the bedroom sitting on the edge of the bed, shaking, stomach churning, the drunken spin returning.

In her cell, Lizzy could feel her body returning to that state; the memories bringing back the adrenaline rush and fear she had felt. She must have sat on the bed for more than an hour trying to gather herself that night. Eventually she'd willed herself to get up and go to the bathroom, her mind blank as she got ready for bed, still unable to process what had happened. Once in bed, she'd promptly passed out, exhausted.

Lizzy remembered how in the morning she'd woken terrified that Reedy would come round. She was on tenterhooks all day waiting for Tony to return, and when he did, he'd had to wait for her to unlock the front door from inside.

He'd come in, dropping his bags where he stood, and asked, 'What's going on babe, why all the locks?'

He'd seen her hands shaking and taken them in his, then wrapped them round him as he'd embraced her. 'Lizzy, what's going on?' His tone had been firm, trying to hide his fear.

Lizzy hadn't been able speak; her face buried in his chest as she clung to him, relieved he was home, tears tumbling down her face. He'd heard her sniffles and pulled her away slightly. 'Lizzy? Oh sweetheart!' He'd embraced her harder and they'd stood there for as long as it took for her to stop crying and pull away. Then they'd walked together to the lounge, Tony watching her, waiting for her to speak so he could find out what this was all about.

Once they'd settled on the sofa she'd slowly gone through it, the first time she'd allowed herself to since it had happened. Tony's brow had furrowed as she'd described Reedy's actions and smiled slightly when she'd said how she'd handled herself. But his response hadn't been what she'd expected, in fact it had left her cold.

'And you're sure this was Reedy?'

'What you on about? Of course I'm sure!'

'Were you drunk, Liz?'

'What you saying, Tony? Of course I was drunk, we all were.'

He'd shaken his head. 'I can't imagine him doing that.'

Lizzy had blinked in surprise. 'Tony, he DID do it, it's not a question or something I imagined.'

'Are you sure that was what he was doing, Liz? That he wasn't just trying to pick you up? You know what you're like when you're drunk, you often fall down.'

Lizzy's jaw had dropped open and she'd pulled away from him.

'What? Why are you defending him, Tony? He molested me! Don't you get that!'

He'd tried to stroke her face but she'd batted his hand away. 'I'm sure that whatever happened, it upset you badly, Liz, but Reedy knows better than to do something like that.'

'What are you saying?'

'I'd batter him if he touched you.'

'He did fucking touch me, Tony! He groped me, rubbed his fucking groin against me and slobbered all over my neck! It was revolting!'

Tony's hands had gone up. 'Alright, alright, calm down. I'll have a word with him.'

Lizzy had stood up and crossed her arms tight across her middle. She'd felt herself shaking again. 'You do what the fuck you want, but don't fucking tell me I imagined it! I'm thinking of calling the police.'

Tony had sighed and stood up too, placing his hands on her upper arms gently. 'Oh, Lizzy, don't do that, let me have a word. There's no point making a whole fuss about it, especially not at the moment.'

She'd eyed him suspiciously. 'What do you mean?'

'Well it's only been a couple of months since you lost the baby, you're still recovering from that, especially with it being the second time, and my modelling is just starting to take off, do you really want to create a whole drama out of this?'

Lizzy had been too stunned to speak. He'd taken her silence as agreement and attempted to hug her again even though she hadn't responded. 'It'll be best this way. I'm sorry this happened to you, Lizzy, I really am. I'm home now and it'll all be fine.'

But it hadn't been. His lack of belief and outrage had left her unable to feel any kind of emotion and by the evening she'd even started to doubt herself; asking herself if it had happened, if it was possible at all that she had misconstrued the whole thing. But in the pit of her stomach she'd known she hadn't and her inability to eat dinner that night had reflected it. She'd gone to bed early and had been asleep when Tony had joined her. She'd ignored his attempts to wake her, even though he had.

Because of Tony's reaction she hadn't felt she could share it with anyone. She'd felt like a fraud, as though she'd made it up. If Tony hadn't believed it, why would anyone else? She hadn't called any of the girls. She'd just done what he'd done and pretended it hadn't happen until the following Thursday evening when she'd waited up for him, knowing that he'd been to meet Reedy at the gym to do some sparring.

She'd been hopeful, keen to receive some kind of retribution, some kind of apology once he'd heard the truth from the horse's mouth. But when Tony had come through the bedroom door he'd just smiled at her, and said, 'Hey Lizzy, I didn't think you'd still be up.'

'I just wanted to know what he said.'

'Who?'

'Reedy.'

Tony had paused while taking his shirt off. 'About what?'

'About what he did to me Saturday night!' Lizzy'd shouted, her fury at his ignorance getting the better of her.

'Oh yeah, that.'

Lizzy's emotions had frozen at his dismissive tone.

'Yeah, THAT!' She'd said through gritted teeth. ' did ask him about it, didn't you?'

'Calm down, yes I did.' Tony had sat on the edge the bed to take off his socks.

'And?'

'Well, not a lot. He said you were both really dru and he couldn't remember much. He said he thought y stumbled through the door and he reached for you, b that was all he could remember.'

Lizzy had searched Tony's face for some sort flicker of emotion: was it a joke? Was he going to laugh i a minute and tell her how he had kicked the shit out o him? But there'd been nothing.

'So that was it then? Fuck what happened to your wife how your mate molested her and made her fear for hel life, as long as you and him are good, then it's all fine!'

Tony had straightened, not facing her. She'd been pretty sure he'd rolled his eyes.

'Lizzy, I thought we agreed to not make a big deal out of this?'

'No, YOU agreed you didn't want to make a big deal out of this. Apparently it's okay for your mate to molest your wife while you're away, as long as there's no fuss.'

'Fucking hell, Lizzy, it's not like that at all! If it makes you happy I did threaten him, I told him if I hear any fucking different I will have him. He knows I wasn't messing.'

'If you hear any different? You have heard different — from ME!'

Lizzy had gotten out of bed and stomped round to his side. She'd stood in front of him with her hands on her hips.

'Tell me to my face, Tony, why you are doing this? Why are you disrespecting me so, and for someone like him?'

'Lizzy, it's not disrespect. You were both drunk, shit happens, but you handled it, and you handled it well. I saw the bruises tonight – nice big blue ones on both of sides of his ribs.' Tony'd grinned.

When they'd first got together, teaching Lizzy self-defence had been important to Tony, it was something he'd been very passionate about, and he'd equipped her for every possible scenario.

Lizzy had thrown her hands up. 'So you know I'm not lying!'

'I never said you were lying, I just think you might have misunderstood what happened. We all do that sometimes when we've had a few. And with Reedy being the wind-up merchant he is, he confuses people with his intentions.'

His last comment had taken the wind right out of her and she'd stood slack jawed staring at him. He wasn't going to change his mind about what had happened. His loyalty to Reedy had left her speechless. She'd stumbled back round the bed and got in, turning her back on Tony and thumping the switch on her bedside lamp, putting her side in darkness. Nothing more had been said.

Chapter Twenty-Three

Lizzy shuffled on her cot, her stomach churning as she remembered the following week and encountering Reedy for the first time after it had happened – in her own home. He'd called round to collect Tony for a night out. The half grin, half sneer on his face when she'd jumped at finding him there, his only acknowledgement that anything had happened. He had said nothing, not that night, or any other night for many months. But she wasn't foolish, she knew it was so he could keep up the façade to Tony that he was a good guy. Tony might have acted like it was all nothing, but Lizzy knew he was keeping a close eye – and so did Reedy.

It was so long after the event that even Lizzy's guard was down when he finally did say something, and even then he had done it in such a way that if she repeated it, it could have meant more than one thing. Tony had been right about that, he was good at confusing people – although she knew it was deliberate.

They'd been in the Peacock, last pub of the evening, and everyone had had plenty. Reedy had staggered out of the toilets and walked straight into her, even though she and the girls were standing a fair distance away. He'd used his whole body, almost knocking her to the ground and causing her drink to spill all down her front. As he'd grabbed her to stop her from falling he'd whispered in her ear, 'Oops sorry Lizzy, almost as enjoyable as the last time, don't you think?' And she'd leapt away from him, brushing at her top, trying to hide the flush on her face, the heat of it burning in her cheeks. Some might misconstrue it as embarrassment, but the shake in her hands and racing heartbeat told her it was much more than that: fear and rage.

Tony had looked over but hadn't moved, although when Reedy returned to him, he'd glanced at her a couple of times with concern in his eyes, especially when Lizzy wouldn't return a smile. They'd met up outside the pub to go home and she'd taken his arm without speaking.

'Is everything alright, Liz?'

'Why'd you ask, Tony?'

'What did Reedy do?'

'He fell into me, claiming it was an accident.'

He'd turned his head to her, but she'd kept looking straight ahead.

'Did he apologise?'

'Yeah, but said it wasn't as enjoyable as last time.'

She'd glanced at him and he'd frowned, but she didn't say anything more. There hadn't been much point, and she wasn't going to get into a row about it again.

From that time onwards Reedy had made snide remarks at every opportunity, initially relating to that incident, and then after her third miscarriage, to her inability to keep a child. Tony seemed to ignore her upset more and more, until he eventually joined in.

Lizzy turned over on her cot again. Only now was she beginning to see the influence of Tony and Reedy's friendship on her marriage – how in a lot of ways it had been poisonous. How so much upset and anger had been caused by Reedy and his scathing remarks, insidious in their delivery. Lizzy pondered the intent behind his nastiness. Had Reedy been jealous, and if so, of who? His friendship with Tony had gone back to their childhood. Lizzy tried to remember what Tony had said about it, and realised, not much. He'd been quite tight-lipped, just saying that Reedy had had it rough and Tony had been there for him – no details or explanation for his loyalty. Had Reedy felt he'd been replaced by Lizzy? Or was it that he felt he had a right to everything Tony had? Lizzy turned it over in her head, but she got nowhere, it just left her feeling sick recalling all the puerile, lurid comments Reedy had made. Going over this stuff was only keeping her awake. His arrival in court had managed to disrupt her again.

Lizzy sat up and shuffled onto the floor in the pitch black cell. Sitting cross-legged she attempted to clear her mind but it was difficult, images of Reedy's slimy grin kept flashing through her mind. With persistence she managed to turn it into Tony's loving smile, back in the early days of their marriage. Her heart ached over what she'd done, but again she just kept repeating the same method of clearing her mind and focusing on one point until her body relaxed and the sweep of tiredness came in. She had no idea what time it was when she crawled back onto the cot but when the lights came on in the morning she felt anything but refreshed.

Chapter Twenty-Four

The meagre breakfast they shoved through served its purpose and Lizzy fell back on her cot, hoping to fall into a deep sleep again, but an hour or so later her door popped open and the word 'Visitor' was shouted round the corner. She dragged herself off her cot and ran a brush through her hair, wondering who it would be this time. The thought of Reedy wasn't far from her mind and she prayed it wouldn't be him. She didn't think she could stand that, not after the night she'd had. But when they brought her along the corridor past the visitor's room, she saw her sister Lucy through the window and tears of joy sprouted in her eyes.

The handcuffs didn't allow a proper hug, so a squeeze had to do, and when Lucy pulled away Lizzy saw the same tears in her eyes.

'I'm so sorry I didn't come sooner, Lizzy. As I said in court, part of me just thought this whole thing would blow over, that you hadn't really done anything.'

Lizzy remained silent as she sat down. Lucy joined her and held out her hands across the table. Lizzy took them.

'Maybe I shouldn't ask this, but why, Lizzy? Why for goodness sake? You loved him.'

Lizzy looked down at their intertwined hands, letting her tears fall onto the table. No one had asked her that and she had no idea how to answer.

'Can you even remember the night it happened?' Her sister prompted.

Lizzy nodded her head in a quick sharp motion, releasing her sister's hands and sitting back, wiping the back of a cuffed hand across her nose. Lucy reached into her handbag and pulled out a tissue, causing the guards to take a step forward. She wafted it around showing them what it was before passing it to Lizzy, who held it to her nose as she spoke.

'Unfortunately, Lucy, I do, every detail.'

'Can you tell me about it?'

Lizzy gave a sigh. She hadn't spoken about it yet, not properly. Her therapist had asked her questions about it in the beginning but he'd given up when she hadn't replied. Her silence had been partly due to the drugs and partly because she was so ashamed she couldn't put the deed into words.

'What exactly do you want to know?'

'All of it, how, why … what actually happened, Lizzy?'

Lizzy took a deep breath. 'He'd been having an affair, Lucy – and not just some fling, he'd been with her for two years! He'd even gone public with her, everyone knew, everyone had seen them together.'

'Oh sweetheart.' Lucy put her hand out again and Lizzy took it.

'I'd gone out and seen it with my own eyes, although that had ended badly.'

'Is that the attack that was mentioned in court?'

'Yeah. And he asked me for a divorce, Lucy, that night.'

'What did you say?'

'Nothing. I just walked out of the room.'

'So he didn't ask again?'

'No, but I didn't really give him the opportunity to.' Lizzy thought about all the nights she had gone to bed early when he was home, sometimes as soon as he walked through the door. 'I started avoiding him whenever he was home, although he was out most of the time anyway, away modelling, or some other event related to it. I didn't really know to be honest, and didn't want to. I sort of stopped caring I suppose.'

'So what kicked this off, then? How did it get to murdering them, Lizzy?'

'I came home one day, early from work. I hadn't been feeling too good, so asked if I could leave early. And when I stepped into the hallway I could hear them – doing it – in our bed. She was screaming away and he was grunting like a pig, it was horrible!'

Lucy's other hand went to her mouth, wide-eyed.

'The noise sort of climbed into my head. It was like some kind of drilling noise you can't get away from. It paralysed me and I stood there at the bottom of the stairs, listening to it. They didn't stop so it was clear they hadn't heard me – although how could they with that racket going on.'

Lizzy's nose had turned up, she could still hear the high pitch screeches Sally had made in a kind of rhythm. The image it had created in her head still visible in her mind's eye.

'It was revolting. It turned my stomach and I could feel myself flush all over. I can't explain it. Lucy, I just went straight to the kitchen and got that knife – you know the one, it was mum's, that freezer knife.' Lucy nodded, her eyes wide in fascinated horror. 'I didn't really think about what I was going to do with it or anything, maybe just threaten them, all I could think about as I climbed the stairs was stopping that noise. It wasn't until I was in the doorway that they paused. There they were, in our bed, him on top of her like an animal, all shiny with sweat. She must have seen me as her next scream was one of shock.'

Lucy whispered, 'What did you do?'

Lizzy looked at her, not really wanting to say it, but knowing she had to. 'As soon as I heard that scream, I dunno, it's like it pushed me forward. I put the knife in his back before he could even turn. And when he fell off her, gasping for breath, her screams got worse. I had to stop them.' Lizzy's eyes left her sister's as she thought about the strike she made, all the blood that had gushed out and soaked the sheets. Lizzy's voice also dropped to a whisper as she said, 'I slit her throat.'

Lucy took her other hand to her mouth, and mumbled, 'Oh Lizzy, no.'

They sat there for a moment, tears pouring down Lizzy's face until she breathed in a tiny voice, 'I'm so sorry, Lucy, I'm so sorry. I didn't want him dead, I really didn't. I just wanted him to stop doing that, in our bed, in our house. How could he?'

Lucy took her sister's hands again, clasping them tight as her own tears fell. 'Oh Lizzy, I'm so sorry too.'

Lizzy sat there crying for a while. She wasn't sure if she could stop the tears but eventually they slowed. Lucy didn't say anything and just let her cry, comforting her as best she could from across the table. Once Lizzy had control of herself she continued.

'It's afterwards that my mind seems to get all foggy. I remember trying to sleep in the spare room, but being woken by some flies that had got in due to the smell. I dunno how long I was like that for before the police turned up.'

'Who called them, do you know?'

'They said neighbours and work colleagues had been calling, concerned because no one had seen Tony or me, or been able to contact us.'

'Didn't anyone come round or try and call?'

'They might have, I don't remember, I only remember being in the spare room. I didn't come out, I didn't eat or anything.'

Lucy squeezed her hands. 'I wish I had known things had gotten so bad earlier. I should have got in touch. I thought of it so many times. It's my biggest regret.'

'You shouldn't feel bad. I'm not sure it would have changed anything.'

'No, but as Uncle Peter said, we all knew things weren't right but we didn't do anything.'

'Uncle Peter? Oh gosh, I hadn't thought about him. How is he taking all this?'

'Shocked like the rest of us, but he's fine. It was his idea to get in touch with Marcus.'

Lizzy scoffed. 'What? Does he think Marcus can change any of this?'

Lucy looked a little offended by her tone. 'No, to rally support. He is your brother and you were close to him at one time. Uncle Peter thought he should at least know.'

Lizzy pulled a doubtful face but didn't say anything. Then she asked a question she had been thinking about ever since her sister had shown up in court.

'How's mum? Does she have any idea about any of this?'

Her sister paused, lifting her hands off Lizzy's and sitting back a little. 'I visited her when I first came up and then again yesterday. She asks after you as she does still remember who you are, although she struggled with me initially. I told her you were going through a hard time at the moment, but I didn't go into details. I don't see what it would achieve at this point.'

'But has she noticed my visits have stopped?'

'I think so, by the fact that she asked where you were. But I'm not sure whether in her current state she's capable of understanding how long it has been.'

'She was already like that when I last visited her. She had no idea of time or even what year it was. But she seemed sort of content in her oblivion.'

'Yes, I noticed that. The nurse I spoke to said she rarely has completely lucid moments anymore, and it actually makes it a little easier because she doesn't get so upset about having missed so much.'

'Are you up here alone or are the girls with you?'

'The girls are at home with their dad. We decided it wasn't a good idea they came too, even though they wanted to. They only have a rough understanding of what has happened. They want to see their aunty.'

'Oh gosh, not while I'm in here. I don't think that would be a good idea at all!'

'No, exactly. Although …' Lucy hesitated for a second. 'Depending on the outcome of this it might be the only way they will get to see you again.'

Lizzy looked down at her hands. She knew that was the truth but she hoped to achieve a glimmer of hope.

'There is a chance, depending on how this goes, that I might get the option of release at some point. Many years down the line, mind you, but that's what I'm sort of trying for.'

'That would be something. I can't bear the thought of you in here for the rest of our lives.'

'Me either.'

Lucy reached her hand out to Lizzy again and she grasped it. The guard stepped forward and said softly, 'It's time ladies.'

Lucy let out a big sigh. 'I'll be here the rest of the trial, you can rely on that, so you'll see me in court. And if I'm allowed, I'll visit again. They don't make it easy.'

'I know. Thank you so much for coming.' Lizzy couldn't hold back her tears of gratitude and her sister pulled her into a hug when they stood up. The guard seemed to ignore the lengthy contact this time, maybe knowing it might be the last.

She watched her sister being escorted out and then waited for another guard to take her back to her cell.

Once there, she fell face down on her cot and cried like she'd never cried before, for everything and everyone and all that had happened and was going to happen. She let it all out until she had no strength left in her and fell asleep.

Chapter Twenty-Five

Lizzy slept the rest of Saturday away. She vaguely remembered the slot opening for lunch but she didn't fully wake up until she heard the doors pop for the exercise hour late in the afternoon. She shuffled herself into sitting and shoved her feet into her sandals. Her head felt groggy and her eyes puffy.

She staggered out of her cell and joined the rest of the women as they went out into the yard. The fresh air caused her to yawn and shiver and she found herself standing in a corner, clutching her arms, only able to watch the others do their rounds. Eventually she was spotted by Carlene, who grabbed her while going round and she fell into pace with the rest of them.

'Someone sobbing their heart out from your end of the block, it wasn't you, was it?'

Lizzy nodded.

'What brought that on?'

'Had a visit from my sister this morning.'

'That's a bit of a surprise, isn't it?

'Not really. I'd hoped after seeing her in court she'd come.'

Lizzy fell silent.

'Intense was it?'

'I went through it all, Carlene, from that night. Never said it out loud before, it was like I was talking about someone else.'

'I can understand that.'

'And then family stuff. Talking about my mum and how she's doing.'

'Has she been to visit?'

'No, she's in a home. Dementia.'

'Probably for the best.'

Lizzy glanced at Carlene wanting to feel reproach, but her expression made Lizzy realise she was probably right.

'I miss her.'

Carlene fell silent this time. They all missed someone.

'Any news on your side?' Lizzy asked.

'No, still waiting for court dates to get confirmed. They're dragging their feet with the children having been involved. It makes it all messy.'

'I can imagine.'

'Bickering over the children's ages and whether or not they are old enough to be responsible. Meanwhile they leave them sitting in here, time ticking on and them getting older. I don't want them tried as adults but it's not like I have a say in any of it.'

'Your solicitor any good?'

'She's trying her best, but it's an uphill struggle. There's no precedent for what happened so it's breaking new ground. She wants to bring in a team to support her.'

'What do you think?'

'I think the more the merrier, if it speeds things up. I don't care about me. But I want the kids out of this as soon as possible.'

'Who will be looking after them?'

'My sister and brother want to take them on. They're pushing their end too.'

'Something's gotta give soon, Carlene.'

'I keep hoping. As long as it falls right for them. I don't mind the delay if it means they get out.'

Lizzy took Carlene's arm and gave it a quick squeeze. She responded by patting Lizzy's hand. They continued round a few more times, just observing the other women and talking about other cases. Eventually the bell rang and

Lizzy was ready to go in, looking forward to when dinner came. She was ravenous.

As Lizzy chewed the bland, functional mush they called food, she thought about her sister and how good it would have been if she'd been around over the last few years. Although it would have meant admitting to Lucy she'd been right about Tony – that would have been hard. Despite being here in prison for murdering him, she still refused to think of him how her sister did: a womaniser who couldn't be trusted. She pondered on whether that was where some of the rage had come from. Did she feel that he had let her down in front of her entire family? That his behaviour reflected her inability to pick good men? That all the naysayers had been right all along? After all the crap she had gone through in her teenage, with her mum and sister saying she was going to be used and abused by every guy she met and be treated like some gullible bimbo, he had gone and proven them right, hadn't he?

She felt the familiar bubble of heat in her sternum, the one she'd felt every time she'd heard his key in the lock over the last few months; the one she'd let consume her. She stopped chewing and sat up straighter trying to get it to settle down. She didn't need to feel that way anymore, it was done: the anger, the revenge, the broken pride.

What was that old proverb? Pride comes before a fall? Oh how she had fallen. She looked round at the bare grey walls, a sight she would now live with for a good many years. The price she was paying for feeling enraged about being worth more, and deserving better. Not just from Tony, but from the world. Why couldn't she have had babies like other people? Why had she lost all her children? No one had had an answer. She'd been to multiple hospital visits, had blood tests, gynaecological checks, and nothing, they'd found nothing. They couldn't explain what was going on, why she couldn't carry a child full term or have a live birth. They just fobbed it off as something chromosomal even though there was no history on either side of her family or Tony's. Everyone had said it was just a matter of time, but that was bullshit. They couldn't carry on, it tore them apart – correction it tore her apart. He just took solace in drinking and bedding lots of women. But in their bed had been his mistake.

She felt sick and put her food down. She sat back on the cot and hugged her knees. What had she done? Why hadn't she just packed a bag and walked out? She could have taken him to the cleaners for what he had done – look at all the witnesses there had been to his adulterous behaviour! She would have been sitting pretty.

But even now all she felt was sadness at the love that they had lost. He would have made a great dad too – just like her own.

Lizzy hadn't thought about her dad in ages. This was the first time he had entered her head since this nightmare had began. She felt him keenly now – could almost smell him: he never went a day without wearing his Aramis aftershave. She inhaled deeply remembering how she would snuggle up to him in the armchair, sitting on his lap with her head in the crook of his neck, watching something on the telly. His arms tight round her, often a hand rubbing her back. Just hanging out, being there together, father and daughter. She missed that comfort, that security.

And Tony had been the only person who had matched it. Tony had kept her strong emotionally and physically. She'd relied on him as she had her dad. She'd been sure he would never let her down – not until those last couple of years. And sometimes even then, just for a fraction of a second, she believed that if she could have managed to get herself together they would have been able to pull through.

She thought back to the days he had given her self-defence lessons. How stern he'd always been and how she would giggle when he'd manhandle her into the positions she needed to be in to show her how to topple him. Some days he would get annoyed and have a go at her for not taking it seriously, and other times he would laugh too. But every time he would reassure her that she could do it. It had given her confidence in herself, in her ability to control herself, and she'd needed that after the years without her dad, where nothing had felt sure or comfortable.

Her brother had tried to bridge the gap when her dad had first died, but he had done so in an overbearing, controlling way, which had affected their close relationship. And then he had left to go travelling, to discover his own life, leaving her feeling abandoned all over again.

They had been turbulent years and then with her mum getting ill, everything had felt like it was coming apart. But Lizzy had remained strong for herself and managed to keep it all together, and Tony had felt like her reward for all that.

She thought back to the heady days of their first few years together, their joy at being together and sharing every moment. From picnics in the fields round where they lived, to expensive weekend breaks in the city to see a show. They had embraced it all, doing as much as they could, knowing they wanted to get it all in before they started their own family, and time and money became short.

They'd watched their friends have children before them and learnt the lesson of valuing time on their own. It was also why they had been so ready for a family. She remembered how excited they had been when they started trying. She bought so many pregnancy tests, confident it could happen every month.

The first time Lizzy had fallen it had been a surprise. They had taken a break as Christmas was coming and they wanted to celebrate it with all the food and drink and would begin again in the New Year. But after they came back from a last minute holiday abroad that autumn, Lizzy thought she had caught something; her insides hadn't felt right. And then when she was late she was puzzled. Sometimes it wasn't unusual, but she thought she'd test anyway, just to be sure. And there it was, two defined strips showing they were expecting.

The cliché had happened. She'd rushed into the bedroom waving the stick in his face while he was still waking up. She had bounced on the bed all excited, but also in shock, a little unbelieving, and the thought of her belly getting enormous terrifying her.

Tony had been all smiles, wanting to celebrate in a whole other way, but she was too restless. She'd wanted to work out how far along she might be for the doctors visit she planned to book and all the other information she needed to gather.

Lizzy's mind now stuck on the thought of how she had feared getting a big tummy that first time, when in contrast, by the time she was pregnant for the third time and past the 12 weeks period she was excited at the idea; finally being able to buy and wear proper maternity clothes and actually look pregnant rather than just having gained weight.

But it had never happened.

Lizzy turned over on her cot and pulled herself into a foetal position, rocking slightly as she did. Images flitted through her mind of the horrors that were ahead for them, and then the last time with their last child, Daniel: the blood down her legs, the sharp pains in her lower back, the sensation to push which she'd tried to fight. And all the time the look on his face through it all: cold, numb, and sad. How they had cried as she lay in that hospital bed, him crawling up beside her as they lay there with their tiny bundle; the nurses leaving the room silently and no one interrupting them for what felt like an age. How that night the pain had been unbearable. But she hadn't been alone, not like she was now, in this cold empty cell.

The tears flooded her again, and she rocked herself, this time crying quietly until she lulled herself to sleep.

Chapter Twenty-Six

When morning came Lizzy was shocked she had slept so deeply. She had a trace of a dream but she couldn't catch it. And despite her puffy eyes and raging thirst, she felt refreshed.

Her mind focused on the following day when her solicitor would be visiting her. She had no idea how she would handle being on the stand and if she would be convincing. And after a day of trying to write some things out on a big notepad she'd been allowed to take into her cell, she was relieved when it was exercise time and could discuss it with Carlene.

'You were put on the stand, weren't you?' Lizzy asked.

'Yeah, it's not much fun, everyone staring at you and judging you.'

'No, that's what I was thinking. My solicitor wants them to see me as a person, someone real, give my side of things.'

'That's what they said to me. And I think it helps, you know, giving your own twopence-worth, at least you feel you get a chance.'

'I can hear a 'but' coming …'

Carlene smiled and patted Lizzy's hand. 'But … it's not gonna change anything, Lizzy. You know you did it, they know you did it. You ain't going to have no epiphany up there, no profound release of guilt or anything. It's just saying your piece, and I hope they don't twist it for you.'

'What do you mean?'

'The prosecution can be bastards. They can twist up your meanings and your feelings and all of it. I struggled with that, especially when they kept going on about my kids, and how I egged them on to help me. It was hard.' Lizzy squeezed her hand. 'But you will get through it. Just be short and sharp with them and follow exactly what your solicitor says. Have you got a good one?'

'I think so. He's been very good so far. He took notice of the notes I make during the testimonies, and passed them to the barrister to use – who also seemed pleased. He seemed positive about me getting an option for release. Something he said he wasn't sure would be possible at the beginning.'

'Why?'

'I was so out of it, so doped up and in shock, I barely functioned for the first couple of court dates.'

'Yeah, I remember. But you seem much clearer now. Do you think you are?'

'I think I'm able to face it better now. It's like my brain has worked through all that I did and is slowly accepting it. And I'm letting myself feel now – something I didn't dare before. Whether sad or angry, or indifferent, I just let it happen, you know?'

'Yeah I know. They've got a good therapist in here, haven't they?'

'They have. He's so patient.'

Carlene laughed. 'He has to be with us. He gets so much flak just for being male.'

Lizzy laughed too. 'True. Wonder why they did that?'

'I'm not sure they thought about it. In the other wing they have a woman. They say she's good, too.'

'What about your kids? Are they seeing someone?'

'Yeah, they've got a whole team over there. God, I hope they come through this.'

'Me too.'

They stopped walking and hugged each other. Carlene had tears in her eyes when they pulled away. They sat on a bench.

'Barbara from two cells down is being moved next week,' Carlene said.

'Where to?'

'Maximum security up north near Durnham.'

'Still in psychiatric?'

'Don't know. But it's where they've got space.'

'It never occurred to me they might move me to somewhere far away.'

'It's not permanent here, is it? Could end up anywhere in the country. Couldn't bear being far away from my kids.'

'Do you think they'll serve time?'

'Probably in a borstal at least. I'm hoping for Grant Waverley, I've heard good things coming out of there.'

'You don't think you're jumping ahead, do you?'

Carlene pulled a face. 'Got to face it sometime. I keep praying they won't serve any time, it's what I'm pushing for in all of my testimony, but it's all down to whether the judge goes along with it.'

'Fingers crossed.'

'Yeah and for you too. Any ideas where you might end up?'

'No idea. Suppose it depends if they consider me a threat. And whether they keep me in psych or not.'

'Do you want to stay in psych?'

'I think you get better attention and a chance to rehabilitate. Not sure how I would feel sharing a cell or being out in a crowded prison.'

'Me either. But it's not like we'll get a choice.'

'No, it's not.'

The bell rang and they gathered themselves up to go back inside. They held hands until the last minute and then went their separate ways. Lizzy was grateful for their friendship.

Chapter Twenty-Seven

Lizzy let her mind settle through the evening, meditating for a long time to clear her head. The coming week was going to be a long one; she needed to muster her strength. But when she lay on her cot afterwards, sleep wouldn't come. She thought maybe she'd slept so much the last couple of days she wasn't really tired.

Her mind wandered, as always returning to Tony and his treatment of her over the last few years. She thought about all the time she had spent tracking and stalking him over the last year or so, finding out where his other woman had lived and sitting outside in the car for hours on end, occasionally following her. She thought about the near misses in public places. One stood out in particular.

Lizzy had risen early on a Saturday morning with the intention of following her. She'd left him in bed, snoring off a hangover on one of the rare nights he had returned home. She'd managed to track Sally down on social media earlier in the week and faked an account to befriend her. Luckily for Lizzy, this woman liked to announce the places she planned to go to; the night before she'd tagged the Chadstone shopping centre in Corrington, along with a couple of friends who'd be joining her. Lizzy knew Corrington well, it was only half an hour away. She'd been shopping there often with the girls.

Lizzy had been swift and quiet and in the car before nine o'clock to make sure she'd miss the worst of the traffic through town. Once she arrived in Corrington it was still early and she had the pick of the parking spots. Inside the shopping centre, she settled on a café overlooking a couple of the shops Sally and her friends had mentioned in their enthusiastic comments about their day trip. She got a cup of coffee and a croissant and sat outside, opening a magazine she'd brought with her.

She'd worried she wouldn't spot them but sure enough they'd appeared. She'd spied the three of them browsing a few shops before going into one. Lizzy had debated going in after them, but it was a small boutique and she hadn't want to risk it – she was sure Sally would know who she was. But when they came out they'd headed her way and she'd had to bring her magazine up to hide her face as they settled in the same café at the table next to hers.

Lizzy had panicked, unsure what to do. Despite her intent to follow this woman she'd had no clear idea why she was really following her. Somewhere in the back of her mind she'd had thoughts about finding out details to maybe scare or threaten her, but at that moment with her just a few feet away, she'd lost her nerve, and thought about leaving.

But it had turned out to be the perfect location to eavesdrop and a few words from one of the girls had frozen her to her seat as she'd continued to pretend to read.

'… Reedy too?'

'I like him, but Tony's who I really want.'

'Rumour has it they like to pair up?'

Sally had smirked as she'd replied, 'Yeah, they do. To be honest it's the only reason I agreed to seeing Stu in the first place.'

'So you've been with them both?'

Sally flicked her hair back. 'Once or twice, but not anymore. It's only Tony now.'

'Bet Reedy's not happy about that!'

'He still hangs round a lot, but I don't let him close – although I've let him watch a couple of times.'

The girls had giggled and Lizzy's mind had spun: Tony and Reedy together? Tony share his bed with a woman AND another guy? No, surely not. She's just mouthing off – teasing her mates. And with that Lizzy had stood up from the table, keeping her back to them, and gone to pay. Then she'd hung back until someone else had entered the café and walked out with them blocking any view of her, until she was passed, and then rushed off in the opposite direction.

Her heart had been racing and she'd returned to her car and sat there wondering what on earth she'd heard, and then what on earth she'd thought she was doing! However enraged he'd made her, she hadn't had the guts for this kind of thing. And what would it achieve? Bring him back to her? If he'd found out about any of it he'd have moved out in a heartbeat. It had been the last rational thought she'd had about her behaviour.

Lizzy turned over again for the umpteenth time in her cot, restless at the thought of her stupidity, and how she'd gone on to embarrass herself later in the pub, when she'd attacked Sally. It had been the final action that had brought it all tumbling down around her and placed the final nail in the coffin of hope at ever rekindling their marriage.

Lizzy sat up, fed up with tossing and turning, and leaned against the wall, tilting her head back to see through the tiny cell window high up above her head. She could make out the tiny square of sky, now dark but with a glow at the edge. Could it be the moon? More like the lights in the courtyard.

She pulled the bedding up to her chin, still thinking about the events that led to their collapse. Had the attack on Sally really been the end or had it been before then, when she'd thrown that first punch? Or when he'd thrown his? Had they both realised they'd reached the point of no return then? Is that why it had continued, even though Tony had been more restrained than she had?

She recalled the look on his face when she'd cracked him one across the jaw; the way his eyes has flown open in shock seconds before it hit, and how he'd brought his own fist up in response, just as fast without a second thought until the impact had sent her flying across the room. It ran in slow motion in her mind, the way he had run to her as she'd fallen, trying to stop her, pleading sorry the second he'd done it. But had it knocked any sense into her? It had for a while when they'd sat on the sofa with cold packs over their injuries. His wedding ring had made a complete mess of the edge of her eye socket; the black and turquoise blue had run all the way round.

He'd insisted on her getting an x-ray, and the two of them had sat in A&E looking a right pair: him with his swollen jaw turning a nice reddish black at the edges, and her with her swollen – barely open – rainbow coloured eye. He'd taken her hand gently in his and brought it carefully to his lips, kissing it, tears standing in his eyes, no words needed to express the shame and remorse he'd felt. She'd done the same, both of them feeling like prize idiots.

They'd expected a grilling from the nurses, maybe even the police called, but the response had been much lighter as though trying to hide their mirth at the two of them clearly having given as good as they got, sitting there holding hands throughout and being all tearful.

But a week later he'd gone out and not come home again, so it had been like nothing had happened; they'd still been miles apart emotionally. And then a stream of incidents with Reedy confirmed that Tony wasn't going to treat her any better.

Reminding herself that it wasn't all her fault brought Lizzy back full circle. She had to stop getting lost in the guilt of what she'd done and what caused it. There were so many factors – Reedy being a significant one. With all this time to reflect, and her head finally clearing after all these years now, she was getting the right treatment, she was beginning to see how big a factor his interference had been. From the time he'd appeared his words had caused upset, the miscarriages giving him leverage, and then his actions had led to fractures in her relationship with Tony. It had been Reedy's comments that had started to make her suspicious, too. Tony had been a fool to keep him as a friend. She wondered why he had: he'd known Stu had lied about many things and had no moral values, and he'd known he was a shit stirrer who liked to cause trouble. Lizzy was baffled why Tony had tolerated it, especially once the modelling had taken off. He hadn't needed people like Stu Reed hanging round him. But Tony had still sought him out. It was something she'd never been able to get to the bottom of; she'd never been able to draw Tony out into a conversation about Reedy, he'd always become too defensive.

Lizzy got up from the cot and relieved herself in the corner lavatory, hoping the ritual might enable her to break this thinking and find some sleep, but once back in bed she thought about a list of points that might be worth considering for her testimony. She wished she had access to some light so she could at least write some of them down. She repeated them in her mind several times hoping she would hold onto some of them until morning, but when morning dawned she could only grasp a few, after a light, fitful sleep had left her groggy.

Chapter Twenty-Eight

Lizzy managed to catch another hour of sleep after her breakfast, and then her door popped open and she was called out to a visitor. Even though she knew it was her solicitor, she couldn't be sure after the stream of visitors she'd had, but there Mark Haygarth was, sitting with his pile of files ready for them to try and work out a strategy.

'How're you doing this morning, Lizzy?'

'Bit tired, but alright.'

'Bad night?'

'Wasn't tired enough, and when you spend too much time alone all you do is think and twist your mind up.'

'I can imagine. Have you been thinking about the trial?'

'A little bit.'

Mark tipped his head to the notepad Lizzy clutched.

'Been making some notes?'

'I had loads last night, but it was too dark for me to write them down so I've only managed to remember a few.'

She pushed the pad over to him. He picked it up and took a look.

'Is this a list of incidents?'

'Yeah.'

'Seems most of them involve Stuart Reed rather than your husband?'

'I know. But the more I think about it the more I realise he was the catalyst for many of the fights between Tony and me.'

'Interesting, but what we need on the stand is your side of how the marriage dissolved, rather than place blame on someone else.'

'It's not blame, it's incidents where a fight or argument was triggered.'

Mark nodded, his eyes still on the page. His finger trailed the list – then it stopped.

'Mr Reed molested you?'

Lizzy had forgotten she'd put that down, and felt her face flush.

'Yes.'

'Did you report it to any authorities?'

'No.'

'Why?'

'Because I didn't think I would be believed. Tony didn't believe it, so why should anyone else?'

'Your husband didn't believe you?' Mark looked up in shock.

'Not entirely, no.'

'What? Did he speak to Mr Reed about it?'

'Yeah, he did. He said he threatened him, said that if he found out it was true he'd batter him, but as Stu denied it he didn't take it any further. He thought making a fuss so soon after us losing another baby wasn't a good idea. He just wanted to let it rest.'

'Wow. How did that make you feel?'

'It caused a huge upset between us; I couldn't believe that he chose to believe him over me. I would say it was one of the key things that fractured our marriage.'

'I can imagine. Did he continue his friendship with Mr Reed?'

'Oh yeah, they were inseparable.'

Mark seemed at a loss for words. He returned to the list.

'I see where you are going with this list, but really I'm not sure this is the direction that would help us. It'll be difficult to bring up something like sexual assault if it's never been reported, it might seem like you are creating something to use as an excuse.'

Lizzy's eyes went round and she sat forward opening her mouth to protest, but Mark put his hand up.

'I know, I know, I don't believe that – having witnessed Mr Reed on the stand the other day I am quite convinced he did assault you. But one: we can't prove it, and two: there's no record of it. It will seem like we're plucking things out of thin air. It might be a trigger point for the demise of the marriage, but– '

'It was more than a trigger, Mark, it changed the entire status of trust and respect. It was a complete game changer.'

Mark put the pad down and sighed.

'Do you really think Tony believed him over you? Or do you think he might have decided that it would be too much for you to go through after the loss of your child?'

'Does it matter?'

Mark frowned. 'What do you mean?'

'Mark, I was violated. Reedy did this in our home, when Tony was away. I handled it – as Tony taught me how to handle myself – but I was still scared for my life until Tony walked through the door again. Tony was concerned, he didn't dismiss me, but I expected more from him. After he knew I was alright and nothing major had happened, he just brushed it under the carpet as though it was nothing and carried on as usual with Reedy. It doesn't matter who he believed, it was that it didn't seem to matter enough to make a fuss over. And one thing Tony had always done in our relationship up until that point was to make a fuss of me.'

'Okay. So it is a factor, and a significant one, but we can't use it in court due to a lack of evidence.' He picked up the pad again.

'What sort of thing can we use then?'

'We need to sort of establish a timeline of events, things we know about for certain and can refer to directly.' He ran his finger down her list. 'These incidents are small, sort of skirmishes. And as you say, they are significant but it's the bigger things like the miscarriages, events like those on the girls holiday, you attacking Ms Bryant, that kind of thing.'

'But the assault was a big thing, it was a HUGE thing!'

Mark looked up. Lizzy was restraining tears, her face burning. He put the pad down and leaned across the table to touch her arm.

'I'm sorry, Lizzy, I didn't mean to upset you, and make you feel dismissed all over again. Let me note this down and look into it, discuss it with some colleagues and see if there is a way we can approach it that we don't have to get bogged down in the details of it. I don't want the prosecution using it against you, that's all, and they could. If they can undermine anything you say, they will. We need to stick to hard facts.' He straightened in his seat and took the pad. 'Okay, I see you've given me a timeline of your pregnancies, and also his modelling career. Do you think these things caused distance between you?'

'Definitely, especially when he didn't have a new baby to show off or talk about. It was hard having it in the newspapers, too, although we were left alone on the whole. But the more popular and in demand he became with photo shoots, the less time we spent together.'

Mark scribbled down some notes on a fresh sheet of paper.

'And you have an incident here at an event you attended …?'

'Yes, the last one I attended with him.'

'What happened?'

'When someone suggested I dance with him, he said he couldn't because I was too fat.'

'What blatantly, just like that?'

'Well, he said he wanted to dance with someone lighter on her feet, and how it would be difficult to move round a dance floor with someone carrying so much weight.'

Mark raised his eyebrows. 'That's pretty blatant. What did you say?'

'Nothing. I left.'

'Right in the middle of it?'

'Yes, I got a taxi back to the hotel, changed rooms, and left early the next morning.'

'What did he say about that?'

'Nothing, not a word. Just came home later and that was that.'

'So there was a complete breakdown in communication?'

'Yes.'

'Okay. We need to ask questions about these. Do you have other incidents of him speaking to you this way publicly?'

'A couple, but after that event I didn't go out much … well not to socialise with him, only to spy on him.'

'Spy on him?'

'Yes, sometimes I would follow him, or her, or him and her.'

'Okay.' Mark scribbled in his pad again. 'And I assume doing that didn't help you, in fact probably made you feel worse?'

Lizzy paused, thinking about it. 'I suppose it did. I didn't really think about it like that, I was just so lost in my rage and hatred. But yes, I suppose it did only make me feel worse, sort of fuel the fire.'

'Was there anything that made you feel better?'

'Only going to the gym and working it out on the machines.'

'Well that's a positive, rather than a negative. You gave yourself some sort of outlet. Did you ever seek professional help from a psychiatrist, or psychologist, about any of your feelings, about the marriage or the loss of the babies?'

'I was offered counselling after I lost the babies, and I did see someone a few times after I lost our third child, Amber.'

'Did it help?'

'A little bit.'

'And the last baby you lost, you also lost late, didn't you?'

'Yes, I was coming up on twenty weeks. It was a little boy, Daniel.'

'Did you see someone after you lost Daniel?'

'No. I couldn't talk about it for ages. I just couldn't. And maybe that was a mistake. But I just focused on trying to think of another way of having a baby, whether fostering or adopting. I felt like time was running out.'

'Was Tony supportive of this idea?'

'No. We had a lot of rows about it, he said he wasn't ready.'

'So another bone of contention; we're racking up quite a few. There's his friendship with Mr Reed, and then the modelling career, and then him not wanting to foster or adopt a child.'

'Gosh that sounds like we didn't come together on anything. It wasn't like that.'

'So how was it?'

'He just felt that I needed to recover more. And I think the loss of our children affected him too – and not just from the viewpoint of his career. Like me, I think he felt judged by the outside world: what was he doing staying with a woman who couldn't carry his children? Reedy in particular used to make jokes about that.'

'How did Tony respond to those jokes?'

'It depended. He might tell him it was enough, or he might laugh if he had enough beer. But he would always end up saying that Reedy meant nothing by it.'

'Do you think Mr Reed meant anything by it?'

'Reedy liked to cause trouble. I think he might have been jealous of Tony – or even of me! – and he wanted to stir the pot. I don't know what his motives were. All I know is that I didn't understand why Tony remained friends with him.'

'Could there have been any other reason behind their friendship?'

'None that I know of.'

'Okay, but it's all speculation anyway, and not any help in our case.' Mark sat back. 'Tell me more about your marriage: was it just you fighting for it alone? Do you think Tony wanted it?'

'Not sure what you are getting at?'

'Why didn't he ask for a divorce sooner, before his affair with Ms Bryant?'

'Because he could have his cake and eat it, I suppose. Someone at home to do all his bidding, and someone to go out and show off with.'

'Do you think that's the truth or do you think it's more complicated than that?'

'Because we stopped talking to each other it's hard to say. I mean after every fight there would always be a truce, or a show of tenderness, and on occasion love-making that would put us back on track. It's sort of how the years flowed after the miscarriages.'

'You use the word tenderness, can you give me examples?'

'Often after a row Tony would pummel a punch bag he had in the basement, and after one really bad row he came back upstairs with his hands bleeding. He let me wash them and bandage them, without a word, knowing it was my way of apologising. And we made love after. And then the first time our rows became physical and I hit him, he struck me back really hard, giving me a black eye. He insisted we went to the hospital to get an x-ray and he held my hand the entire time. He took complete responsibility. There was still love and caring, but it was getting lost in everything else.'

'How often did your fights become physical?'

'Not often, it was only after I knew about his affair with Sally. I started it really. I hit him, punched him right across the jaw, and he reacted by punching back. I think we probably had about four or five fights like that.'

'Did you end up with many injuries? Did you have to go to the hospital again?'

'No. He always came off worse, because he tried not to hit me back. Usually he was trying to get hold of my arms and pin me down to stop me. I might have had a few bruises, round my wrists or where he had to climb on me to hold me down, but he never punched me in the face again. He was a better man than that.'

'Okay. So you wouldn't say it was domestic abuse then?'

'Oh gosh no – well, unless it was him being battered by his wife! I left him with bruises across his torso a couple of times – cracked a rib once too. We went to the hospital for that.'

'Did you feel remorse?'

'Always.'

'But you couldn't stop yourself?'

'Not in the moment. Our fights were mostly screaming, and either one of us would walk out. But every now and then I would just lose it completely.'

'This was more towards the end you say?'

'Yes, the last year, sort of like a build-up. And the fights were always about him being out with her.'

'Did you ever speak about divorce?'

'Yes, the night after I attacked her in the pub. He asked for one then.'

'What did you say?'

'Nothing, I walked out.'

'And he didn't bring it up again?'

'No. But then it wasn't long after that I killed them.'

Mark stopped; his pen paused in mid-flow on the page. He looked at her. Her eyes shifted. 'What?'

'I've never heard you say that, Lizzy, so blunt, so cold. I'm not sure I like it.'

'It's a fact Mark, it's what I did, I have to face and accept that.'

'Yes, but make sure you don't say that in court, Lizzy, it might make it hard for us to convince them it wasn't intended.'

He continued writing.

'Aren't we going to talk about it in court then?'

'What?'

'That night, and what I did?'

'Yes, but I hope Mr Davis will elicit a more emotional description. More on what went on inside your head. He's going to ask you questions about what happened that day, how you found them, what you thought, felt, and your actions. Do you think you will be able to handle that?'

She nodded. 'I went through it with my sister. It was the first time I had ever said it all out loud, so hopefully I can. But it won't be easy.'

'I know that, Lizzy. I don't expect it to be. And neither will the jury.'

Mark put his pen down and sighed.

'It's going to be tough, but Mr Davis will lead you through it, Lizzy, and he'll make sure you don't digress too much. The most important thing is making sure the prosecution have nothing to feed off, to give any suspicion that you thought about killing them before that day.'

'But I didn't. Right up to that day I still hoped we might find some kind of way or reconciling everything; that he would stop his affair and give us another chance.'

Mark quickly scribbled her words down. 'That's good Lizzy, he can ask you about that, we can get that across.'

The guard stepped forward. 'Sorry Mr Haygarth, but times up.'

'Really? That was double the time?'

The guard nodded.

'Okay.'

Lizzy felt a pang of fear in her belly. 'Is that it then? Do you think we're ready?'

'I've asked for them to bring you an hour early on Friday, so we have some time before the court session starts, with Mr Davis too, just to do a quick run-through. I'll have the questions fully prepared.'

Mark stood up collecting his papers and putting them into his briefcase.

'Will I be first?'

'There'll only be you, Lizzy. This is your day.'

'Oh.' Lizzy found the idea daunting. 'And will the verdict be the same day?'

'I hope so, unless they make us wait over the weekend.'

Lizzy stood as he moved towards the door.

'Thanks Mark, you've been great.'

'I'm doing my best for you, Lizzy, let's hope the effort will be worth it.'

Lizzy didn't reply, just waved him goodbye as the guard escorted him out and another came in to take her out.

Chapter Twenty-Nine

Lizzy returned to her cell for lunch and then was called again for her visit to the therapist. As she settled into the chair of the tiny office he smiled at her.

'How's Lizzy?'

'Not too bad.'

'And how was Friday in court?'

'Interesting – and upsetting. A couple of Tony's friends testified, then one of mine and my sister.'

'Which were interesting and which were upsetting?'

Lizzy sighed. 'All of them I suppose, although all for different reasons. Reedy had to be the most upsetting. He was one of Tony's best mates: slimy, nasty piece of work, always shit-stirring between us. He came out with a string of lies, but my barrister managed to discredit him. And Hayley, bless her, one of my old friends – we used to be quite close – stood up for me on the stand, but it didn't quite turn out so well, painted me as someone suicidal and falling apart …'

'In light of your diminished responsibility plea, is that wrong?'

'True. I was probably near breaking point, but I wasn't as bad as she made out – well, I didn't think so anyway. But she sort of made out that I was driven to murder him, sort of out for revenge. I wouldn't say that was accurate.'

'What would you say was accurate?'

'Maybe I was falling apart in the sense that I was letting it all consume me, and desperate to stop my husband having an affair. I was obsessed and driven towards ending their affair – but not in that way, murder never crossed my mind.'

'Did you have a plan of any sort do you think?'

Lizzy pulled a face. 'No, not really. I just wanted to find out as much as I could, so I didn't feel like I was being kept in the dark. No, no plan. I was just consumed with anger.'

'What do you think the anger was mostly about?'

'Betrayal. That I was worth more than that. That I deserved better after everything I had gone through after trying to have a family. That it wasn't fair that she was getting all of his attention.'

'So you wanted his attention?'

'Yes.'

'What did you hope to gain from his attention?'

Lizzy frowned. 'I'm not following you.'

'You were already his wife, you had a home together. What kind of attention did you want from him?'

'I wanted him to talk to me. To love me again. To be tender and loving and reassuring.'

'Did you ever say that to him?'

'I might have.'

'In a calm rational way?'

Lizzy thought back to all the rows. 'No probably not.'

'Was he ever like that?'

'Oh yes, definitely.'

'When did it change?'

'After we lost Daniel, our fifth baby.'

'Do you think you might have changed then, too?'

'Yes. I think I shut down after we lost him. It was so different from the others.'

'The pregnancy?'

'Partly because it was the furthest I'd ever gotten. But no, after. It was like it took the wind out of us – him too. We had our hopes so high that time, we were convinced we would finally have a child and then all our hopes and dreams were pulled out from under us.'

'Did you talk about it after?'

'No. That's what was different. There was this silence that neither of us knew how to fill. None of the old lines of comfort worked for either of us anymore.'

'What did you do?'

'After a while I looked into fostering and adoption but Tony didn't want that. He said it was too soon.'

'Did you think it was?'

'I don't know, maybe. I just needed something to focus on, something positive, some way of salvaging our hopes, I suppose. But he wasn't up for it. We had big rows about it.'

'How did they end?'

'Usually with him walking out.'

'He refused to talk about it?'

'He just kept repeating that it was too soon and he wasn't ready to think about it and if I pushed him he would definitely say no to it.'

'How did that make you feel?'

'Desperate. I so needed something good to focus on, some action I could take to change the fact that I couldn't give us a child. I needed there to be a happy ending. But he just wouldn't help me take any steps towards that.'

'Did you feel let down by Tony?'

'Yes a little bit. He wasn't giving me a chance to make up for losing the babies.'

'Make up for losing the babies? Did you feel he blamed you?'

'No, he never blamed me. But it was my body that didn't work, wasn't it? Not his. His end worked. We got pregnant often enough, but it was my body that failed to carry them full term.'

'And you felt you had to compensate for that in some way?'

'Well, yes. We always planned on having a family; it's what we both wanted. I had to find a way somehow.'

'Do you think he wouldn't want to stay with you if you didn't have a family then?'

'He said that our marriage was never about whether we had kids or not, that it had always been about us.'

'But you didn't believe him?'

'I wanted to, but then he was with her, wasn't he?'

John let out a big breath. 'I see. How was it seeing your sister in court? I understand she came and visited you on Saturday, too?'

'It was good, really good. She surprised me up there on the stand, supporting me. I didn't expect that. And then her turning up.'

'What did you chat about?'

'All sort of things, but mostly the murders.'

'The murders?' Her therapist raised his eyebrows.

'Yes. I went over the night I killed them.'

John look stunned for a moment. 'The night you killed Tony and Sally?'

'Yes.' Lizzy felt a little embarrassed by his surprise.

'What prompted that?'

'She asked me why I had done it when I had loved him so much. And she asked me if I remembered it. I told her I did, in perfect detail.'

John sat up a little. 'So you recounted it all?'

'Yes.'

'Did you find it hard?'

It was Lizzy's turn to take a deep breath. 'It's a bit like ripping off a plaster. It's hard thinking about it and you pick at the edges of it, but once you get a hold of it and pull it off you feel a whole lot better and it wasn't nearly as painful as you thought it would be.'

John didn't speak for a moment, so Lizzy continued.

'It was the first time I'd ever said it all out loud. It felt like I was talking about someone else doing it.'

'I can imagine.'

'But it was therapeutic in its own way. I cried myself to sleep that night. I haven't cried like that since I lost my dad. And things feel a little clearer now than they did before.'

'In terms of what happened?'

'Yes, and what's ahead of me.'

'Are you worried about the conviction?'

'I know I'm going to be in here a long time, but I'd like to think I might get a chance at starting over again outside these walls.'

'You want that?'

'Yes. I didn't for a while there, but I think I do.'

'Wow, Lizzy, this is great. You seem to be coming to terms with what happened, taking responsibility for it, and finding a way to live with it.'

'I'm not there yet though, Doc. I've still got to take the stand.'

'Does it scare you?'

'Definitely.'

'Do you really think there is anything that you can say that would be wrong?'

'If I come off all cool, calm and collected about it, I don't think it'll go in my favour.'

'Do you feel all cool, calm and collected about it though?'

Lizzy thought back to her endless night of tossing and turning and all the thoughts she had about Reedy and all the events that had happened.

'No, not really. There's still stuff spinning around in there.'

'What sort of stuff?'

'Stuff about Reedy, Tony's best mate. How much trouble he caused, how nasty he had been, and how Tony had sided with him sometimes.'

'Sided with him over what?'

'Reedy would make rude remarks about me not being able to carry a baby full term, and make sexual innuendos about him maybe taking over from Tony to give him a rest. He even sexually assaulted me one night, too.'

John's eyebrows went up again. 'Did you tell Tony about it?'

'Yes. But he didn't want to make a fuss about it.'

'So he didn't even speak to his friend about it?'

'He says he did, says he threatened him, told him if he found out it was true he'd beat him up. But he didn't want to take it any further.'

'If it was true? So he didn't believe you?'

'He believed something happened, but he thought I was drunk and had misinterpreted it.'

'Were you drunk?'

'I was until he did that. I'd never sobered up so fast!'

'What did you do?'

'I assaulted him right back, elbow to ribs, knee to groin and shoved him out the door.'

Her therapist smiled. 'Sounds like you handled it well.'

'That's what Tony said. But it really shook me up.'

'Did you report it?'

'No, because Tony didn't want me to; he thought it was too much after the miscarriage earlier in the year.'

'Did that upset you?'

'I wasn't fussed about reporting it, but the fact that he remained friends with Reedy bothered me a lot. I didn't understand that. Why would you remain friends with someone who sexually assaulted your wife?'

'Did it affect things between you?'

'Definitely. It was never the same after that. It was like I couldn't trust him anymore. He became someone I could no longer be sure of.'

'Did you have many people in your life you could be sure of?'

'No, not really. Tony was it really. All my family lived far away – well except mum and Uncle Peter, but mum was in the nursing home by then, and Uncle Peter popped round from time to time but our relationship wasn't like that. I had a couple of friends I was close to, although later on I stepped away from everyone.'

'Why did you step away, do you think?'

'Nobody could relate to anything I was going through, and they were sick of me talking about it. Losing the babies and stuff, people expect you to get over it and move on, and the first couple of times I could, but after that it just became too hard. And then with the troubles with Tony – people got sick of me talking about that, too.'

'Even your friends?'

'Yes, even my friends. All they could see was this guy who was becoming a celebrity. Some of them thought I was jealous or sour grapes, or something; others thought I had nothing to complain about. They'd say "So women look at him, so what? He's a model, it's what they're supposed to do." None of them got it; none of them understood how much he had changed.'

'Do you think you changed too?'

'Oh yes, definitely. I used to be the life and soul of the party. It's what made my friendship with Hayley so special; we were the two wild ones everyone had a good time with. That all stopped after the babies.'

'Do you think you could have changed anything that happened?'

'Maybe. Maybe if I'd had more help, you know, like gone into therapy sooner.'

'At any time did you and Tony sit down and talk about getting some counselling – even for your marriage?'

'What? Tony try marriage counselling?' Lizzy laughed. 'No way, he wouldn't have a bar of it. No. He wasn't that type of guy. He wasn't about to talk about his feelings with a stranger.'

'So he didn't come with you when you went to counselling after you lost the babies?'

'Well, he came to a couple of the sessions about the grief counselling, after I lost Amber – our third. But counselling about our marriage? No.'

'Do you think it would have helped him?'

'I don't know. His way of dealing with it was getting on with life, and trying again. He wasn't someone who would give up easily on things.'

'You don't feel he gave up on your marriage, then?'

Lizzy paused. She'd never looked at their marriage that way. 'He didn't walk out – well, not permanently, so no. I don't think he gave up. I sort of felt like he was waiting.'

'Waiting? For what?'

'For me to settle down, calm down, pull through whatever I was going through.'

'So you felt it was all down to you?'

'Yes.'

'He wasn't responsible for anything?'

'It was me who got all upset after the babies, me who gained weight, me who started shouting and screaming, me who went off the rails.'

'And he had no hand in it?'

Lizzy stopped. She looked at John like he had asked a rude question. 'I murdered *him*, Doc, not the other way round.'

'No, I'm talking about the lead up to it. You think everything was all your fault, the entire marriage, Lizzy? Have you ever considered that it takes two? That he could have been more supportive, tried harder?'

'Yes, sometimes, but …'

'There's always a but, isn't there?' John smiled. 'I'm not saying he was responsible for your actions, but he could have changed the outcome with some of his.'

Lizzy gave a small smile. 'I don't expect to hear people defend me, not after what I did, or after how I behaved over the last couple of years, but yes, deep down I think a lot of my anger started because I felt he wasn't doing anything to help our marriage. I was angry at him for that.'

'It's okay to be angry, Lizzy, to feel betrayed, even let down by your husband. All those emotions are okay. But it's the action we take in response to them that matters.'

Lizzy looked at her hands in her lap.

'Our times up for today, Lizzy, but I think we've had a really good chat. Would you like to come again before Friday?'

'Can we?'

'Sure, although it might have to be a short one. How about Thursday afternoon?'

'Okay.'

Lizzy stood up. 'Thanks, Doc, you help me see things from another angle.'

'It's what I'm here for.'

Chapter Thirty

Lizzy was taken back to her cell, her head buzzing with the conversation she'd had with her therapist. She wasn't sure what to make of it. She wasn't used to people defending her. She'd always thought the failure of their marriage was down to her. It started with losing the babies, but then she'd let herself go after not being able to recover from losing Daniel. His little face etched forever in her memory. The little boy they'd both so desperately wanted. She'd tried to suppress her grief with food. She'd gained excessive weight and lost all interest in going out. But had she given herself a chance? Had anyone given her a chance? She felt like she'd only been allowed to mourn for a limited time before moving on. It hadn't just been her friends that had made her feel that way, but Tony too. She didn't think anyone had been surprised when he'd gone off with another woman, but her friend's testimony in court had shown her that wasn't true. How many other assumptions had she made that were wrong?

People had cared but they hadn't known what to do. She wished someone had reached out, it would have made such a difference, but they had backed off.

Her thoughts were distracted by the exercise bell. She plodded out, not really paying much attention, walking round the yard lost in thought.

'Lizzy? Eh, Lizzy!'

Carlene's voice penetrated the swirl inside her head. Lizzy spotted her on one of the benches and headed over.

'You've got your head in the clouds this afternoon.'

'Yeah, the Doc gave me a lot to think about.'

'Good stuff?'

'Different stuff. He suggested that it wasn't all my fault – you know the build up to the murder? That maybe Tony added to it, too.'

'You telling me you've never thought that before?' Carlene sounded incredulous.

'No, not really. I always saw that it was me driving him crazy, not the other way around. I was so full of rage. I mean, I knew that he had treated me badly and he was off with another woman, but I didn't make it easy for him at home, and after we lost the babies and stuff I just sort of let myself go.'

'Are you blaming yourself for his affair?'

'Maybe if I'd had my shit together, and looked after myself–'

'Stop right there!' A few heads turned at Carlene's raised voice. Lizzy was startled by her anger.

'You went through hell losing those babies, don't you dare blame yourself for not bouncing back and being the perfect wife! Did he help you? Did he encourage you?'

Lizzy's eyes were wide. 'Maybe not, but–'

'No! No buts!' Carlene wagged a finger in front of her nose. 'You know damn well that he didn't support you the way you needed him to. And then he started fucking someone else – in your house!'

The yard had stilled. Carlene glanced round and took a deep breath, smoothing down her skirt as she did so. Seeing no fight, the other women carried on.

'I'm sorry, Lizzy, but women make excuses for abusive men all the time. And it might not have been physical, but often emotional is much worse. Refusing to talk, treating you like shit in public, and then parading another woman around behind your back? You've got to be crazy to think that it was all your fault, you really have!'

Lizzy was stunned into silence. In her own mind she knew all the things he had done to upset her and break her heart, but she had also come up with reasons behind him doing it: her screaming and shouting, the embarrassment of having a wife who couldn't keep a baby, and then having a fat wife. But no he hadn't been helpful or supportive. He hadn't said much, and what he had said had rarely been complimentary or reassuring.

'Lizzy?' Carlene put her hand on hers. 'I'm sorry for getting angry. I didn't mean anything by it.'

'Oh no, Carlene, it's fine, really.' Lizzy patted her hand. 'You're right. I haven't made him responsible for his part, not in my mind. I've always taken it all on myself. I know all the things he did wrong, but I always thought I did worse. I did do some dreadful things – and then I murdered him! I can't blame him for that now, can I?'

'No sweetie, you can't, you have to accept that that was a step too far, but at the same time, it was a result of many things. Not all murder is black and white, in fact for most of us in here it's the exact opposite – really messy. It's a process, Lizzy, and we are all going through it. But ease up on yourself and putting yourself through it mentally, okay?'

'Okay.' They gave each other a hug.

As she walked back to her cell, Lizzy's mind continued to go over all the things she'd done, particularly in those last few months. How the fights had escalated, how her stalking had escalated. She hadn't talked to anyone about those things.

The one night she would never forgot was the night she'd feigned illness. He'd asked her several times that week if she was going out. She had been undecided until Friday when she said she felt tired and not up to it. She couldn't tell if he was relieved or not.

Once he had gone out, leaving a pungent trail of aftershave behind him, she had moved fast, getting ready herself, but not in her usual get up – oh no. She'd bought a wig earlier in the week, a jet black one, in a sharp bob cut – a complete contrast to her dish-water blonde mess of long split ends. It made her face look pale, and she'd used dark eye make-up with brilliant red lipstick to top it off. She looked like something out of the 1920s, no one would know it was her.

But Lizzy wasn't one for drinking alone, so she'd asked one of her new friends to meet her. Sharon had barely recognised her, which is what she'd wanted, and they'd had a good laugh about it. Lizzy had explained that she wanted to cut loose and pretend to be someone else for the night. Sharon had been more than happy to go along with it.

Lizzy had known which pub Tony would start in, and sure enough, he'd been there. He'd surprised her though by only being with the lads, but she'd bided her time, knowing better.

Her new look had attracted a bit of attention at first, some of the lads had looked over, interested in 'the new girl in town', so she'd kept to the corners with Sharon until eventually as the night had worn on and more people had come out, she'd been able to merge into the background and observe what was going on.

And in the second to last pub of the night her stealth had been rewarded: Tony's new woman had joined him. Lizzy had been shocked at how open they were. Adrenaline had pumped round her system and her hands had trembled as she sipped at her drink, but she resisted the urge to make a scene – that night anyway – due to Sharon.

Sharon was such a new friend she hadn't known who Lizzy was married to. They'd met through work; Sharon had joined the company and moved into the area only six months earlier. Lizzy had offered to take her out and introduce her to some of her other new friends. They always met in town; Sharon had never been to Lizzy's home. It was refreshing to be with someone who didn't know about all her problems. Plus it gave her a chance to hear the gossip she wouldn't normally hear.

'Here, Lizzy, do you know him?'

'Who?'

'Him over there, the one with that bird all over him?'

Lizzy played along. 'I've seen him about, his name's Tony.'

'He's married I heard, but that's not his wife.'

'Really? You don't say!'

'I know. He's got quite a reputation. He's also a model apparently; I saw some of his pictures in one of those men's mags, for some aftershave or something.'

'Yeah, I know. He's becoming quite the celebrity round here.'

'Wonder if his wife knows he's out with another bird.'

'I doubt it; otherwise she wouldn't be his wife anymore, would she?'

'That depends. I heard she never comes out anymore, used to be quite the socialite, but now she stays at home. They lost a baby last year apparently.'

'Really? That's sad.'

'Yeah it is. He doesn't seem to care though, does he?'

Lizzy hadn't replied, she'd just kept sipping on her drink, and watched them canoodle, her stomach in knots, the drink starting to churn. She hadn't been drunk enough to handle this scene.

'Shall we move on to the Peacock, get in before the rush?' she'd suggested.

Sharon had nodded and they'd drunk up and left. Lizzy accidentally bumped into his woman on her way out – giving her a harder shove than necessary and shouting sorry over her shoulder with a giggle. The woman had given her a sharp look but Lizzy had ignored it.

In the Peacock, Lizzy had asked Sharon if she wanted to go on to the nightclub, but she'd said no, having to get up early the following day. Lizzy had been relieved. She hadn't thought she could handle seeing them there, too.

Although when the pub emptied and they'd been queuing for a cab, Lizzy'd seen them walk in the opposite direction. Clearly they hadn't been planning on going to the club after all.

The taxi had dropped Sharon off first, so Lizzy had redirected him to where she thought they'd gone. She hadn't known the woman's name at that point, but had a rough idea where she lived, having known who some of her friends were. And sure enough, as the cab pulled down one of the side streets, she'd spotted them turning a corner at the end.

She'd told the cabbie to pull over and paid him while getting out, waiting for him to drive off before making her way to the corner they'd just gone round. She knew the layout of these streets well and she'd walked with purpose, not planning on slowing when she turned the same corner. But her heart had been racing and her hands sweating, so she'd crossed to the other side of the road to avoid coming face to face with them if they'd stopped. She needn't have worried, they hadn't been there; they'd stopped much further down the road outside one of the houses and were leaning against the small garden wall slobbering over each other.

Lizzy had wondered why they hadn't gone in until a car had pulled up, causing Lizzy to hesitate. Out jumped Stu Reed and some woman he'd managed to snag for himself. Then the four of them had gone inside.

Lizzy had carried on walking, pacing herself and slowing down as she'd passed the house, feeling safe in the darkness on the other side of the road. The lights in the downstairs room had been on and the curtains wide open. She'd been sure she'd caught a glimpse of a woman straddled across Tony on a sofa. The sight had sparked another flood of adrenaline, but this time one of upset. Tears had flooded Lizzy's vision, causing her to stumble as she'd tried to rush away.

Even now, in her cell, Lizzy could feel the sensation: the drop in her stomach, the sharp pain in her gut as though someone had stabbed her, and the tightness round her chest. All of them had remained as she'd rushed home, the walk across town seeming to go by in a flash as her mind kept showing her images of the two of them together.

Once home she'd rushed upstairs and stripped everything off, climbing into the shower, trying to wash herself clean of those images. It'd felt the same as when Reedy had molested her. But much like then, no matter how long she stood under the shower head, they'd refused to be washed away.

She'd ended up climbing into bed and curling up into a tight ball, sobbing herself to sleep.

Lizzy found herself lying in the same position now, on the cot in her tiny cell. That had been just the beginning of her stalking trips, which had escalated over the months and weeks to follow until the ultimate night when she could bear it no more and had attacked his floozy.

Chapter Thirty-One

Despite the shame she felt about that fateful night, Lizzy could still feel the rage. This was the juxtaposition she lived with, and it was what had driven her past the point of no return.

Lizzy had gone out wearing the same black wig, but had been on her own, tailing them from pub to pub, sitting in the corner, supping on her beers. She'd already consumed half a bottle of wine before she'd left the house, so by the time she'd slipped into the Angel she'd been in a misty zone of alcohol-induced intent.

Her mind had been a cesspool of furious thoughts and seething retorts as she'd run through all the things she would say if she confronted them. But she still hadn't quite had the nerve, despite her skinful. In the end it had been their actions that had triggered her: Sally's hand had fallen to Tony's arse and squeezed it, and he'd responded by putting his arm round her to pull her in for a kiss. All sense had left Lizzy.

She'd flown out of her corner and rushed the woman, going for the hair. She hated the perfect shiny blonde locks that cascaded down her back like something out of a magazine. Lizzy had dreamt of grabbing hold of them and now she did, yanking as hard as she could, pulling Sally back, causing her to scream.

Lizzy couldn't remember if she'd made a sound, maybe a grunt as they'd landed on the ground, then Lizzy had been on top of Sally, throwing punches left and right.

Hitting her face again and again. Lizzy had been in the grip of an adrenaline rush and barely noticed all the hands grabbing at her, trying to pull her off. She'd resisted, throwing herself back at her time and again. But in the end there'd been too many and she'd been dragged off her and thrown out of the pub, into the street outside.

She remembered lying there, trying to catch her breath, bringing herself up on her arms, her wig all askew. She'd pulled it off and crawled to the pub wall, and sat back against it. Then she'd realised someone was watching her.

She'd looked up to find Tony staring at her with a look of disgust on his face. He'd said, 'Get up' in a low voice. She hadn't been sure if it was anger or embarrassment – or both.

She'd done as he'd said, and once standing he'd gripped her arm and led her to the taxi rank. They'd climbed into the back of a cab and sat in silence for the journey home.

It was only once there that he'd spoken, tainting her rage with shame and turning it all back on her. And then the ultimate: speaking about divorce. That was when she'd known she'd pushed it as far as she could and she wasn't going to win the battle she'd created. That was when she'd realised she'd driven him away.

He hadn't come upstairs after her that night, when she'd run away from his words, instead she'd heard the front door just a matter of minutes after, and known he'd gone back to her.

From that point on Lizzy had shut down. It was over and there was only herself to blame. When he'd arrived home later the next day she hadn't spoken and he didn't make her. And from that point on there were no more words. It had in fact been their last conversation.

Lizzy hadn't allowed herself to think in terms of him being to blame, not since she had murdered them and gone into a state of shock and drug-induced stupor. In the clearing of her mind she could only see that she had brought herself to this point, and she had to accept it. Was it right to think differently now? How would it help her?

Then the answer came: It gave her freedom to grieve, both for her marriage and for the man she had killed. She'd held it all so firmly in check with her rage and then her shame. If she removed those emotions all she was left with was the chasm of heart ache she felt for all of it: the loss of their marriage, their children, their love, and for him, Tony. She would never see him again, or touch him again. The dream and hope of their marriage and family was gone.

Lizzy wept for their children and for the heartbreak it brought – hers as well as Tony's. She wept for all the times he'd rejected her, insulted her and publicly degraded her. She wept for his indifference to her pain and the struggle to find some kind of emotional support.

And then she wept for what she'd done, the images running through her head on an endless loop that would haunt her for the rest of her life.

Chapter Thirty-Two

Lizzy had no idea at what point she fell asleep, but the sound of the food slot being opened the following morning grated on the headache that was now blossoming, her eyes puffy and swollen.

She managed to get up and shuffle to the tiny basin in the corner. Soaking a flannel with cold water, she laid it over her hot eyes. She shuffled to the door and picked up the food tray and took it back to the cot, where she half sat and half lay, working her way through the meagre food, trying to muster some strength for another day.

She was startled by the sound of her door locks being released, and even more at the call of 'Visitor'. She stood up and looked at herself in the metal mirror on the wall. She tried to make herself look a little presentable. She had no idea who it could be this time. Who else was there to come? She ran through different options in her head as she made her way to the visitor room. But the little petite figure sitting in the room hadn't been one of them.

Hayley greeted Lizzy with a tentative smile, her demeanour unsettled as she glanced at the guard and tried not to appear shocked at Lizzy's appearance. She stood to give her a brief hug.

Lizzy gave her a genuine smile, grateful for the hug as they sat down to face each other.

'Thanks for coming, Hayley.'

'After I saw you on Friday in court I had to come. I felt horrible about how it went down, I didn't mean to make out you were some kind of nut job! I'm so sorry.'

Lizzy put her hand out across the table. 'You mustn't be sorry. You didn't have to speak at all.'

Hayley took Lizzy's hand after a furtive glance at the guard, and gave it a quick squeeze.

'I had to speak after I heard what had happened with Sue. I couldn't believe she dared show her face in there, particularly speaking against you.'

'She always had a thing for Tony, as was made clear on our holiday,' Lizzy said. 'What was more shocking was when she turned up in here the next day asking for forgiveness!'

'She never!' Hayley's dramatic exclamation made Lizzy smile, reminding her of the old days.

'Yep, she said that my solicitor had made her see it all differently.'

'Wow.' Hayley grinned too, but then her smile faltered. 'How are you doing in here? They treating you alright?'

'Yeah, I'm okay. Locked up in my own cell most of the day, although this last week I've been out more than usual with all the visitors and court visits.'

'And how's that going? With the case? What do you think will happen?'

'Either way I'm going to do some serious time, but I'm hoping for the chance of release.'

'Is it looking good?'

'Hard to tell. People like Reedy giving evidence against me doesn't help.'

Hayley's nose turned up in disgust. 'He was always slime. Everyone knows that.'

'Except Tony. He never seemed to see it.'

'I dunno. I think he knew, I just think he felt sorry for him.'

'Felt sorry for him? Why would he do that?'

'Because of what happened when they were kids.'

'When they were kids? I know they'd known each other before, but I didn't think they became mates until Reedy moved here from Petersford?'

'No, Lizzy, they grew up together, but Reedy had to move away in his teens, when his parents split up. Didn't you know?'

'No. Tony never mentioned it.' Lizzy frowned.

'I forget you didn't grow up round town. You were out in one of the villages, weren't you?'

'Yeah, out Cottingslowe way. But Tony didn't grow up round town either, he was in Barton.'

'Yeah, but he went to school in town.'

'So they were mates at juniors?'

'Yeah, Reedy left at the end of high school. Thick as thieves they were.'

'I find it hard to imagine.'

'Reedy had it rough at home. His stepdad used to hit him. It was Tony that brought an end to it.'

'How? I don't follow.'

'They used to hang about a lot – Reedy mostly at Tony's. But one day Tony went round and interrupted a beating, he went home and told his mum and dad who called social services. It's what made Reedy's mum leave his stepdad. They moved in with his nan. After that happened Tony and him became really close, always looking out for each other.'

Lizzy was stunned. She knew how protective Tony could be, but Reedy had such a big mouth – such a filthy mouth. It didn't explain why Tony had put up with it.

'I don't get it though, Hayley, why would Tony let him be so disrespectful towards me, if they were such close friends? He said so many really sickening things in front of Tony: innuendos, perverted suggestions, all those rude comments about me losing the baby and not being worthy of him.'

'I think he started out feeling sorry for him, Lizzy, and

then, well I dunno. When they were teenagers they were a right pair – totally inseparable: if you saw one, the other wasn't far behind. They developed quite a reputation for doing dodgy things, you know, with girls and stuff. All sorts of stories circulated, some of them really bad: things they'd do to girls, you know? Then Reedy's mum got a job over Petersford way – some say deliberately to split them up. Tony seemed a bit lost when Reedy left.'

'I can imagine.' Lizzy was dumbfounded by this new information. 'I know Tony had a reputation, but I didn't think it was that bad.'

'I know. But they were kids, so it didn't seem to matter. I think when Reedy returned Tony just went back to the same way it had always been between them. Tony always stuck up for Reedy. It's just the way it was.'

Lizzy paused. 'But why didn't Tony ever tell me any of this?'

'Maybe he thought you already knew.'

Lizzy tried to think back to any conversation about Reedy, other than ones of her just getting annoyed with Tony for defending him, she couldn't think of one. Reedy had been the one to tell her he used to live in the area and about his divorce, not Tony – although he'd never mentioned they'd hung out as kids. This put a whole different slant on things.

But Lizzy didn't want to waste her visit talking about it. 'Maybe he did. But anyway, how are you? How have you been? What's new with Hayley?'

'Well, this happened.' Hayley brought her left hand out from under the table and displayed a very impressive engagement ring.

'Oh wow! Mike finally proposed!' Lizzy grasped her hand and took a good look at the ring.

'Yeah.' Hayley almost bounced in her seat with excitement. 'I've been dying to tell you. He went down on one knee on my birthday in front of my family and everything.'

'Oh sweetie, that's great. I'm so excited for you. You set a date yet?'

'We don't want to wait long, maybe before the end of the year – depends if we can find a venue.'

'Oh I'm sure you'll have a wonderful day.' Lizzy tried to remain enthusiastic as the thought struck her that she'd be missing out on the big day.

Hayley's sudden silence indicated she realised the same. She slowly removed her hand, putting it back under the table.

They both seemed to pause for a second, before Hayley spoke again.

'You're doing better than you were before … you know before the … the …'

'You can say it, Hayley, the murders.'

'Yeah, before them.' Hayley's shoulders slumped and she sighed. 'I can't believe you did it, Lizzy. I'm sorry, maybe I shouldn't say it, but I can't believe you took his life. What possessed you to do such a thing?'

Hayley's eyes welled up with tears, and Lizzy gave her a sad look. 'I'm not sure I can ever explain it to you, Hayley, I'm not. I struggle with it myself. But when I came home that day and heard them fucking upstairs in our bed … I just … the sound of her screams every time he … you know …' Lizzy put her hands up to her ears. 'I just couldn't take the sound of it. It just did something inside my head.'

Hayley winced. 'You heard them? In your bed? How awful? And she was a screamer? Yeah, she looked the sort.'

Lizzy burst out in hysterical laughter at this comment, alarming the guard who took a few steps forward. Hayley looked surprised too, but smiled.

'Oh I'm sorry, Hayley, but only you could come out with something like that: 'She looked the sort.' You're so funny.'

'Glad I can still make you laugh, even in here.' She

giggled. 'But she did. Always dressed up, showing off, like she was a queen. I hated her.'

'Do you think she knew it?'

'Oh yeah, don't you worry about that. We all let her know it, strutting about with someone else's man. But she didn't care.'

'No, she really didn't.' Lizzy thought of how, even after the attack, she'd still carried on with Tony. 'She just seemed to do what she wanted.'

'Yeah, much like him.'

'What do you mean?'

'Well, we all spoke to him, Lizzy, we all told him it wasn't on: me, the other girls, the lads. But he just told us to butt out, that it wasn't our business. The only one who seemed alright with it was Reedy, but that was no surprise, was it?'

'Why did he do that to me, Hayley? I just don't get it. After all we went through, after all we'd had together, how could he just disrespect me like that?'

'I don't know, I really don't.'

'I had no clue everyone knew though … well, that anyone cared at least. That's been a big surprise to hear.'

'I know, and I feel bad about that, as all of us do – the lads too. But you were unreachable, Lizzy, you shut yourself away, you never returned my calls. You just didn't seem to want to know. And I dunno, I thought that eventually something would give and it would all blow over – whether you guys would split up or finally sort it out. But I never imagined this. Not this.'

'I'm sorry.'

'What?' Hayley frowned as though she'd misheard.

'I said, I'm sorry. I didn't mean to shut you all out. I didn't mean to drive you all away. I didn't mean to drive HIM away. It's all such a mess!' Lizzy couldn't stop her flood of tears.

'Oh, Lizzy!' It was Hayley's turn to reach across the table with both her hands, and they sat there for a few moments, both in tears, until eventually Hayley hunted through her bag for a tissue to mop them up.

The guard took the opportunity to step forward and tell them their time was up.

Hayley sighed and did up her handbag, in no rush to go. But Lizzy stood up knowing it would only be a matter of minutes before she would be asked again. Hayley stood with her and gave her a long hug.

'I'll be there on Friday, giving you moral support. And I'll make sure I visit as much as I can.'

'I don't know if I will be close by or not.'

'It won't matter, I'll still come. I miss you, Lizzy. It's not the same without you around anymore.'

'Shhh, don't say things like that, you'll set us off again.' Lizzy struggled to contain her upset at the thought.

Hayley stepped forward and kissed her on the cheek, squeezing her hand as she did so. 'You take care of yourself, and I'll see you soon.'

'Thanks for coming.'

Hayley gave her a tight smile before hurrying out, putting a tissue to her nose at she went.

Chapter Thirty-Three

When Lizzy was brought back to her cell she sat there staring at the wall, her mind processing Hayley's visit. She'd missed her friend a lot. It had been hard handling everything on her own and feeling like there was no place to turn, although she'd become used to it after her dad had died and mum got sick, so moving into Kettleby had been a life changer for Lizzy.

Through her first job, as an office assistant at a security alarm manufacturer, Lizzy had met Hayley. Then when the company moved and they were all made redundant, even though they had gone on to work in different places, Lizzy as a secretary at an accountants, Hayley in the sales office of a tools manufacturer, their friendship had prevailed. They'd always gone out a lot together – until those last fateful years. Hayley had been born and raised in the town and knew everyone. She'd brought Lizzy into her life there. Lizzy had been eternally grateful for that. Even meeting Tony had been through Hayley. She had been the one to introduce them.

Lizzy smiled at the memory, and the standard line Hayley would use when she saw someone she fancied: 'Just look at it!'

'Who?'

'Him, over there with his back to us!'

Lizzy saw a guy with a blonde ponytail across the pub.

'Who is he?'

'Who is he? You don't know?! That's Tony Dyson. Hottest thing in town.'

Lizzy laughed. 'You say that about a lot of guys.'

'Oh no, not Dyson, he's extra special. Everyone wants a piece of him.'

'So you haven't been there, then?'

Hayley laughed, her eyes sparkling. 'Oh no, I can't touch that, he's mates with Rob.'

Hayley kept to a strict code of not dating lads who hung around in the same group. Rob had been a guy Hayley'd been off and on with for a while. Lizzy hadn't thought anything was going to come of it. Rob hadn't seemed to be able to get his shit together enough to understand that you didn't mess about and leave someone like Hayley hanging, she wouldn't wait around forever. (And she hadn't).

'Arh.'

'But that doesn't mean YOU can't.' Hayley had given Lizzy one of her wicked grins.

'What? Me? I shouldn't think I'm his type of girl.'

Dawn had cut in. 'Oh don't worry about that, every girl is his type of girl!'

Hayley had giggled at that, but said, 'Oi, we'll be having none of that sort of talk! He's alright, very tasty, but yes, he does like the girls. Although he'd been off the market for a while, so you never know he might have changed.'

They all roared with laughter, knowing the unlikelihood of that.

'Off the market? Was he serious with someone then?' Lizzy studied the back of him, imagining the front.

'Yes, Sandy. She was alright, nothing special to look at, but he got it bad for her and they lived together for a while.'

'But not anymore?'

'No, not anymore. Not sure what happened, heard they were arguing a lot, and now he's sharing a house with

Eddie. Not sure what went down. But the fact he's out round town is a good sign.'

There'd been silence for a moment as they'd all observed him. He must have sensed it because he'd started to turn round slowly. When he'd turned far enough his eyes had fallen on Lizzy, and he'd given her a broad grin, showing a line of perfect white teeth, his blue eyes sparkling. She hadn't been able to resist and returned the same. Then he'd winked, and turned back.

The girls had let out a joint gasp, their eyes wide.

'Oh my god, you're in there!' Dawn had breathed on her left.

'He definitely likes you!' Hayley had exclaimed on her right.

'I'm not so sure.' Lizzy had been a little unnerved by the experience. He'd definitely been something special, but out of her league. 'I can't see him going for me. He's far too good looking.'

'Don't talk rubbish. Tony knows a good thing when he sees it,' Dawn had stated.

'Yeah, don't put yourself down; you could have your pick of the guys in here.'

Lizzy had laughed. 'I don't know that.'

'You had Phil after you last week …' Dawn had used her fingers to count.

'And his brother Lee the week before.' Hayley had doffed her beer bottle at her.

'Yeah, but they were drunk and just wanted someone to take home. I'm not that sort.'

'But that's my point, Lizzy, Tony'll know that: the lads talk. If he's interested he'll know it will be more than that.' Hayley had gotten all serious about it.

Lizzy'd had butterflies at the thought and wondered if she could really get a guy like that.

As the night had gone on Lizzy had caught Tony looking at her several times in the different pubs they'd gone to. And then down the nightclub he'd done the same there, although more intensively, and even said 'Hi' as they'd passed by each other. Then at the end of the night as the slow songs had come on he'd made his way over to her. She'd thought he was going to ask her to slow dance, but he hadn't. He'd just asked her how she was doing and what her plans were after the club. She'd said she was just going home. He'd offered to walk her. Who had she been to refuse?

Hayley had hugged her goodnight as they'd come out of the club, the sparkle in her eyes giving away her excitement. And Lizzy had been surprised at the conversation she'd had with Tony while they'd walked: talking about books, films, life experiences. She'd been surprised by the depth of this charmer, and when he'd left her at her door with a gentle but perfect goodnight kiss, she'd known it wouldn't take much to fall for him.

The slot in her cell door announced the arrival of lunch and she was grateful for the break in her thoughts as she picked up the tray and took a hungry mouthful. Reminiscing over their early days wasn't good for her. It made her yearn for what once was, which was then crushed by the realisation that it would never be again. He was gone – at her own hand. A thought that now caused the food to stick in her throat. She swallowed some water to shift it.

Her mind skipped over the rest of her conversation with Hayley and settled on the discovery of Tony's childhood friendship with Reedy. She could not recall a time that Tony had ever mentioned it. She found that odd. But it did explain his defensiveness on the topic, and why he'd refused to shut him out of their lives.

An involuntary shudder shot down her back at the thought of Reedy touching her that night. The skin on her neck crawled as though remembering his slobbery tongue. Her shoulders came up in a reflex action of rejection as though it had just happened. She thought back about what Hayley had said and what had happened to him as a child.

She couldn't muster any sympathy for him. He was grown up now, he wasn't a victim anymore.

Lizzy spent the afternoon thinking about the up and coming trial. She didn't like the idea of two more days with all this noise in her head, although seeing her therapist again on Thursday would help. She tried to imagine what she might say in court, or what she might be asked. Would she be too cold now she was feeling less guilt-ridden? Would they believe she hadn't planned it? And what difference would it make to her sentence? At the end it was all down to the judge; it was out of her hands. She didn't dare think about what sort of prison she might be put in. She doubted she'd be as isolated as in here. Now her meds were working and her head was clearing, she was beginning to feel the isolation, but what would it be like in general population? Would it be as rough as the telly programmes made out, or would she be okay? So far all the women here had been fine, but then she only saw them for an hour a day. What would it be like being amongst them all day, every day? She had no experience to base it on.

The bell rang and her door popped open. She was more than ready to stretch her legs. And out in the yard she did rounds with Carlene.

'You had another visitor?'

'Yeah, how'd you know?'

'Heard it up the line. You know how it is. So who came this time?'

'One of my old friends, Hayley. We used to go out drinking a lot back in the day. We had a lot of laughs.'

'She giving evidence on your behalf?'

'Already has done. It didn't go too well, the prosecution managed to twist up her words.'

'They're good at that.'

'Yeah.'

'Any news?'

'Only that she's getting married and I'm not going to get to see it.'

'Yeah, those kinds of things are off our agenda for a few years.'

'It's hard.'

'It's meant to be.'

'But I did get one bit of interesting info: she explained why Tony had always been so loyal to his slimy mate, Reedy.'

'You mentioned him before?'

'Not sure. But he used to shit-stir between us, and once he tried it on with me – well, molested me if I tell the truth.'

'Shit! What did your husband do?'

'Not much – "had a word", but that was all. It became a real sore point between us. But I've just found out they were old childhood buddies, something Tony had never mentioned. Tony had been his sort of protector, after finding out he'd had it rough at home, with an abusive stepdad.'

Carlene pulled a face. 'Sounds like a nasty story.'

'Yeah, not pleasant. Doesn't make up for his vile behaviour though.'

'No, and so it shouldn't. But does it change anything?'

'No, not really. Just explains why they were always thick as thieves and why Tony wouldn't cut him off. Strange he didn't mention it.'

'Maybe he thought you knew.'

'That's what Hayley said.'

'You can't dwell on these things, Lizzy, you'll drive yourself crazy. It's done now, and it makes little difference in the end.'

'Yeah.' Lizzy sat on the bench as they came to it, and let out a breath. 'All this sitting around in cells is making me so unfit. I'm out of breath.'

'Yeah, life inside does that to you. How long you got now?'

'Two days before I take the stand, and I think there'll be a verdict too.'

'They can linger over the sentencing though in some of these cases.'

'Doesn't that depend on appeal?'

'Maybe. You think you'll need to appeal?'

'Not sure I can.'

'Yeah, it gets all a bit technical.'

'What about you? When are you up next?'

'The kids are going up in front of the judge next week. Not sure if I'm going to get to be there or not. My solicitor is trying.'

'I really hope for you, Carlene. I do.'

They fell into silence and observed the others in the yard. There was a skirmish between two women that the guard split up and Lizzy was reminded that life in prison might not always be as easy as this. Then the bell went and it was time to return to the cells.

For the first time since arriving here, Lizzy didn't look forward to another twenty-four hours alone.

Chapter Thirty-Four

After having her dinner, Lizzy tried to settle her mind. It was a struggle. She had Reedy floating around in there now. Was he going to show up at the final trial? Would she have to look at him when she spoke on the stand? Could she bear to see that sneering face of his again?

It occurred to her that she had moved her rage to him now instead of Tony. But after going over so much of what had happened she realised that he'd been a huge part of it. He'd always been there with the snide remarks in public that led to rows between her and Tony later. And he'd instigated so many of them. Why? It was like watching previews for movies as each incident popped into her mind. He seemed to have focused a lot on the loss of their children, seeming to enjoy taunting her about it – but always her, never Tony. Had he been jealous? She'd always thought that he'd wanted what Tony had, but maybe he hadn't, maybe he'd been jealous of her, maybe it was Tony he'd wanted. Maybe he'd resented their closeness, their love, the successful marriage. Maybe that was why he'd tried to sour it, and maybe that was why he was so gleeful to find something that hadn't worked for them.

But why had Tony given him so much ammunition? Why had he told him so much about their private life? And that was it, wasn't it? Reedy had liked to provoke her with the fact that Tony had confided in him; told him things that should have only been between the two of them and no one else. It was like he'd been gloating. But the one that had really upset her – and there had been many – was the one that hadn't even been true.

When Lizzy had lost their fourth child she'd only been 6 weeks along, and Tony had wondered if she'd been pregnant at all. She knew she had been but he was unconvinced, suggesting it was just a heavy period. But being a man he had no clue how different a "heavy period" and the loss of a baby actually was. She'd argued that they'd lost their first at the same stage and he'd believe that, but he'd said they'd had a pregnancy test to confirm it that time.

She hadn't bothered doing one. She hadn't seen the point until she was further along and confident there was a chance it might actually stay. Maybe part of her knew it wasn't going to or maybe she no longer believed any would. But she hadn't seen the point in wasting the money on a test – or the hope either. But she had skipped a period and her breasts had swollen. He'd tried to claim all that could be psychosomatic – a phantom pregnancy. It had been an upsetting disagreement, one that he'd conceded, thankfully, being that it was her body and she knew what she was experiencing. But it hadn't been one he'd kept to himself.

It had been a Friday night out, one of the last with the girls in fact, and looking back now, Lizzy wondered if this had been why.

She'd been in Henry's with the girls when Tony and Reedy had walked in. Tony had given her a winning smile and a wink on his way to the bar, and then brought a drink over, giving her a kiss as he did so, before returning to the lads. The girls had all made romantic gushy sounds and she'd smiled. She'd known he'd already had a skin full, having knocked off early that afternoon, and that he was just warming her up for later when they got home. But she didn't mind. It wasn't often he took the time these days, but then it wasn't often she was out either.

But Reedy had managed to shatter the warm glow on his pass through to the toilets when he'd started making strange noises at them. The girls had giggled but looked puzzled at his strange behaviour, which he seemed to think was so funny. They'd asked him about it on his way back.

'I'm a ghost. Ask Lizzy, she'll know what I'm on about.'

They'd all turned to her expecting an answer, but she'd shrugged, being as oblivious to the meaning as them.

'I have no idea what he's on about.'

'You gonna ask him?' Dawn said.

'No. It's what he wants. He's just attention seeking like a little child.' Lizzy had taken a swig from her beer to drown her own curiosity. A sick feeling in her stomach indicated it couldn't be anything good.

But of course he hadn't left it alone: in the next two pubs he'd done the same. The girls had tried to ignore him, thinking he was just being stupid, but by the last pub everyone was drunk, especially him, and when he'd repeatedly walked past making pretend ghost noises, Jen had given in.

'What are you on about, Reedy? You trying to be scary or something?' She'd turned to the girls, giggling and said, 'It's not Halloween, is it?'

'No Jen, I'm a ghost, you know, those things some people believe in and others don't. They could be there or they could be a figment of your imagination.'

'We still don't get what you're on about.' Dawn rolled her eyes at him.

'Ask Lizzy, she knows all about phantoms, don't you darlin'?' Reedy put his arm round her and gave her a squeeze.

She'd pushed him away. 'Get your filthy fucking hands off me, right now!'

'Calm down, it doesn't matter anyway. It's gone now.'

She'd turned and slapped him hard across the face, the

crack loud enough to be heard over the music in the pub. A few people had looked over, including Tony.

Before Reedy had been able respond, she'd attempted to elbow him in the stomach, but he'd jumped back in time to miss the worst of it.

'Whoa, whoa, easy tiger!'

'Keep your fucking hands off me, you disgusting piece of shit!' Lizzy spat at him.

Tony had rushed across the pub and tried to placate her.

'Easy, Lizzy, easy.'

But she wasn't having any of it. She'd jabbed a finger in Tony's face.

'And you can keep your big fucking mouth shut! How dare you speak to this arsehole about our private life! How fucking DARE you!' She'd chucked her drink in Tony's face and stormed out the pub.

When the fresh night air had hit her, she'd staggered slightly, but when she heard the door open behind her she'd kept on walking as fast as she could. She thought it would be the girls, but it wasn't, it was Tony.

'Lizzy! Hey, Lizzy, hold up.'

'Fuck off, Tony, leave me alone.'

He'd run up behind her and caught her arm.

'Stop. What the fuck was all that about?'

'Why don't you ask your precious friend back in there? Go on, ask him, 'cause I ain't gonna fucking tell you. I'm going home.'

She'd yanked her arm out of his grasp.

'Leave me alone!'

He'd taken her advice and let her go. The walk back home had helped her work off her rage. By the time she'd got home all she'd had left were tears. She'd collapsed on the sofa in the lounge and sobbed, trying to mop her face up with her sleeve but ending up going into the kitchen to wash it instead.

By the time she'd finished Tony had arrived, and he'd stood in the kitchen doorway looking drunk and bewildered.

She'd glanced at him as she used the kitchen towel to dry her face off.

'Well?'

'I'm sorry, Lizzy. I didn't think he'd do something like that.'

'You don't know him well then, do you? What did he have to say for himself?'

'He'd scarpered by the time I got back; one of the girls told me what he'd been saying all night.'

'You gonna speak to him about it?'

'I guess I'll have to.'

'Have to? You don't think it was out of order, then?'

'Stu just does it to wind you up and it works. You have to learn to ignore him.'

'So you're not gonna say anything?'

'I'll try, but he'll just laugh it off.'

'Why did you tell him in the first place, Tony? Were you laughing at me behind my back?'

Tony had sighed. 'Oh Lizzy, don't start that.'

'Start what Tony? Is it my fault you've got a big mouth and that you go round slagging me off behind my back?'

'I didn't slag you. I just mentioned to him that it had happened.'

'What had happened Tony?'

'The pregnancy.'

'You didn't say pregnancy though, did you? You said phantom pregnancy.'

Tony had sat down in one of the kitchen chairs and chucked his keys on the table. He'd brought his hands to his face and pulled them down it, leaving his finger tips on his lips, letting out another sigh.

'It was part of a conversation about my week. I had no idea he would pick it out and make something of it.'

'Do you know how bad it makes me feel that you

don't believe I was pregnant at all? Do you know how shitty it is to have someone like him say things like that in front of my mates? Do you know how fucking humiliating that was? Do you?'

'Lizzy, come on, you're getting yourself all upset for no reason.'

'No reason? My husband's out there disrespecting me and humiliating me –'

'I didn't humiliate you, Lizzy, it was him not me.'

Lizzy had given a sarcastic laugh. 'Not you? It was you that said it to him, and you know damn well how much pleasure he takes belittling me and taunting me. It's not like this is the first time.'

'Is this about me or him?'

'It's about the both of you: him for doing it and you for letting him do it.'

'Letting him? I have no idea he's doing it half the time. It's all in your head.'

'What like the pregnancy?'

Tony had glared at her.

'I just don't get why you're friends with him.'

'Oh here we go again.' Tony had put his head in his hands.

'Oh fuck you, Tony!' Lizzy had stormed out the room and gone up to bed. She hadn't thought she would sleep, but she'd gone straight off – not even waking when he'd finally joined her.

Chapter Thirty-Five

Lizzy's mind wandered to the following morning and how they had made up; his way of saying sorry. Although he hadn't been that sorry, seeing as a few months later it had happened again, until eventually he'd joined in.

She tried to stop her mind following that thought. She turned over on the cot and attempted to divert her thoughts to something else, but there wasn't anything. Her whole life was consumed with the court case and what she had done that afternoon, when he'd taken the final step and sealed his fate. She couldn't believe he had brought his woman back to their house – their bed. She was still shocked by his nerve. And had it been the first time? That was what had haunted her at the time. How long had she been taken for a mug? How many times had he and that Sally fucked in their bed? How many times had Lizzy lain in their dried sexual sweat and secretions? Her skin crawled even now, thinking about it. Had he had the decency to actually change the sheets to cover it up? Surely she would have been able to smell it? Smell her?

The burning rage that bloomed in her stomach made Lizzy curl up tighter. She felt her dinner start to rise and swallowed, taking deep breaths as she pushed the thoughts away. Then tears started to form as she wondered if she would ever recover from it and be able to recall it without any emotion. She wished for the drugged up fog she'd been in when they'd first brought her in here, so she didn't have to think or feel anything.

Her mind had jumped to the afternoon she'd discovered them, because in some ways it was less painful than all the crushing moments that had led up to it, so many of them instigated by Reedy. They'd been the reason she'd stopped going out, and this particular stream had started shortly after they had buried Daniel. Reedy had at least avoided any remarks about their son's death, knowing that Tony wouldn't have tolerated that, and focused on her weight gain instead. He'd given her nicknames starting with 'chubby', making lurid comments about how Tony had more to hold onto, and then moved onto 'porky' relating it to the sound of a pig making love, and then he'd settled on "Lardy Liz", claiming its appeal to chubby chasers.

Tony, who had become quiet and disinterested at home, had laughed at these comments and told her time and again it was just a joke when she'd repeatedly complained about it. Often she'd give up and walk away, until one night when Tony did speak up, but not in support of her.

'You just gonna stand there and let him speak to me like that?'

'Yes, I am Liz, it's just a joke.'

'It's not a joke to me.'

'No, nothing is anymore.'

'What's that suppose to mean?'

'What it says: you're a miserable bitch who can't take a bit of ribbing.'

Lizzy's mouth had opened in shock. She hadn't known what to say, but Reedy had. 'Trouble is you can't see those ribs anymore.'

Tony had thrown his head back and laughed really hard at this.

Lizzy gaped at Tony.

'Oh come on Liz, you have to admit he's funny.'

'No Tony, he's not. He's insulting – and so are you.'

'What for telling the truth?'

'Truth?'

'Yes, truth. You're fat Liz – lardy as he says. And it seems to have smothered your sense of humour, too.'

Reedy had laughed then and Tony had joined him. Lizzy had been so furious she'd left the pub and gone straight home. That night she'd debated walking out on him. And now, lying in this tiny cell, she wished she had.

He hadn't apologised the next day or even made reference to her going home early. And when she'd started to turn down going out, he'd stopped trying to change her mind. And after her early return from the modelling event in London, he'd never asked her if she was coming out again. It was what had made the stalking much easier.

Lizzy didn't want to think about that again and got up from her cot. She washed her face in an effort to cleanse her mind. She sat and meditated and finally managed to clear it enough to allow her tiredness in. She returned to her cot and slipped into a fitful sleep.

The next morning she remembered strange snippets of her dreams. They contained Reedy chasing her down street after street, and every window she ran past displayed images of Tony with a woman, seemingly a different woman each time.

When her breakfast was pushed through the slot it came with an envelope. She opened it up and found a letter inside with a list of questions sent by her solicitor. "These are some of the questions that will be asked. Have a think about them, Lizzy," it said.

She reviewed the list as she ate her breakfast. Mark had grouped the questions into categories: The marriage, The miscarriages, After the miscarriages, and The murder.

The questions about their marriage were standard: How they met, Tony's reputation, how soon they'd got married, their plans for a family, other people's reactions to their relationship. And the miscarriages too, even though they were hard to think about: How far along she had been, the gap between, medical treatment received, where was Tony during them, what support she received. And then after the miscarriages: any counselling, whether it helped, how it affected their marriage, how it affected her friendships.

The questions pertaining to the murder were the toughest: take them through what happened that day, how she had found them, what had she been thinking, what was her intention, what had happened afterwards.

Mark had added a note afterwards saying, "These are general, Lizzy, we'll talk about specifics on Friday morning with Mr Davis, but just so you have an idea of how it will go. He will also ask about all the people who have testified, and who you feel had the most influence on your breakdown. This might direct to Mr Reed, and if the topic of the sexual assault arises organically then we will tackle it, but we want to be careful not to digress. We want it solely as a marker towards your breakdown."

Lizzy read the word "breakdown" as though registering it for the first time. Her therapist had used the term too, but only now seeing it written in black and white did she name what had happened to her: a breakdown. And it had resulted in the death of her husband – by her hand.

Lizzy had always considered herself to be strong, emotionally. She imagined having a breakdown would mean breaking from reality and no longer being coherent or lucid, or being able to function on a day to day basis, whereas she had – or thought she had. Although looking back now maybe she hadn't functioned as well as she had thought: she'd cut off all her friends and her only conversation with her husband had been screaming rants. And she had broken from reality after she'd murdered them.

When she thought back now, it was like a sort of cloudy span of thoughts and images. She had no concept of time or events. In fact, she couldn't clearly remember how she had ended up here in the psych ward of the prison. She must have gone before a judge, but she had no recollection of it.

A breakdown; she finally connected it to the plea of diminished responsibility, a term she felt was a cop out, or an excuse for what she had done. Now it made more sense. She'd had a breakdown and she had been unable to control it or take any responsibility for it.

It was a new thought for her and she pondered it until her door popped open and the call of "Visitor" came. She frowned wondering who it could be this time, and again the fear that it could be Stu Reed crept into the edge of her thoughts.

Chapter Thirty-Six

As soon as she saw their faces Lizzy rushed into the room and launched herself into her brother's arms. She held onto him tight, the wave of emotion overwhelming her and she cried. He held her tight too, stroking her hair and apologising for not coming sooner. Finally she released him and stepped back. He handed her a tissue to wipe her face. She hadn't seen Marcus for over ten years, but it didn't change how she felt about him; their bond could never be broken. She searched his face, noticing how it had aged, along with the grey flecks in his hair. But it was still her brother smiling back at her, with a tinge of sadness in his eyes.

Then she acknowledged the man next to him, her Uncle Peter, whom she embraced too. He was the stalwart of their family who tried to keep it all together for them. The lines on his face showed Lizzy the toll this was having on him. He wasn't a young man, having retired a couple of years ago, but since she'd last seen him he'd aged considerably.

'I'm sorry I haven't been before now, Lizzy.'

'It's okay, Uncle Peter.'

'I just didn't think it would come to this. I thought there had to be some mistake until Lucy confirmed it.'

'It's okay. I didn't really want anyone to see me in here anyway, not at the start. But now … well, it seems it's going to be the only way you're going to be able to see me for several years to come.'

'So it's true then?' Marcus said, as they all took a seat round the tiny table.

'Yes, it's true.'

There was a moment of awkward silence which Lizzy broke. 'When did you fly over?'

'A few days ago, but I had to apply to visit you and wait for a slot to come free.'

'Yes, it's been pretty busy this last week. How was your trip over? Did you come alone?'

'Yes, the kids are in school. It was all a bit last minute.'

'I'm sorry.'

'No, don't be, I should have come over more regularly, but I just got so caught up in my life over there.'

'Well you have children now.'

'I know, but that's no excuse. I'm sorry I didn't come over when I heard about your problems. I should have. I haven't been a very good brother.'

Lizzy gave him a small smile. 'Have you been to see mum?'

'Yes, daily.'

'Does she recognise you?'

'It's taken a while to convince her of who I am. She keeps showing me pictures of me when I was young and telling me that's her son. She's not in a good way.'

'And she still has no clue I'm here?'

'No. I don't think she would be able to comprehend it.'

'It's probably for the best.'

They all looked at their hands not knowing where to go from here. Lizzy could sense they were holding back.

'If there is anything either of you want to ask, you can, you know. I don't want you to dance round any of it. Time is short.'

'Lucy told us some of what you told her during her visit. I still can't get my head round my little sister doing that. Lizzy, you've thrown your life away for what? Revenge?' Marcus sounded confused and Lizzy didn't know how to placate him.

'Oh Marcus it was so much more than that. I'm only just starting to understand it all myself. I just … after we buried Daniel, I just … came apart.'

'Daniel, who's Daniel?' Marcus glanced at Uncle Peter.

'Daniel was Lizzy's fifth child. She lost him at 20 weeks, Marcus. There was a funeral.'

Marcus' face flushed. 'Oh, I'm sorry. I didn't know you had named him.'

'Yes, I did Marcus. And Amber who we lost at 16 weeks and had a funeral for two years before that. There are three others I wasn't able to name because they didn't get far enough along, so I wasn't going to leave the two I did manage to see and hold, without names.'

'I'm so sorry, Lizzy. I'm sorry I wasn't there.' Marcus put his hand out across the table and she took it. 'I know how precious my three are, I can't imagine the horror of losing them.'

'Do you have any photos?'

Marcus looked surprised. 'Yes, I do. I wasn't sure you would want to see them though.'

'Oh yes, definitely. I'm still their aunty, and you never know, hopefully one day I might get to meet them.'

Marcus took his wallet out of his coat and showed it to the guard, who nodded. He took out some photos and passed them to Lizzy. She looked at their tiny happy faces, all tanned from the Italian climate: two girls and a boy.

'Which one's which?'

'That's Isabella and Abby, and that's Roberto.'

'They're gorgeous.'

Marcus smiled and Lizzy handed the photos back.

'How long do you think you'll have to serve?' Uncle Peter asked.

'I'm not sure, it depends whether they accept my plea of diminished responsibility or not, and whether I get an option for early release. But even with that I'll probably serve a minimum of ten to fifteen years.'

They both looked shocked at this.

'I'll be lucky if I don't serve a full life sentence of twenty-five years or more.'

Marcus took a deep breath. 'That's a long time Lizzy.'

'Yes it is, but I committed murder – twice.'

There was silence again.

'Do you think you'll stay in a psych ward or be in an open prison?' Uncle Peter stayed focused on the possibilities.

'I really don't know at this stage. I have no idea where I will be transferred to from here. I hope I do continue to receive treatment though.'

'Surely if they recognise you had some kind of breakdown, they will?'

'I hope so.'

'We'll be there on Friday, Lizzy, to support you.' Uncle Peter reassured her.

'Thanks. It's going to be a heavy day.'

'Have you been prepped to give evidence yet?' Marcus asked.

'Yes, my solicitor sent me some questions to look at yesterday, and I'm going to be at the court house early for a chat beforehand.'

'The press is going to be a nightmare.'

'I know, there seem to be more and more of them each time I go.'

'Oh they're definitely ramping it up; even my arrival back in the country got noted in the papers.'

'I'm sorry.' Lizzy felt tears sting her eyes again.

'Oh Lizzy, don't apologise. It's okay. We'll get through this.' Uncle Peter put his hand out to her and she took it, while still holding Marcus' with her other hand.

'I just wish I had turned to people for help rather than push them away. I needed help after losing Daniel, I realise that now.'

'We should have all seen it too, Lizzy. I mean, I saw you regularly but I didn't realise it.' Uncle Peter squeezed her hand.

'I was good at hiding it. Plus you were busy with mum.'

'Not so busy I couldn't make time for my niece.'

'It's okay. I don't want anyone to feel responsible for what I did. I chose to shut everyone out over the last few years, and I also chose to pick up the knife that night instead of walk out the door.'

'Why didn't you?' Marcus asked softly.

'I …' Lizzy looked at her hands, her fingers intertwined with her brother's and her uncle's, no one letting go. 'I couldn't stand it – the sound of it, of them upstairs. It made me so angry that they were there, in our bed, doing it. I had to stop it. I couldn't walk away. I felt like if I did I would have given in somehow, like she had won.'

'Sally Bryant?'

'Yes. He was my husband – mine. I couldn't stand the idea that I had lost him to someone else. It just hurt so much.' Lizzy still felt the pain cut through her. Tears streamed down her face, and Marcus let go of her hand to get out another tissue for her.

'I wish you'd told someone how much you were hurting.'

'I didn't believe anyone cared by then. People were sick of hearing my woes: losing the babies, Tony playing up behind my back. They thought I was wallowing in my own misery. Several people told me to snap out of it, or get over it – including Tony. It's why I shut them out.' Lizzy blew her nose. 'I'm sorry I'm such a mess.'

Both of them said, 'No, don't be silly.'

'I would have been more worried if you weren't.' Uncle Peter gave a small laugh.

'Yes, if you were all calm and collected I think I'd be far more concerned.' Marcus smiled.

The guard stepped forward and tapped his watch. 'Sorry, but it's almost time.'

'Okay.' Marcus gave his sister a sad look. 'I'm staying until we know the outcome and where you're going to be. And I'll try and see you again before I go back.'

'I'd like that.'

'And I'll make sure I come and see you more regularly,' Uncle Peter said. His eyes sparkled with unshed tears. 'Maybe even be able to bring you some treats, depending on what's allowed.'

They all stood up, taking turns in giving her a hug.

'Give mum a hug from me when you see her, won't you?' Lizzy said to her brother.

'Definitely, sis.'

'Now you take care of yourself, Lizzy.' Uncle Peter put his hand to her cheek and stroked it.

'I'll try, Uncle Peter.'

She watched them walk out of the room and waited to be taken back to her cell before collapsing on her bed and weeping.

All these people coming to support her now; all these people who hadn't before; and the uncertainty of ever seeing them again was overwhelming. Would she see her brother again? Would she ever meet her nieces? It all hinged on what happened on Friday. Would they believe she hadn't planned it? Would they believe that she had lost her mind? Would they see how broken she had become?

Lizzy exhausted herself with all the questions spinning round her head, and fell asleep, not waking until her door popped open again with another visitor. This time one she never would have expected.

Chapter Thirty-Seven

It took Lizzy a moment to recognise the top of the head she could see through the high, visitor room window as they brought her to the door. He was the last person she'd expected to see here.

'Eddie? What are you doing here? Is everything alright?'

'Hey, Lizzy. Yeah, it's fine. Hayley thought I should come. She wanted me to come and talk to you about Tony and Stu. She said there were things you needed to know.'

Lizzy felt her stomach tighten. She took a seat at the table and Eddie sat down opposite her.

'Things I need to know? Should I be worried?' Eddie's pause concerned Lizzy.

'Hayley said Tony had never mentioned how he and Stu had been mates as kids or how they'd grown up together – let alone what they got up to.'

'No, he never talked about it. Although I knew they had known each other, but not that they were close. I think Tony didn't talk about him because I didn't like him.'

'None of us liked him, Lizzy, not now and not then when we were kids. He was trouble. Always was.'

'But he had problems with his stepdad, didn't he? That's what Hayley said, that he used to hit him and stuff.'

She felt strange having this conversation with Eddie. He was a big, soft, gentle natured bloke – when he wasn't provoked. When she'd come on the scene, he and Tony had been best mates. They were considered the hardest guys in town. No one messed with either of them. And with Lizzy he'd always been the perfect gentleman: always polite, always respectful, always considerate. Nothing harsh, rude or inappropriate, that wasn't who he was. He was the exact opposite of Stu Reed. It didn't surprise her that Eddie didn't like him.

'Yeah, I remember when it happened. I remember how upset Tony had been about walking in on that situation. It really bothered him. I always thought Stu milked it for all it was worth though. And I think it's probably why he went so wayward. It was a shame he had to drag Tony with him.'

'What do you mean by "wayward" Eddie?'

Eddie's eyes flicked across hers. This clearly wasn't something she was going to like.

'It started out innocent enough. You know, early teens, interest in girls, embarrassing them in school and stuff. And then when we were about thirteen or fourteen, stories started to circulate about things they'd done to girls in the toilets. It wasn't always clear if they were consensual either. Then into sixth form their rep was one of always sharing.'

'What girls?'

'Yep, girls. They bragged about it. And then there was the incident in Great Thornton at the campsite, when they were on a school trip. A girl left in a bad way in the woods. Stu and Tony had been questioned about it by the school and by police. I think that's when Stu's mum decided it was time to leave.'

'And this was Tony, too?

Eddie nodded.

'Did you ever ask him about it?'

Eddie shook his head. 'By the time I became close mates with Tony it was all over. It wasn't something you bring up. I remember someone else asking him when we were out. He'd had a skinful and I hadn't liked his response. He'd said, 'Some girls say they're up for it and then chicken out at the last minute. We didn't give her the option.' The guy who'd asked hadn't liked it either and they'd almost kicked off. I'd had to take him home to cool off.'

'And you didn't ask him about it after, like the next day or something?'

'Lizzie, he was a mate. I wasn't going to grill him about it. I just wanted to pretend it hadn't happened. Without Stu around he turned into a decent bloke. And then when the two of you got together I didn't think he'd ever look back. If Reedy hadn't shown up again we wouldn't be here, Lizzy, I'm sure of that.'

'You and me both, Eddie. You and me both.'

They were silent a minute. Then Eddie sighed. 'But that's not all, Lizzy.'

'Oh god, there's more?' Lizzy swallowed, not sure if she wanted to hear it.

'Well, that wasn't really what I came to tell you. It's about the affairs.'

'Plural?'

'Yeah, although really they were mostly one night stands until Sally came on the scene. It was always Stu who found the girls, but he used Tony as bait.'

'Bait?

'Yeah, you know: the looks, the modelling, to reel them in. You know how he was, Lizzy, always liked playing up to the girls.'

Lizzy nodded. He always loved being the centre of attention where the women were concerned.

'And they'd always go twos up with them.'

'Twos up? You mean a threesome – Stu, Tony and some girl?'

'Yeah. And that's also how it happened with Sally. But she didn't want Stu after a while, she only wanted Tony. None of them really wanted Stu. I think that's why he got fresh with you that night.'

Lizzy held her breath. Did she hear that right? 'What do you mean, Eddie?'

'That night he tried it on with you, when he walked you home, when Tony was away.'

'How do you know about that?'

'He told me – Tony did. He was upset about it, obviously, and he wanted me with him when he confronted Stu about it.'

Lizzy took in a sharp breath. Eddie paused. 'And? What happened?'

'Stu squirmed to begin with and then he got angry. Told Tony that it wasn't right he wasn't sharing you. I couldn't believe my ears. I think what made it worse was that he managed to turn it round on Tony, make it his fault – and Tony let him.'

'But Tony never agreed to share me … did he?' Lizzy's mouth dropped open, her eyes felt like they were bulging.

'No, Lizzy, he didn't do that. He just kept shouting that you were his wife and Stu was to keep his hands off. That the girls they were picking up were enough.'

'Thank goodness.' Lizzy's mind raced. Eddie fell silent letting her process it. 'So they shared that Sally too, then?'

'At the beginning, yes.'

A thought crossed her mind. 'Do you know whether it ever happened at my house?'

Eddie looked at her as though she was asking confidential information, then he sighed. 'Yeah, a couple of times. That's when I spoke up and had a go at Tony. It didn't end well.'

'So I gathered.'

'Sometimes I wish I'd told you about it … you know, before.' His glanced at his hands.

'I'm not sure it would have helped.'

'No. That's what I thought. None of us knew what to do.'

'Everyone knew all this then?'

'Only a couple of us knew the extent of it. I told

Hayley. I asked her if she would approach you, but it was a lot.'

Lizzy sighed. 'I wasn't very approachable, Eddie, not back then. Please don't blame yourself for any of this.'

'We're all responsible, Lizzy. We all had a hand in how this went.'

'You can't think like that, Eddie, you can't. I did this, not any of you. I should have just left him.'

They were both silent. The guard stepped forward and said, 'It's time.'

Lizzy gave Eddie a small smile. 'I'm so pleased you came and told me though. It's helped me understand things better.'

They stood up. 'Yeah, Hayley said it was time. That you needed to hear it.'

'She knows me well. Thanks so much, Eddie.' She reached up to his huge stature and gave him a quick hug. He was smiling when she stepped back.

'I'll see you in court on Friday, okay?'

'Okay.'

He clenched a fist at her in solidarity and the guard showed him out.

Lizzy waited to be taken to her cell where she could process this new information, but it was still exercise time, so she was let out into the yard instead.

Chapter Thirty-Eight

Out in the yard she sat on the bench breathing in the fresh air. Her head full of all she had just heard after having had two visits in one day. Carlene was doing rounds and stopped after her fourth, sitting down beside Lizzy.

'You not walking today?'

'I might in a bit, fell asleep after a visit this morning and got woken up to another one.'

'Blimey, you're popular.

'Tell me about it. My head's spinning.'

'Powerful visit then?'

'Yeah, the first was my brother – not seen him in about 10 years, he lives in Italy. He came with my Uncle.'

'Wow, he's come a long way.'

'Yeah, he has.'

'And who was the other one?'

'Eddie, an old mate of Tony's. They fell out over the affair. He came to tell me the details. It answered a few questions.' Lizzy wasn't ready to go into it.

'They're all coming out the woodwork now.'

'Tell me about it.'

'Shame they hadn't before it all happened.'

Lizzy glanced at Carlene and smiled. 'I thought the same, but didn't dare say it out loud. But it's not like it's their fault or anything.'

'No, but it's a factor.'

'I don't need to say it, they all feel it anyway.'

'Yeah, people do after a murder. Sometimes it's the only thing that makes them stop and think and check in on their own families.'

'I'm grateful they all came. They could have turned their backs on me.'

'Also true. How you feeling about it all?'

'Alright. Just so much to process.'

'Worrying about Friday?'

'A little. It's like I feel too clear-headed.'

'What do you mean?'

'Well, I feel like I'm getting my head together: thinking clearly, realising stuff, putting it all together. I'm worried that I'm going to come off too cold.'

'Cold?'

'Yeah. You know, I'm pleading diminished responsibility, but now I feel like I am actually taking responsibility for what I've done. And maybe if I come over as though I've got my shit together they won't believe I didn't before.'

Carlene gave her a long look. 'You are really over thinking this.'

'Am I?'

'Oh yes. You're in here all safe and sound, snug as a bug and got all this time on your hands to reflect. And just because you realise what you've done, doesn't mean you intended to do it before – if anything it means you weren't thinking about it before. The fact you didn't realise before now means it couldn't have been premeditated – if that makes sense.'

Lizzy laughed. 'Yeah, it kind of does. My solicitor sent through a list of general questions they're going to ask at the trial, and he said how he wants to use some things as markers of my breakdown. I didn't realise I'd had a breakdown. I didn't have a name for it, but I didn't know that's what happened to me.'

'Oh it definitely was. Your first couple of weeks in here, I could hardly get a word out of you, let alone anything coherent.'

'I feel like this sort of fog has lifted off my brain.'

'Yes. I get that. I had a fog of rage.'

'Yes! Yes, that's exactly it.' Lizzy felt relief sharing her feelings with someone who could relate. 'I was so caught up being angry all the time it was like I was blind to everything around me, and everything I was doing.'

'It definitely consumes you. I can't believe I roped my kids into helping me. How sick must I have been? I should never have done it. Those poor kids.'

Lizzy saw the shine of tears in Carlene's eyes and put her arm round her. She tried to think of something to say. She wanted to say it would be alright, but she couldn't. She didn't know if it would be.

Lizzy was saved by the bell and they walked back inside together, giving each other a brief hug before returning to their solitude. Lizzy lay down on her cot and waited for dinner, her mind processing everything she'd heard from Eddie.

She felt vindicated somehow. She didn't expect that. She had always believed there was something unhealthy about Reedy's association with Tony and now it was confirmed, although she'd had no idea of the depths it had gone to. She'd known that Sally was sleaze, and lacking in any moral conscience. How else could a woman so openly cavort with another woman's husband, in front of a whole town? It came as no surprise to her that she'd started with Reedy – they were the same type of people. And it now made sense of what she had overheard in the shopping centre that morning. But the thought of Tony sharing women with Reedy … it made Lizzy's toes curl and a shudder of revulsion ran through her. Thank goodness Tony never asked her to do that – although he never would have done. From the very beginning she had disliked Reedy and Tony had never questioned it. He'd known the truth about Reedy, always had, but why had he gone along with it? Why had he rekindled their old friendship? He could have kept his distance. Lizzy didn't like to think that Tony could stoop as low as Reedy, but he had. She'd known Tony had had a reputation but she hadn't imagined one that bad. Would it have put her off him if she'd known before? She liked to think it would. It was a shame no one had mentioned anything about Reedy earlier, too. Why hadn't anyone told her about them two before? Did they think she already knew? She tried to think of any discussion with the girls about Reedy and when he used to live there, but there'd been none. She'd known he'd come from Kettleby but never considered it meant he had also gone to school with them all.

Their history shone a new light on Tony and his behaviour. It calmed her to know more about where it had come from and that it hadn't all been created by her. Although she'd always wonder if he'd have been so easily turned if they'd had children. Would he have turned away from his family? She didn't think so. She wanted to believe that Tony wasn't a natural cheater, that he'd been goaded into it, influenced by someone as crass as Stu Reed. Lizzy felt no sympathy for him about his childhood. He chose to turn out the way he did. He chose to treat women like pieces of meat, just there for his pleasure. He disgusted her!

The sound of the food tray being pushed through the slot froze her in mid nose scrunch. Fortunately her hunger was such that it killed all further thoughts until it was satiated, and with a full belly her mind calmed. She thought about her brother's visit instead, and how great it had been to see him.

Chapter Thirty-Nine

The following morning Lizzy felt rested. Despite having slept half the afternoon the previous day, she'd fallen asleep without any problems the night before. Her visit with Eddie had helped put some missing pieces together, and her chat with Carlene had made her realise there was someone else in the world that understood what she had gone through. It had a calming effect on her; she didn't feel so lost anymore.

She explained the same to her therapist that afternoon.

'This is good news, Lizzy. It might be a good time for you to return to group therapy.'

'Don't rush me, Doc, I've only just got here. One person is one thing, but I'm not sure about a whole group.'

'You'd be surprised at how many understand your feelings, Lizzy, it's very common.'

'So Carlene's right about a lot of women being in here due to their rage about a man?'

'Well, maybe not about a man specifically.' John shifted in his seat and Lizzy smirked.

'Sorry, Doc, didn't mean to make you feel uncomfortable. I don't mean to tar the entire population of men with the same brush.'

John smiled back. 'I know, and in this wing there are a lot of women who are here due to an offence involving a man. But I was thinking more about the feelings of rage and how they cloud your thinking, and that they are a prime symptom of a breakdown, and often depression.'

'What angry people are depressed?'

'Often the two come together. When someone can't resolve what they are angry about, they turn that anger on themselves. It can create hurt and sadness on such a deep level that they can't shake it easily.'

'I was a bit of both I suppose: angry at myself and sad that I couldn't change it.'

'Change what specifically?'

Lizzy thought for a moment about what she most would have liked to have changed. 'My ability to carry a baby. It's like my body had failed me – failed us, Tony too. And no amount of tests seemed to provide a solution.'

'Did they come up with any reason why they thought it was happening?'

'Some said too little progesterone when the egg was implanting, some said chromosome issues, but no one knew. It was nothing obvious. They couldn't find anything wrong with my womb or cervix. My cervix wasn't dilating too early, the babies weren't being starved of any nutrients, and they couldn't find any kind of genetic disorder. It seemed to be a mystery.'

'And would it have felt different if you had known?'

'Definitely. Then I would have had something to work with. We might have been able to solve it, or at least not keep on trying, and turn to adoption or fostering earlier.'

'So you were angry at your body. Were you angry at Tony, too? Did you feel you blamed him for it in any way?'

'I think I started to resent him. He wasn't the one having to go through the grilling each time. It wasn't his body failing. And then when he stopped being sympathetic that made me more angry.'

'Why do you think that was?'

'I'm not sure. I thought how dare he! How dare he think I should just get over it. How dare he call me fat, and make me feel worthless. How dare he after all I had been through. How dare he stop being loving and supportive.'

'Did you feel he abandoned you?'

Lizzy blinked. She'd never thought about it in those terms before.

'Yes. It was like he was there in person, but not in spirit. It was like part of him had gone away and I couldn't get him back.'

'Have you ever felt abandoned before?'

'Yes, by my dad – although he died. He was sick, there was nothing he could do about it. It's just how I felt at the time.'

'Anyone else?'

'My brother. When he up and left to go travelling and then never came back. It took me a long time to accept that. I felt cheated for ages.'

'Did you ever tell him?'

'I never had the chance to. He was barely in touch.'

'But he came in to visit you yesterday, didn't he?'

Lizzy paused. It always caught her by surprise that he already knew who had been to visit. 'Yes he did.'

'How did it go?'

'It was fantastic to see him. It was like no time had passed.'

'How long had it been?'

'Ten years give or take.'

'Will you see him again?'

'I don't know. It depends where they send me after here.'

'Are you worried about the move?'

'Yeah, of course.'

'Why?'

'I don't know where I will be going, let alone how long for, and whether I will be in a psych ward of a prison, or out in general population.'

'What would you like?'

'I'm not sure. I am now at a point where I don't think I could cope with being locked up for as long as I am here. But out in a general population, fending for myself? I just don't know.'

'I'll be recommending you still have treatment, but I think you would benefit from socialising too.'

'It scares me.'

'What being around other people?'

'Being around strangers who might be dangerous.'

John smiled. 'It's not always as it's portrayed in the media or on television, and considering what you are in here for, you could be dangerous too.'

Lizzy paused, and then gave an embarrassed smile. 'Yes, I suppose I could be.'

'Bearing that in mind, do you think the women you mix with here are dangerous?'

Lizzy pulled a face. 'A few of them could be.'

John tipped his head from side to side. 'Maybe you're right. But mostly they are just people, just other women going through similar things to you. I think being in group therapy would show you that.'

'So you think I'm worrying about nothing?'

'Not nothing. It's understandable, there are still lots of things that are unknown, there could be difficult situations ahead. But you don't need to focus on them at this point. Just one step at a time. Are you ready for tomorrow in court?'

Lizzy took a deep breath and let it out. 'Ready? Not sure I will ever be ready, but my solicitor has given me a list of questions he's going to ask, so I think I'm prepared as much as I'm going to be. He's meeting me tomorrow before court to go through it.'

'What are you hoping for, Lizzy?'

'Best case scenario?'

John nodded.

'A chance at release, hopefully after fifteen years.'

'What do you think it will take to get that?'

'Me showing I was a mess back then, that I didn't think about killing them until that moment. I hope I can get them to believe that.'

'Are you worried they won't?'

'A little. I feel so much calmer now, so much more together.'

'Why do you think that would work against you?'

'Maybe they'll think that it wasn't true that I had a breakdown – that I was like this all along.'

'What do you believe?'

'I know I had a breakdown. I know I wasn't in my right mind.'

'Do you believe you are in your right mind now, then?'

Lizzy paused, wondering if he was trying to suggest something, but John's face was open and quizzical, solely trying to unearth what she was thinking about herself.

'I feel like I am waking up after a long, exhausting nightmare. I mean, the nightmare isn't over, but it's a different nightmare now, one where I have to face the consequences of my actions. It's like I was blind or had fogged up vision, and now I can see again. I mean, I'm not completely there yet, it's early days. But I feel like I'm facing what I have done and owning up to it.'

'That's great, Lizzy. You've come such a long way in such a short time.'

'Thanks Doc. It's like I lost a part of myself and I'm just getting her back.'

'Good. Hold on to that.'

'I will.'

'I'm going to wrap things up. Depending on the outcome of tomorrow depends how much longer we will see each other. I'm going to pencil you in Monday and we'll talk then when we know more. But I'm really pleased at your progress, Lizzy. I was worried at the beginning that we might never get here.'

'Me too.'

Chapter Forty

Lizzy still had a whole afternoon to reflect on the questions her solicitor had given her. One of them was about Tony's modelling career and how it had affected her marriage. She'd never considered it a factor before, although of course it had affected Tony. If nothing else he'd taken more time over how he looked. He'd become more self-conscious when out in public, even when it was just around town shopping. It had changed his priorities.

Before Tony had been signed up to the big modelling agency in London, he'd take small modelling jobs in his stride, considering it just a bit of fun and extra money, nothing major. But after, he'd started to reschedule things to suit the dates they wanted him, even if they weren't confirmed until the last minute. He'd talk about the earnings and how maybe he could give up his day job, something that he'd never cared about before. He'd started to take himself more seriously. And it had meant he took Lizzy more seriously – or more specifically her role as his wife and how she dressed when they were out together in public. Several times he'd said, "You're not going out wearing that, are you?" And even if she was just popping out he'd ask her to change. "We've got to keep up our appearances," he'd say, "even if it is just to the shops. You never know where there might be a camera." And a couple of times he'd been right.

The local newspaper would occasionally snap a nasty one of her and run it. And then the nationals would pick it up. And the more popular he became, the more often it happened. They didn't print anything hurtful about her losing the babies, even though it did make news, but they did comment on her weight gain. This had put her under pressure, not just from him but from the outside world too. Although it wasn't as big a pressure as the pressure now – now she'd murdered him and his other woman.

And that was something else that bothered her: in all this the focus had remained on her, there'd been hardly anything about the affair. Lizzy still had access to newspapers, all be it fleeting glimpses during her exercise time, and even though the double murder had been splashed about in the first few weeks of the case, little had been said about the affair. The viewpoint they'd taken was one of pity; everyone felt sorry for the other woman. But no one had asked what she was doing with him in the first place? No one had questioned their behaviour. No one had asked whether what they'd been doing was wrong. It had all been "Poor Sally". It made her sick.

And if Tony had been out with her so often round town, how come no one had taken a picture of them together? He was a celebrity, so how come it hadn't been in the papers? Lizzy would have seen it if there had been; she'd read them every day to see what they had to say about her and Tony. Had Tony paid someone to keep it quiet? How had he managed to get away with it? It didn't seem fair that she was being vilified in the press and he wasn't, after everything he'd done. Especially now, in light of everything Eddie had told her. But the little voice in her head reminded her that she was the one who had taken a knife to them, not the other way round. It was normal for people to feel sympathy for the victim.

Lizzy sighed and picked up the notepad they'd allowed her and started writing out some thoughts in response to the questions Mark had given her. She spent the rest of the day going through them.

She discussed a bit of it with Carlene during exercise time, but she didn't go into depth. Carlene had plenty of her own stuff on her mind, with her children's case being moved up to the next week. Lizzy realised that she might never know the outcome for Carlene if she got moved to another place. She made a note to herself to ask if it was possible.

That evening she spent a long time meditating, gathering her energy for the day ahead. She needed everything she could muster. And fortunately it enabled her to fall asleep without any problems.

Chapter Forty-One

In the morning Lizzy woke before her breakfast arrived. She felt tense and restless, pacing the floor. Once the food arrived she was given half an hour to eat it before they'd take her to the showers. Usually showering was a whole process: every couple of days everyone would line up and take turns in the ten cubicles available, with only fifteen minutes allowed. But today she was alone, and no one seemed to hurry her. She felt an odd twinge of privilege.

When she returned to her cell, Lizzy found her court suit hanging ready for her, having been sent to the cleaners. Again a sense of something surreal crept across her as she dressed and readied herself. This was it, but she felt detached from it, almost numb.

Handcuffs were put on her before they took her out to the van as usual, which always seemed to negate the entire dressing up.

The journey to the court was uneventful and they drove round the back rather than pulling up in front. She had no idea if there was a crowd out there and didn't want to know. It felt strange entering the courthouse without being spat on.

Two courthouse security guards led her to a side room where her solicitor was waiting. Mark stood up as she entered and smiled.

'How are you doing this morning, Lizzy?'

She let her eyes take in the wood-panelled walls, the high windows, and the long mahogany conference table in front of her. It would be her final time here.

'I'm doing okay, Mark.'

He swept an arm out as though presenting the table. 'Please take a seat. We need to get through as much as we can before we're called.'

'Who else is in the stand today?'

He pulled his head back slightly and frowned. 'No one Lizzy, today is only about you. This is it, the final testimony – your testimony.'

'Oh, yeah, of course.' Lizzy blinked.

'You knew that, didn't you?'

'Yes, I just forgot. I thought there might be some other people first, kind of warm up the crowd if you know what I mean.' She smirked, trying to lighten the mood.

'No, we've heard from everyone. They just need your take on it now. You nervous?'

'Oh yes.'

'Just look at Mr Davis when you're on the stand, okay? Keep your eyes on his face and focus on his words. The prosecution will also cross examine you, but really I can't see they will have much to ask.'

'Will there be a lot of people in there?'

'I think so, yes.'

'Press too?'

'No, no press. The judge made that decision early on. They don't think it's appropriate, especially as you pleaded guilty.'

Lizzy took a deep breath. 'Well, that's something at least.'

'Yes it is. Now then, how did you get on with the questions?'

'Okay, I thought they were fairly straight forward and general. But I made some notes too. I listed a few things I thought might be worth touching on to support the breakdown.'

Mark opened a folder the security guard had handed him. He scanned through Lizzy's notes and immediately starting making notes in his own paperwork.

There was a light tap on the door and Mr Davis appeared, already dressed in wig and gown. He briefly shook Lizzy's hand and took a seat next to Mark, who shared the paperwork with him.

'Mrs Dyson, I'm going to try and lead you through some questions to bring out the things you and Mr Haygarth have discussed. Okay?'

Lizzy nodded. They went through the questions and how he'd formulate them: what he would be driving at and the points he would try and make. Lizzy still didn't feel like she was really there in the room, in her own body. It was all so calm and collected – the complete opposite of the crime she had committed.

In what felt like no time there was a knock at the door to let them know it was time to go in. Lizzy stood and stroked the skirt of her suit down as best she could with handcuffs on and took a deep breath.

'Ready?' Mark put a hand on the middle of her back.

'As I'll ever be.'

They walked to the courtroom in silence, Mr Davis and Mark going through the door first, obscuring Lizzy's view of the crowd beyond. The shuffling silence of a hushed courtroom greeted her, and she struggled not to bow her head and stare at her feet as she walked to the dock. Instead she looked to her left to see who would be sitting on her side and she was met with the smiling faces of her support group: Lucy, Marcus, Uncle Peter, Hayley, Eddie, Sue, Dawn and even Jen. She attempted a smile but it felt fake, her anxiety robbing her of the joy at seeing them there. She stepped up into the dock, and stood waiting for the judge to enter before sitting down.

A few moments later she was called to the stand. She walked to the witness box still in handcuffs, and when she sat down, she did as Mark had said and kept her eyes on

Mr Davis, watching him push his chair out and stand, taking his time as he prepared the papers and made his opening statement. She could feel her legs shaking, and her hands remained damp no matter how many times she wiped them on the side of her skirt.

She could sense the jury to her right, twelve people with their eyes on her – or at least she assumed they would be. They might also be on Mr Davis, but she wasn't going to turn to look, not yet, and maybe not at all.

Mr Davis walked towards Lizzy as he ran through preliminary questions, enabling her to get her bearings and find her voice. He started with standard stuff: her name, what she did for a living, how long she'd been married. Then he started asking about her marriage.

'When would you say problems started to arise in your marriage?'

'It's difficult to pinpoint, but I suppose when the miscarriages started.'

'From the very first one?'

'I'm not sure. If I look back I would say there were signs after the third miscarriage.'

'What were those signs?'

'His attitude towards me changed; he became less respectful.'

'Is this around the time his modelling career started?'

'Yes.'

'Did you support his modelling career?'

'Oh yes, I'd nagged him about it for years. He had the face for it.' Lizzy smiled remembering the first headshots Tony had had done for his portfolio. She'd pulled faces at him the whole time and his laughter had worked wonders on the photos; they'd been perfect.

'But from that point forward he was less warm and loving?'

Lizzy frowned. 'I wouldn't say that, it sort of ebbed and flowed. It seemed to be more in social settings.'

'Can you give an example?'

'One night I was out with my friends and Tony was with his. One of his friends came over and made a rude remark about how I didn't need to have a big car anymore seeing as there weren't going to be any children. Tony told me not to get upset and that it had just been a joke.'

'But it wasn't to you?'

'No. Not at all. It was very upsetting. But Tony didn't seem concerned it upset me.'

'Was this a close friend of his?'

'Yes. Mr Reed.'

Lizzy's eyes went straight to Reedy's face. She knew where he was sitting; she's spotted him out of her peripheral vision over her solicitor's shoulder. He seemed startled by the identification. Mr Davis also glanced at him, encouraging the jury to do the same.

'Did Mr Reed make many of these types of comments?'

'Oh yes. He always took the opportunity to make me feel uncomfortable whenever I was out socially.'

'Did he always focus on the miscarriages or were their other comments?'

'Mostly the miscarriages and my inability to carry a baby full term.'

'Would you like to give the court some other examples?'

'He offered to have sex with me, if Tony wasn't satisfying me, and said I wouldn't have to worry about getting pregnant because I wouldn't be able to keep it anyway.'

'Was Mr Dyson aware of this?'

'Oh yes, it was said in front of him.'

'And he wasn't concerned about it?'

'No, he would laugh, tell me it was just a joke.'

She could sense movement to her right, the jury resettling in their seats not liking what they'd heard.

Mr Davis paused, as though seeming to debate his next question. Lizzy waited, wondering if he would bring up the assault even though Mark had said it wasn't relevant.

'Did Mr Dyson ever ask Mr Reed to stop?'

'I know Tony told him to stop coming round on Sundays. But if he did ask him to stop making comments it didn't make any difference, he continued.'

'Would you say this caused problems in your marriage?'

'It began to, yes. It was the cause of many arguments.'

'Was Mr Reed aware of this?'

'Yes. Tony confided in him about our marriage – that also caused rows. I personally felt that was what Mr Reed intended.'

'He wanted to break you up?'

'I think so, yes.'

'Why would he want to do that?'

'Jealousy.'

'Of Mr Dyson being with you?'

'Partly. I believe he thought Tony should have shared me with him.'

'Shared you with him? As in sexual relations?'

'Yes.' Lizzy hadn't been sure whether Eddie's information would be useful, but Mr Davis seemed open to it.

The entire courtroom seemed to shuffle in their seats at hearing this – except Reedy who she could see over Mr Davis' shoulder, glaring straight at her.

'What led you to believe this, Mrs Dyson?'

'A friend witnessed a conversation between the two of them about it.' Lizzy made sure she kept her eyes fixed on Mr Davis this time. She wasn't going to expose Eddie.

'Between Mr Dyson and Mr Reed?

'Yes.'

'Did Mr Dyson agree to this?'

'No. As I understand it he thought it was a step too far.'

'But this didn't stop Mr Reed from making things

difficult between you?'

'Not at all, no. I think it made him worse. He seemed to encourage Tony to disrespect me. I don't think he liked us being happy or someone else being close to Tony. They'd been childhood friends and he wanted Tony to himself.'

'Mr Reed had moved away, hadn't he?'

'Yes, in his late teens. But they'd been very close before then and had been known to share girls back then.'

Mr Davis paused letting the new information sink in. The courtroom and the jury remained still. Lizzy wanted to glance at Reedy but didn't let herself.

'So you believe Mr Reed used these comments as a way to cause a rift between the two of you?'

'Objection!' The prosecution barrister didn't bother rising to his feet. 'Speculation. Is the defence trying to make Mr Reed accountable? I don't see the relevance of this line of questioning.'

The judge looked at Lizzy's barrister.

'I'm trying to establish what contributed to Mrs Dyson's breakdown, Your Honour. Her state of mind was already fragile due to the miscarriages. I am trying to clarify what events for her, personally, may have increased it further.'

'Sustained. But Mr Davis remember, Mr Reed is not on trial. Mrs Dyson is. Kindly rephrase the question.'

'Yes, Your Honour, thank you. Mrs Dyson, do you think Mr Reed's taunts and remarks contributed to the problems in your marriage?'

'Yes. It showed me that Tony's loyalty was split and I was no longer his confidante. I didn't feel I could fully trust him anymore.'

Mr Davis walked back to the desk and moved a few papers around before continuing. Lizzy knew he was regrouping and trying to find another way in.

'You said you supported Mr Dyson's modelling career?'

'Yes, wholeheartedly.'

'Did you attend functions with him?'

'Yes, I did.'

'Did that ever become difficult?'

'Yes, after we lost Daniel.'

'That was your fifth miscarriage?'

'Yes, and the last.'

'And you lost him at twenty weeks?'

'Yes.'

'What became difficult?'

'I gained a lot of weight and Tony became unhappy about being seen with me in public.'

'Did he say that?'

'Not initially. The first couple of events we went to after having Daniel he just sort of manoeuvred me out of the press photos. But at the last one I attended with him, he bluntly said he didn't want to dance with me because I was fat.'

'He said this to you before the event or at the event?'

'At the event, in reply to one of the other guests asking if he was going to dance with me.'

'He said this to another guest?'

'Yes.'

'And you heard it?'

'Yes, I was sitting at the table with several other people too. We all heard it.'

'Did anyone say anything?'

'Yes, the gentleman said it was uncalled for in light of our recent loss, but Tony said that I had to get over it and get on with life and not let myself go.'

'In front of the other guests?'

'Yes.'

'Did you say anything?'

'No. I was too embarrassed, but I left shortly afterwards.'

'Alone?'

'Yes. I changed rooms at the hotel and then went

home alone the next morning.'

'Did you talk about it when he got home?'

'No. You could say that was sort of the beginning of the end. We were never right after that and I never went with him to any of his modelling events again.'

Mr Davis referred to his papers again. Lizzy could feel the tension building as he approached the more difficult topics.

'When did you first strike you husband, Mrs Dyson?'

There were audible gasps in the courtroom, and a ripple ran through the jury, but Lizzy kept her eyes on Mr Davis, looking him in the eye.

'We had a row after I found out about his affair and I punched him in the face.'

'Did he hit you back?'

'That time, yes.'

'That time? How many times did you strike your husband?'

'I dunno, four or five times over the last year or so. It's hard to remember, we had a lot of rows.'

'And he didn't hit you again?'

'No. Hitting women wasn't Tony's style. It's not who he was.'

'Did he hit anything else instead?'

'Only his punch bag in the basement, after the rows.'

'Did you row a lot? Was that normal?'

'Towards the end we did, it became the only way we communicated.'

'What triggered the rows?'

'They were mostly about him going out all the time.'

'Did the rows ever resolve anything?'

'Not really, but sometimes they connected us again.'

'Connected you? In what way?'

'We both knew that things were getting out of hand, and afterwards we would forgive each other.'

'What, like kiss and make up?'

'Sometimes, or just do something sweet for each other, a token gesture: a cup of tea, a home cooked meal, a bunch of flowers. When he hit me, he held my hand the whole time at the hospital and even cried. Neither of us was happy about what was happening.'

'Did you ever seek counselling?'

'After we lost Amber, our third child, we had some counselling together.'

'Did it help?'

'A little.'

'What about after Daniel?'

'No. It was offered, but we both sort of shut down. We didn't speak for the first week after the funeral. We just couldn't.'

'In what way did this contribute to the difficulties you were having?'

'We struggled to find our way back to each other after that. And then when Tony refused to talk about fostering or adopting, it shut us down. I couldn't pick myself up after that.'

'He didn't want to foster or adopt?'

'I don't know that he didn't want to, he just wasn't ready to talk about it, but I needed to. I needed to see a way forward and I pushed him on it. We had a few rows about it, and I think it drove us further apart.'

'How long was this before you found out about his affair with Miss Bryant?'

'About 18 months or so. It was about three or four months after we lost Daniel. He'd been having an affair about a year before I found out. I don't know exactly when it began.

'How did you find out about his affair?'

'I found a comb in his coat pocket. It was lilac. It wasn't his.'

'Did you ask him about it?'

'No. I knew he would lie about it.'

'So how did you find out for certain?'

'I followed him.'

'When he was out?'

'Yes.'

'Didn't he see you?'

'I would dress up and disguise myself with wigs and stuff.'

'So you stalked him?'

'I suppose so, yes.'

'Did you ever stalk Miss Bryant?'

'A couple of times.'

'Did you ever attempt to speak to her?'

'No.'

'You attacked Miss Bryant in a pub. Do you remember that night?'

Lizzy took a breath. She could feel all eyes on her, especially from the jury. 'Yes.'

'Can you tell us about that night?'

'I was out alone, following them.'

'Did you plan to attack Miss Bryant?'

'No. I thought about confronting them, but I didn't know what I would say.'

'What caused you to attack her?'

'I'd had a few drinks, trying to pluck up the courage, having followed them around a few pubs already, and in one of the pubs they started kissing. She put her hand on his arse. That's all I can remember really, until after.'

'What happened after?'

'Tony took me home in a cab.'

'Mr Dyson? What did he say?'

'He asked for a divorce.'

'What was your response?'

'I walked out of the room and went to bed.'

'Did you want a divorce?'

'No, I didn't. I wanted my husband back.'

Mr Davis gave Lizzy a small smile.

'Did you love your husband, Mrs Dyson?'

'Yes, very much.'

'Did you plan to kill him?'
'No, I did not.'
'Thank you, Mrs Dyson, that's all for now.'

Chapter Forty-Two

Lizzy watched the barrister for the prosecution, Mr Romford, stand up and slowly straighten his gown. She hadn't really paid any attention to him before. He didn't look much older than Mr Davis, maybe in his late 30s, but he had a look in his eye that made her uncomfortable: a sort of glint as though there was something amusing him about all this. It reminded her of Reedy. It wasn't good.

'Mrs Dyson, you say you didn't plan to kill Mr Dyson and Miss Bryant?'

'No.'

'Can you tell us a little about what happened that night?'

Lizzy shifted in her seat.

'I came home early from work because I didn't feel well, so Tony didn't know anything about it, and when I entered the house I could hear screaming coming from upstairs.'

'Screaming?'

'Yes, a woman screaming. It startled me for a minute, but then I heard grunts too, male ones, and I realised they were having sex upstairs.'

'You knew it was Mr Dyson and Miss Bryant?'

Lizzy gave him a sarcastic look.

'Who else would it be?'

'You didn't think someone had broken into your house?'

'No.'

Mr Romford walked towards the stand. 'What did you do?'

'I remember standing there taking my coat off in sort of shock as they continued. They hadn't heard me come in, which wasn't a surprise with the noise they were making. It was a bloody awful noise too. I couldn't stand it.'

'And that's when you decided to kill them?'

'I didn't 'decide to kill them', I had no such thoughts, I just wanted the noise to stop, *needed* it to stop.'

'So you thought you'd get a knife from the kitchen to stop it?'

Lizzy didn't like the way he was leading her.

'No. I went into the kitchen to put the kettle on, but the noise was getting bigger and bigger inside my head. I don't remember opening the drawer and getting the knife out, I just remember the knife being in my hand as I went up the stairs.'

'It was a particular kind of knife, wasn't it?'

'I don't remember.'

'A double edged freezer knife, the type you use to cut frozen meats with, is that right?'

'You'd have to ask the police, I don't remember.'

'You can even use them for cutting through bone, can't you?'

'I don't know.'

'So you didn't select this knife for any particular reason?'

'No. I didn't select it at all. I don't remember grabbing the knife.'

'Yet there was a carving block full of knives on the counter and you opened the drawer to get this one out?'

'No, as I said I don't remember getting it out.'

'You just remember it was suddenly in your hand?'

'Sort of, yes.'

'So even though you had a knife suddenly in your hand, you still had no intent to kill?'

His incessant attempts at get her to say yes were grating on Lizzy's nerves.

'No. It wasn't like that; the thought didn't cross my mind.'

'What thoughts did cross your mind?'

'Angry thoughts: at him, at her, at their nerve –'

The prosecutor cut her off. 'So what did you plan to do when you got upstairs?'

'I didn't plan to do anything.'

'You must have had something in mind when you grabbed the knife?'

'No, as I said, I didn't remember grabbing the knife.' Lizzy struggled to keep her voice calm.

'So you went upstairs with a knife in your hand for no reason?'

'Yes I had a reason.'

'To kill them?'

'No! To stop them *fucking* in our bed!' Lizzy shouted.

The entire courtroom went still and Mr Romford smiled. Lizzy could feel her face burning and tears threaten to fall. He strolled back to his desk, and said, 'I have nothing further, Your Honour.'

Mr Davis popped up from his seat. 'May I redirect, Your Honour?'

'Go ahead, Mr Davis.'

He walked round to face her.

'Mrs Dyson, you talked about the sound of them having sex getting inside your head, what do you mean by that?'

Lizzy wasn't sure where he was going with this, but she went with it.

'It was like one of those noises that gets louder and louder the more you focus on it – like flies buzzing. There was so much of it, it was so loud. It was like they were in the room in front of me having sex, as though they were taunting me with it: with their pleasure, with their desire.'

'Did it remind you of anything?'

'It reminded me of what I'd had with Tony in the early days, how much we had desired each other.'

'So it represented what you had lost?'

'Yes.'

'And at that point did you feel you had lost anything else?'

'Yes. I had lost everything: our babies, my friends, my self-respect. I couldn't trust anyone or anything.'

'And how had this affected you up until that point?'

'I'd cut myself off – although I hadn't realised it at the time. I couldn't cope with interacting with people. I went to work and I came home and that was it. I was convinced they were all talking behind my back about what a failure I was, how much I had let Tony down. And when I found out about the affair I was sure everyone was happy about it, that they thought it was what I deserved. It made me so angry, and so exhausted at the same time. Everything was going wrong and there was nothing I could do.'

Tears were falling now and she couldn't stop them. Mr Davis handed her a tissue.

'Mrs Dyson, what did you see in the room that night that made you commit murder?'

The image of them came into Lizzy's mind. She could see his long blond hair sticking to the sweat on his back, her legs wrapped round his waist, as his hips moved up and down, thrusting into her.

'I saw him fucking her in *our* bed, in *our* bedroom – OURS!' Lizzy tapped her chest with her finger as tears rolled down her face. 'We'd picked that bed out special before we'd moved in. We'd conceived all our children in that bed – well except one. And the sheets that were on it, I'd ordered from an expensive catalogue. Special Egyptian cotton they were, they felt lovely. And they were sweating all over them, putting their stink all over them!' Lizzy's nose wrinkled.

'Did they hear you come into the room?'

'No. They didn't stop. Not until I used the knife.' She

looked down at her hands, her fingers tearing at the tissue.

'What did you do afterwards?'

'I went to sleep in the spare room. I was so tired.'

'How long did you sleep for?'

'I'm not sure. According to the Police it was three days.'

'According to the police?'

'Yes, they worked it out from when I'd last been at work. I don't remember any of it.'

'You don't remember anything from the time you killed them to the time the police came to the house?'

'No.'

'You lost three days?'

'Yes.'

'Do you remember being taken into custody?'

'Vaguely. Just snatches, some images.' Lizzy felt her mood slump as she recalled that state of mind, a blanket of calm falling over her.

Mr Davis moved closer to the witness box.

'Mrs Dyson, if there was one thing you could change about that night what would it be?'

'That I hadn't come home early. If I had come home at my usual time I wouldn't have found them.'

Mr Davis gave her a sympathetic look. 'The defence rests your honour.'

Chapter Forty-Three

When they led Lizzy out to the side room she could only sit and sob. She felt people moving round her, in and out, and she heard Mark's voice, but she couldn't stop the tears. It was like she'd opened a box inside that held all the pain from that night and she couldn't shut the lid again.

Then a different voice arrived, whispering words of comfort in her ear and an arm came round her. Mark had brought Lucy in to sit with her and help calm her down. It worked.

She brought her tears under control and was allowed to visit the toilet. Then they waited. Lucy remained in the room sitting next to her, holding her hand tight. They didn't speak, they just watched the clock and the people who came in and out, until they were called for the final verdict. The jury had only needed a couple of hours to deliberate; there'd been no request for the weekend. Lizzy didn't know if this was good or bad. But the moment had arrived. Would she have to serve multiple life sentences or would she get a chance at life again? She didn't want to think about it anymore. She just wanted it all to be over with.

Lucy was ushered out of the room before her, insisting on a quick hug first, and then Lizzy was taken to the dock. The judge came in and everyone was allowed to sit, except her. Lizzy was to remain standing while the judge spoke. When he did, Lizzy tried hard to concentrate on his words but they felt alien to her as though he was speaking another language. She watched his lips move, waiting to hear the number of years, imagining it forming on his lips, but something else came out, something she didn't expect to hear.

'Mrs Dyson, you entered a plea of diminished responsibility and never have I presided over a case in which it is more fitting. The series of events and circumstances coupled with the lack of support that led you to undertake such a heinous crime are overwhelming. However, despite this, you have not hidden behind them or used them as an excuse; you have not shied away from taking responsibility for your actions or from showing remorse, and that gives me hope.

'Therefore, I am going to make a recommendation that you receive as much help as necessary to enable your rehabilitation, and to be held in an open facility where you are to serve a minimum of ten years. I don't believe that you are a risk to the public. I believe this was a single act; a cry for help, one that ended in the loss of life of two innocent people. Please don't prove me wrong, young lady.'

Lizzy couldn't stop the tears from streaming down her face when she said, 'Thank you, Your Honour. I won't, Your Honour.'

Lizzy sat down with a slump. The tears had begun again and she couldn't stop them. She couldn't speak. She couldn't smile. Only once everyone was out, except the security guards and her solicitor, did she manage to turn slightly and smile at Mark, who had sat down next to her.

He leaned in and put his hand on her shoulder. 'It's alright, Lizzy, it's over now. You were great, and we couldn't have got a better verdict if we tried.'

'I thought when that guy made me angry we had lost.'

'No, in fact I think it did the opposite, it worked in our favour; it showed it was a crime of passion.'

'Passion?'

'Yes passion. Where your actions were anything but premeditated, they were incited by rage in a desperate situation.'

'Would that have made a better defence?'

'I wouldn't have trusted it. Not in this case. Lizzy you had a breakdown, a break from reality. Now it's time for you to find your way back.'

Lizzy took a deep breath. 'Ten years inside will give me plenty of time to do that.'

Mark gave her a sympathetic smile.

The security guards came to take her out of the courtroom.

'If there is an appeal, which might happen with how his family responded to the verdict, you might get to see me again, but if not Lizzy, good luck.'

'Thanks Mark, you've been great.'

Mark remained seated while they led her out and she glanced back giving him one last smile. Despite her immediate destination being unknown, Lizzy was relieved it was over.

Epilogue

Lizzy tried not to fidget as she waited for them to finish processing her release. Ever since she'd been informed of the date she'd been counting down and now the day was here she could hardly believe it.

She was a mixture of excited and anxious at the thought of coming out after ten years. She'd been safe in here. She'd become part of a community. She'd made strong, deep friendships she would miss. She was also so used to living in a small space she was scared at the prospect of a whole house – although it wouldn't be her own house, it would be her Uncle Peter's. Her house had been sold years ago. She also couldn't imagine what it would be like to have all her things back. It would be like opening Pandora's box: on the one hand joyous at seeing all her treasures again, on the other fearful of the memories that it would bring up. Being in here for ten years meant she'd had time to process many things, but in here they were also kept at a distance; she couldn't reach them. Now she was going back into the thick of it and would be tested on everything she'd learnt.

There was a lot of paperwork, which was no surprise, and Lizzy watched the wardens nervously as papers were shuffled around. Two of them took turns signing corners here and there. Then they pushed it toward Lizzy and she put her initials where they indicated, hoping that would be the end of it. It was, and two more wardens appeared to take her outside. But rather than exiting out the main entrance, they took her through the prison to a side entrance for the more notorious prisoners.

Hayley had warned Lizzy during her last visit that the press knew about her release date and there'd been a slew of articles about Tony's death, asking questions about whether it was right she should be allowed out. And this morning, the main warden, Mrs Prentis, had told Lizzy there had been a gathering of journalists and protesters overnight and there would be no chance of her getting out without problems. So a Plan B had been organised and Hayley notified of the change of pick-up location.

When they led her through the courtyard on her way to the side entrance, it was exercise time. This gave her one last chance to wave to a few of the inmates that had become close friends – especially Carlene, who had joined her there two years after she'd arrived. Carlene's trial had been a lengthy affair with the kids being involved, but fortunately they'd been let out into their aunt and uncle's custody after only serving a couple of months. Carlene still had four years to go. Lizzy was confident they would stay in touch and meet up once she was out.

When they brought her to the large metal door that led out onto the side of the prison, she expected someone to step out with her, but they didn't: They stepped back from the open door and left her to make her own way out.

She felt like a rabbit coming out of a warren after a predator attack. She cautiously looked out before taking a step. She could see Hayley's car off to the left, parked up on the edge of the woods that surrounded the prison.

As she stepped over the threshold Lizzy saw Hayley get out of the car and walk round it, opening the back passenger door to indicate it was clear. The side of the prison was shielded from view due to the front extending out either side, so she rushed forward, running across the scrap of grass area to the car, giving Hayley a quick hug before slipping into the back seat, and lying prone as the prison staff had suggested. Hayley covered her with a blanket, giggling a little.

'I'll pull over once we're a distance away and you can join me in the front.'

'Okay,' Lizzy replied, her voice muffled by the blanket.

She heard Hayley put her small bag in the boot, and they set off, Hayley turning the car round to head back towards the front of the prison. Lizzy could hear the muffled sound of people as they passed the gathering at the front.

'Are there a lot of them?' she asked.

'Yeah, tons of them. Plus some arseholes with placards too – can't catch what's on them though. Honestly it's like they've got nothing better to do on a Friday!'

'Any of them seen you?'

'Yeah, but this isn't my car, and I've put a cap on in case they recognise me. We'll be past it in bit. I want to make sure there's no chance any of them are following us.'

They travelled on in silence. Lizzy had been up at the crack of dawn and was tired. This would be a perfect opportunity to take a nap, but she was too hyped up so lay resting her eyes, her mind running through what was ahead: arriving at Uncle Peter's and settling in. Would there be a crowd to greet her there too? She hoped not. Why were there so many of them? Yes, the case had been high profile due to Tony's modelling career, but really were people still so outraged about it? Was ten years not enough?

As her mind continued to chatter away, she felt the car slow and Hayley pulling in somewhere.

'Okay, it's clear, no one has come after us, come and jump in the front.'

Lizzy wasted no time doing so, and Hayley beamed at her. 'It's so good having you here with me. I've been waiting for this moment for YEARS!'

'I know, tell me about it.'

'Are you okay though, it's not too overwhelming, is it?'

'I didn't expect all this attention from the press. I don't get why they're still so interested? Or is it that they think that ten years isn't long enough?'

Hayley glanced at her. 'I didn't want to tell you at my last visit, 'cause I didn't want to worry you, but that's your friend, Reedy's doing.'

Lizzy's stomach clenched. 'What do you mean?'

'The press knew about your release date and started approaching people asking questions, but no one would have a bar of them except him.'

'Of course.' Lizzy rolled her eyes.

'He made quite a bit of money off them too, from what I gather. He's been telling all sorts of stories, talking about that Sally woman and Tony and making you out to still be a psychopath.'

'How the hell would he know? It's not like he's had anything to do with me since – thank god.'

'He doesn't care about that. He only cares about the money and getting attention. That's all he's ever been about.'

'Great! Does that mean there'll be a ton of press waiting for me at my Uncle Peter's then?'

'There weren't this morning, and I'm hoping that as they didn't know what time you were released, they won't be there when we get back, so we should be alright.'

'Yeah, but tomorrow they probably will. I'm gonna be a prisoner in his house instead.' Lizzy felt sick. This wasn't how she'd imagined her release. She knew it wouldn't be easy, they'd even counselled her about it in prison. It wasn't just getting work, but how people would respond to her in general.

'People aren't against you, Lizzy, not those that know you. We're ready for them if they show up.'

'What do you mean?'

'A few of the lads and some of the girls have agreed to come over this afternoon and tomorrow, and longer if needs be. People aren't impressed with what Reedy did.'

'There's no stopping that arsehole.'

'I wouldn't be so sure about that.' Hayley glanced at Lizzy again, this time with a twinkle in her eye.

'What do you mean?'

'I don't want to say too much, 'cause I'm not yet sure of the outcome. But he dared to show his face round town last night, mouthing off about your release and stuff. The lads didn't like it.' Hayley paused.

'And?'

'And he's in hospital. That's all I know. I don't know how bad it is yet.'

Lizzy was stunned, but couldn't suppress a smile. Then there were tears. She had no real idea why, they just started falling, and she found herself having to catch her breath. Hayley put her hand on her leg.

'It's okay, Lizzy. It's okay.'

She managed to whisper through her tears, 'I never thought anyone cared that much. I never thought, not for a moment. And he was so awful, Hayley, so awful. If he hadn't come back to live in Kettleby, if he'd just stayed away in Petersford ... I'd still have my Tony.'

'Oh, Lizzy.'

'He'd never have done all that shit without Reedy about.'

'Maybe. But you guys weren't in a good place, were you? Otherwise he'd never have been able to come between you.'

Lizzy was silent. Hayley was right. But being out again and hearing about all of this, it was like ten years hadn't passed at all.

Hayley had to take her hand off Lizzy's leg to change gear. She revved the engine, pushing the gear stick in hard. 'I so didn't want all this to happen for you today! I so didn't! That tosser can't even let you have one good day! I hate him so much!'

Lizzy looked at her in surprise. 'I thought it was just me.'

'Oh no. These last few weeks with all those articles, he's done nothing but stir up trouble, pissing everyone off, raking it all up again. He should have been sent down too!'

Lizzy thought about her time inside. It hadn't been easy, and she'd had to find her place, there was a hierarchy and people were kept in their place, especially if they stepped out of line. But Reedy was wily, and a good manipulator, he would probably have got on fine, even been a top dog.

'No, I prefer the lads' method, that way he gets his just desserts.'

Hayley smiled. 'True.'

They were approaching the outskirts of Kettleby now, and it was starting to look familiar. Lizzy thought she might find it all too much after being inside for so long, but it was wonderful to see the hills surrounding her hometown again.

Hayley had caught Lizzy up on all the local gossip: who was doing what with who. Lizzy had forgotten how the town ran on this kind of stuff and was amused by it, even though she knew she was one of the main topics. It was something she had to learn to live with and not be fazed by. The therapy she'd had while inside had helped her build herself back up, now it was time to put it to the test.

Hayley made sure not to drive past Lizzy's old house even though it was on the way to Uncle Peter's, and Lizzy was grateful for that; she wasn't quite ready to deal with those memories just yet.

When they pulled up to Uncle Peter's terraced house there was no sign of any paparazzi, but there were banners welcoming her home and her heart rose. The front door opened and out came her uncle and her sister, Lucy. She got out and embraced everyone as they went into the house. Inside there were more banners and balloons and two more friends, Dawn and Jen, waiting in the lounge, along with a buffet on the table in the walk-through dining area. Lizzy hadn't expected any of it and was again tearful at the support she was being shown, support she'd believed was non-existent last time she was here. It felt strange, but elating.

She sat down on the sofa and looked round at them as they chatted among themselves. It was like nothing had changed, but everything had changed; like ten years hadn't gone by, but yet she'd been away forever. She had expected to feel anxious around them like she had before she'd gone to prison, but that was all gone. It reaffirmed all the work she had done to come back to herself.

She smiled at Lucy, who sat down next to her. Lucy hadn't been able to visit as much as Hayley over the years, due to living so far away, and Lizzy noticed how her sister had aged: the greying hair at her temples and wrinkles round her eyes and mouth, but it was wonderful to be sitting next to her again. She took her hand and squeezed it. Lucy smiled at her.

'Marcus wasn't able to come over then?' Lizzy glanced round the room to confirm she hadn't missed him.

'No, he tried, but it's the wrong time of year for his company. He hopes to come over soon though. You could even go out to stay with him.'

'I'd love to, but I don't think my probation will allow that just yet.'

'You could request it?'

'It's a bit soon for that, I need to check in regularly and establish I'm trustworthy.'

'True. I forget that really you aren't truly free yet.' Lucy brushed a piece of Lizzy's hair out of her face.

'I may never be.'

'Don't be silly, in four years they'll review it and see that you're no longer a threat.'

'I mean inside.' Lizzy put her hand on her stomach.

Lucy squeezed her hand, but didn't say anything.

The doorbell rang and her uncle peeped out of the front window.

'Is it reporters?' Lucy asked.

'No, just the lads.' Uncle Peter hobbled out of the room to let them in.

'How's he doing?' Lizzy asked Lucy. 'I see he's stopped using his walking stick, but I hope me being here won't be too much for him.'

'He's much better. The hip operation was a huge success. He's been quite excited about having you to stay actually, I think he could do with the company. Since mum died, he seems to have lost a sense of purpose, you know, now he's not visiting her every week. I mean he has his mates and stuff, like he's always had, but living alone's not much fun.'

'No, it's not. I'm glad I'm a welcome intrusion though. I don't know yet how I'm going to get on my feet and buy another place.'

'You've still got the money from the house, they couldn't take that away from you.'

'True, but it won't last me long if I'm living off it too. I need to find work.'

'Give yourself some time to adjust first. That's why I thought a trip out to Italy might be an idea, get away from everything for a few weeks.'

'That all depends if Italy lets me in! I've got a record now, remember? And not for some trivial thing.'

'True. But we can look into it.'

'Maybe.'

The lads consisted of three of Lizzy's male friends, or really Hayley's as she had introduced Lizzy to everyone in town many years ago: Nathan, Leigh and Dave. They'd kept in touch while she'd been inside. She'd been surprised at Leigh's letters; she'd never thought he'd be the writing sort. They each gave her a quick embrace and peck on the cheek before heading for the food and drinks.

'Have you been up there this morning?' Jen asked Nathan.

'Yep.' He popped a piece of cheese into his mouth.

'And? Come on, don't leave us in suspense,' Dawn said.

'He'll be in a while. He's quite a mess apparently, bit of internal damage and stuff.'

'Is he conscious?' Jen asked.

'Yep.' Leigh cracked open a can of beer.

'Is he talking?' Dawn took a sip of her drink.

'Not to the coppers. He daren't.' Dave glanced at Nathan with a smirk.

'What do you mean?' Jen was looking from one to the other.

'We went in earlier. There's a copper on his door who knows me and let us in to have a chat.' Nathan was also resisting a smile.

'What have you two done?' Jen's eyes were wide but their smiles were contagious.

'Nothing. Just reminded him that talking to the press was what got him into this in the first place, and if he dares say anything we have a girl ready to claim he tried to sexually assault her that night and that was why he got a beating.'

No one in the room spoke for a minute, then Lizzy did.

'I can't say I'm unhappy about what you lads have done–'

'We didn't do anything!' Dave interrupted. 'It wasn't us that gave him that beating.'

'No, but you know who did, don't you?' Lizzy eyed them one by one. They had the decency to look uncomfortable and break eye contact with her. 'As I said, I'm not unhappy about what happened to him, it's long overdue in my opinion, but I've just got out of prison. I know what it's like and I'm telling you, it's no party. Don't get yourselves in trouble – not for scum like him. You're better than that.'

No one said anything. Lizzy continued, 'I lost everything – including my mind if I'm honest, and he was a part of that, but I let it happen. Don't do the same – don't let him goad you into becoming something you're not. Plus it's only going to provoke the papers and make him a celebrity and he'll lap that up, as you well know.' The lads avoided eye contact. 'Is there even a girl?'

'Yeah, Beth Loveday, and he did assault her, last week.' Dave's smile had dropped and he looked Lizzy straight in the eye. 'And there are two others that said they will step forward with her if needs be.'

Lizzy raised her eyebrows. She knew her. 'If needs be? She's not going to bother otherwise?'

'You know how it is, Lizzy, it's more trouble than it's worth, hardly anyone believes the woman, especially if they're out drinking. Plus he's good at spinning stories – you know that more than anyone.' Dave was never one to shy away from the truth. Lizzy nodded.

Leigh settled down on the sofa next to Lizzy. 'Cath said to me last night that we need to get him out of town, and she's right.' Cath was Leigh's wife and another of Hayley's friends. Everyone nodded in agreement.

Uncle Peter got up and went to the window.

'What is it, Uncle? Paparazzi?' Lucy got up to look too.

'Yeah, a couple of them.'

'The banners make it clear where I'm staying,' Lizzy said.

'No we took them down when we came in,' said Leigh.

'Those people have been here before; I recognise their faces. They know who lives here.' Uncle Peter returned to his chair. 'But Eddie and Mike are coming up the path.'

Hayley got up and went to the door before they could ring the doorbell, opening it just enough to let them in, all three ignoring the shouted questions from the journalists. Eddie and Mike greeted Lizzy in the lounge and pulled up dining chairs, taking beers proffered by Dave.

'Do you think we should call the police yet, Uncle? There's more arriving.' Lucy didn't like the publicity.

'I spoke to the police this morning. They said to call if they weren't gone by five this afternoon. When they realise they're not going to get a photo, they'll give up.'

'But they'll be back tomorrow.'

'Maybe. There's not a lot we can do about it, Lucy. It goes with the territory I'm afraid.'

Lizzy flushed. 'I'm sorry Uncle.'

'None of that, Lizzy, you've done your time, as all of us in this town know. I agree with Leigh's wife. We need to get that Stuart Reed out of here.'

'We can't force him to go, Uncle.'

'No, but we can make it really unpleasant for him.' Eddie took a swig of his beer and it was then that Lizzy noticed the plasters on his knuckles. He saw her notice, but didn't look away. 'He's stirred up a hornet's nest. There's bound to be backlash. He's not got Tony to help him through this time.'

There was silence, and in that silence Lizzy felt Tony's loss, maybe for the first time. Since his death she'd been on a sort of rollercoaster ride, then closeted away in prison, not experiencing a normal day to day without him. She hadn't been to the funeral – she didn't even know where he was buried. She hadn't had to pack up their things and go through any of the memories of their life together, or even sell their house. It was like none of it had really happened. In some ways she'd been protected from it all. Now she was out and here among all of their friends, it struck her. After the elation of being released, it was like someone had punched her in the gut.

She wanted to cry hysterically; instead she fumbled a tissue out of the box on the coffee table and squeezed it against the sides of her nose, forcing herself to hold in the sounds, even though her eyes were gushing tears.

'I'm sorry, Lizzy,' Eddie mumbled, holding back tears himself.

She waved a hand at him to indicate he wasn't to feel bad about it. She gasped taking in a much needed breath, and managed to choke out, 'It's not your fault Eddie, it's just ... I'm registering for the first time he's actually gone ... now I'm here, with all of you.'

More silence followed while Lizzy gathered herself, and then the lads started talking about the previous night out, which slowly led back to reminiscing about some of Tony's antics, this time jolly rather than sombre, sparking laughter and good feelings, like a belated wake.

By the time they were all ready to leave only two journalists were left outside. Lizzy's family and friends had been dealing with this kind of thing since she'd been arrested, so none of them were concerned, taking no notice of them or their questions as they walked out, acting as though they weren't even there. And once Lucy, Lizzy and Uncle Peter had eaten dinner they had cleared off completely.

Lucy stayed the weekend to help Lizzy settle in. Lizzy hadn't imagined she'd need help, but now she was here, just being able to move freely from room to room was peculiar, and not having to ask permission to do things; being able to eat whenever you liked, and whatever you liked. It was liberating, but a little terrifying at the same time. It took a little adjustment. People came and went, all sorts of friends Lucy had forgotten about, all of it helping her feel more normal and less of a pariah in their midst.

Lucy left to return to her family Sunday night, and Lizzy's first week of freedom began. The press had reduced but not given up entirely. The first time she left the house it was to meet with her probation officer. Eddie escorted her and she was grateful, because they didn't let up until she was safely inside the probation building and the same when she came back. Shouted questions ranged from being about the murder and her life in prison, to Reedy in hospital. She remained silent throughout, keeping her head down.

As the week went on, it only abated after Uncle Peter made repeated calls to the police, who then moved them on. Dave had agreed to take her food shopping at a huge store on the outskirts of town and that was the first time she was outside without the press at her heels, experiencing day to day life again. A few people stared at her, and some even went out of their way to avoid her, but no one said anything to her, which was a relief. It showed her that life could return to normal if it wasn't for the press. And the press were only there because of one person: Reedy. An idea started to form in her head.

Lizzy had been kept up to date on Reedy's progress, if only to warn her when he might be out, but there were no signs of that happening any time soon due to complications arising from his injuries. This gave her time, not only to adjust, but to come up with something that might work for everyone.

One evening towards the end of her third week of freedom, she called a cab to take her up to the hospital. She'd called ahead to make special arrangements for her visit, because she wouldn't be attending during normal visiting hours when there were likely to be other people there, especially press. She was surprised at how accommodating they'd been, but then Reedy didn't have any family in the area and she'd been able to leverage that. Plus they knew who she was, so she was able to give them a sob story about her reasons behind the visit, leading them to believe she felt responsible for his predicament and this was part of her atonement.

When she arrived, she was able to get up to his room without any problems; the corridors were empty of people besides the staff who didn't pay her much attention. Due to the nature of how Reedy came about his injuries he'd been isolated and kept in a private room, another factor which served Lizzy's plan well. No prying eyes or ears.

He was awake when she knocked and opened the door, his telly on. He'd mumbled a 'come in', assuming it was a nurse, and Lizzy delighted in the expression of shock on his face when she stepped in.

'Weren't expecting me, were you Reedy?'

'What the bloody hell are you doing here?'

Lizzy was surprised to hear fear in his voice and witness the flustered manner in which he tried to pull himself up to sitting – or move himself away from her. His face was still coloured from the beating and he was going to have some serious scars from the stitches.

'I thought it was time we had a little chat, don't you?'

'No I fucking don't. Get out! Nurse!' He started pressing a button by his bed.

'They know I'm here, Reedy. They thought it would be a good idea. And so did I. We need to clear the air.'

A nurse popped her head in, glanced at Lizzy then at Reedy. 'Everything alright?'

'No, it's not. I want her out.'

'But she's only just arrived. You don't get many visitors; I thought it'd be good for you.'

'No, not her.'

'Give her a chance and see how you feel. I'll be back in a little while.' She winked at Lizzy and left the room.

Lizzy had never imagined Reedy as someone who scared easily, but what had happened had certainly terrified him. He looked at her like she was some crazed demon.

'What do you think I'm here to do, Reedy?'

'I don't know. You're a fucking lunatic! You murdered your own husband easy enough, and poor defenceless

Sally. You've probably come to finish the job.'

Lizzy pulled a face. 'It's certainly a thought.' She was enjoying having the upper hand. He was always so patronising and contemptuous, it was her turn now. 'But I've just done a lengthy stretch, and you aren't worth another. Tony was, and taking that smirk off her face was too, but you? Nah.'

There was something cathartic about finally saying that out loud. She'd thought it a few times, but never admitted it to anyone – not even her therapists, and she'd told them all sorts of dark secrets. She'd never felt guilt about Sally, only Tony.

'Thing is, Reedy, I don't need you dead, I just need you out of my life – for good. And I don't need to soil my hands to do that.'

'What the fuck you on about?'

'You're not welcome here, Reedy. Kettleby is not your home. It never really was. People don't like you round here, never have. The only person who tolerated you is gone. And he only tolerated you out of pity.'

A smirk slithered across Reedy's bruised face. 'That's what you think, is it? You think you knew him, did you? Knew what made him tick?'

'I knew him alright, far better than you. I knew what he really thought. Why do you think he didn't want to share me with you? Why do you think he got so angry when you tried to take advantage of me that night?' Lizzy was pleased to see his smirk falter. 'But it wasn't really me you wanted, was it Reedy? It wasn't about sharing the girl, was it? It was about sharing Tony with them, going to bed with him?'

'You're fucking off your trolley.' But Reedy's smile was gone, and a shiftiness in his eyes confirmed what Lizzy suspected.

'He was your saviour, wasn't he? Your hero, that night he brought about the end of the nightmare you were living with your stepdad. It started then, didn't it? The crush you had on him. Only it didn't stay a crush did it? It grew.'

'You're loopy.' But his eyes were wide, like his big secret had been blown.

'You see, I've had a lot of years to think things over, and read up on how people respond to their rescuers, especially traumatised people. It made sense. But you never dared let on, even to him, did you? 'Cause you knew he wouldn't have a bar of that. No way. Not his thing at all. And you didn't want to mess things up with him. And then you moved away and you moved on, but then when things turned to shit, you came back and you thought you could pick up where you left off. But you couldn't, 'cause I was there and he was with me now. And you couldn't wheedle your way in, so you tried to break us apart instead. But it didn't work. He wasn't going to let go of me that easy; he wasn't going to give up our marriage and everything we had without a fight – even if he did sleep with other women. You didn't manage to kill it.'

'No, you managed that all by yourself,' Reedy sneered.

Lizzy paused. 'Yeah maybe I did. But he's gone now, and there's nothing for you here, nothing but bad memories. It's time you moved on.'

'And you're going to make me, are you?' He attempted a tone of bravado but she could still hear fear.

'I don't think I have to, do I? I mean, look at you. Do you think it's going to get easier? Do you think any of the lads are gonna start liking you? You don't have any friends here, Reedy. Do yourself a favour and leave. Make a fresh start, reinvent yourself somewhere else.'

Lizzy stood up. She was surprised when Reedy flinched, then realised what he'd been through.

'You've had enough beatings for one lifetime, Reedy, give yourself a break.'

She waited for him to speak, but he didn't. He just looked at her. He wasn't going to say it but he knew she was right.

'I got another chance at life, and so did you. Don't waste it.'

She turned away and didn't look back as she walked out the door. It was the last time she saw him, and a week later, when he was discharged, the last time anyone did. He might occasionally haunt her dreams, but she knew he'd never step foot in her life again.

Author's Thanks

There are many, many people who have supported me with my writing, including a wonderful group of writer friends online I wouldn't be here without. But there are a few people that deserve a special thank you:

One of the main supporters of this book from the beginning, and who has provided me with peptalks when I flagged, encouraging me to keep going, and given me crucial feedback when reading earlier incarnations, is SJI Holliday. Susi without you, this book would never have been finished.

Michael Wombat, a fellow indie author, who has been my stalwart supporter through every step of this book, giving me feedback on the story and proofreading, plus encouraging me with the cover and the new pen name, always making me feel that what I am creating is something special. I couldn't have done it without you, Wombie.

For their unwavering support as my betareaders and cheerleaders: Victoria Pearson, Laura Jamez, Angela Lynn, Lisa Shambrook, Nonna Furman, Debra DeVita, Michael Sands.

To Sara Mickleburgh for her conscientious proofreading and support.

And, of course, thanks to my husband, Ron who allows me to sit at home and conjure up these tales around taking care of our two children, while he goes out to work.

About the Author

M K Boers spent her early childhood in Surrey, in the south of England, and her teens moving round the UK, but currently resides in the Netherlands.

She also writes under pen names Miranda Kate, where she has been featured in several Flash Fiction anthologies, and has published many books in Horror, Sci-Fi Fantasy and Dark Paranormal Fantasy genres.

Books under author name: Miranda Kate

Collections
Mostly Dark
Nocturnal Nibble
Slipping Through

Novella
The Game – The Jester Book 1

Novels
Pool of Players – The Jester Book 2
Dead Lake, Tricky's Tales Book 1
Unsailable Sea, Book 2
Blood River, Tricky's Tales Book 3

Find out more about Miranda and where to buy her books on her website:
www.mirandakateboersauthor.com
Subscribe to her newsletter to receive an exclusive subscriber-only novella.

Leaving a review

If you enjoyed this book – which I sincerely hope you did – please leave a review on whatever platform you bought it on, or Goodreads if you have an account there. It makes a HUGE difference to the author, raising their visibility online, furthering their reach and making writing future books that little bit easier.

www.ingramcontent.com/pod-product-compliance
Ingram Content Group UK Ltd.
Pitfield, Milton Keynes, MK11 3LW, UK
UKHW042154060625
6286UKWH00001B/19